The Encounters

J. R. Rauschert

Copyright © 2018 J.R. Rauschert

All rights reserved.

ISBN: 1986852032
ISBN-13:9781986852036

For Elaine

The Best Encounter of my life.

CONTENTS

Acknowledgments

Amber Dreams—1

Skye Gazing—11

Those Eyes—19

Zina, Aragon—23

Karaoke Night—29

Bench Buns—35

Quick Impressions—39

The Park—47

Art Perspectives—55

Peaceful Days—67

Balancing Act—75

Lost Loves—83

First Year—89

The Fan—99

Old Woman—105

Aisle Encounter—115

Two Men—125

Last Visit—131

Country Living—139

The Bridge—145

Best Seller—153

New Girl—161

Quiet Rietta—173

The Ravine—181

Match Play—191

Amen Point—201

ACKNOWLEDGMENTS

Deep gratitude to the members of the Delta Writers Roundtable who have helped me to learn so much about writing. Also, thanks to the members of the creative writers of Lansing area who have read several of these stories. Special appreciations to Bill Koons, whose suggestions have been invaluable. Most of all I want to thank anyone who reads and appreciates literature. Without an audience, a writer creates in a vacuum, so thank you to anyone and everyone who takes the time to read these stories. You are the best.

Amber Dreams

It *had* been a quiet night, but Joel Proust doubted it would stay that way. The calm often came before the quake. With a local tournament nearby, Joel hoped the Bobcats, the softball squad he sponsored, would enliven the place with a triumphant and contained celebration. Boisterous victors drank more—but got less rowdy. Losers spent less, whined more, and, sometimes became bellicose. It didn't help that one of the bar regulars, the bitterly loud, low-level accountant named Kreegan, hated sports and athletes—and everybody else—and would not mix well with the team.

The miscreant had been warned last month and earlier in the week. One more disturbance would lead to being banned from AMBER DREAMS forever. Joel hated to deny anyone the opportunity to buy drinks and help pay the mortgage on the place, but Kreegan had no more chances to waste. Next time he caused a problem, the book-keeper would be tossed out.

Several TVs broadcast baseball games with volumes low to allow conversation. The steady clink of glasses pleased Joel. It meant customers. As he chatted with his best mixologist, Evie, at the mahogany bar, Joel heard the Bobcats arrive.

The captain and best player, Jones, entered first and angrily denounced the umpire, who had cost the team the game, eliminating them from the tournament. With uniforms smudged with dirt and grass stains, the players dragged into the bar. One or two stomped to tables, snarling with long faces and clenched fists. The long, grueling contest meant they needed to drown their sorrows in cold, amber refreshments—

the silver lining for the setback. They hoped to soften the blow with excuses, alibis, and curses at the miserable gods of fate.

Joel sighed, knowing he would have to be on alert. While he didn't mind the efforts to exonerate themselves, he hoped they wouldn't get crazy. Then he relaxed. This group had shown themselves to be more mellow than other teams he'd sponsored. The Bobcats, seven men and five women, always paid their bar tabs, and, helped keep the place looking lively. And, with history as a guide, he expected their worst behavior would prove as feeble as their sporting prowess.

A recovering alcoholic, Joel had fought his love of booze by watching the dysfunctional behavior of his clientele. He managed his establishment with the wisest of the Seven Habits by wandering around, which satisfied his guilty pleasure of observing human behavior and reaffirmed his own need for sobriety.

In his role as a spectator of life's escapees, he could drown out the din and the revelry to fixate on individuals of interest. He could discern a customer's depression, or when someone needed a listening ear. That night, he noticed a player sat alone at a table near the back. Not a regular, she had joined the team only once before, and like that time, she did not participate in the elbow exercises. Likely a designated driver, she slumped with head resting on a hand and an untouched glass of water in front of her. Something, vulnerability or uniqueness, made him want to know about the recluse.

Before he approached her, Kreegan's arrival diverted Joel's attention.

The gaunt numbers-cruncher growled at Evie. "Martini, I need a damn martini."

Joel gave a hesitant nod to the publican, who had the drink ready before Kreegan settled onto a stool and loosened his tie. The surly customer took a sip, and then inhaled the rest of the drink as the barkeep served one of the Bobcats who wanted a second pint of Guinness.

With the empty glass in front of him, Kreegan barked, "Another!" He scowled as Evie finished filling the glass of draft, before slowly returning to mix another drink for him. "Make it a double!" He turned to look around at the other clientele. "Looks like a lot of losers to me. Got your asses kicked."

Several players stood and stared at the accountant. Joel stepped in front of them and held up a hand to assure he would take care of things.

He waited until they sat down before turning and striding toward Kreegan. "Quiet, or you're gone." With force, he slammed a fist on the bar making the martini glass jump. "Settle down."

Kreegan dropped his shoulders and avoided eye contact with Joel. "Just having a drink, here. No need to get nasty."

Joel's thoughts screamed, "You ain't seen nasty, yet," but his head merely nodded. Satisfied to have cut off an incident, he circled through the tables, exchanging small talk with the team members, and commiserating with them about their hard luck in the loss.

Motion at the bar interrupted talk of a bad call at third base. Kreegan jumped off his stool and approached the lone woman at the table in back. Joel saw her make herself smaller as she shook her head at something the man said. When Kreegan sat at her table, she pushed her own chair away.

"I said no." Her voice rose.

Joel picked up his pace. "Is something wrong?" The barked question had clear effect: Kreegan jumped up. She offered a relieved smile.

"The—" Kreegan shrugged, and his eyebrows swept downward. "She and I were just getting acquainted—planning to buy the lady a drink. Why don't you get us each a Michelob?" He straightened himself in a failed attempt to look bigger.

Joel towered over the bookkeeper. "I think she'd like you to leave."

"Yes." Her voice cut through the air between the two men. "I'm just waiting for my friends,"

Kreegan took a step back and stumbled momentarily. "Just being pol—"

"Leave her be." Joel fisted a hand into a palm. "There's a couple of seats at the bar. Go."

Kreegan's nose flared. "What's your problem? There's no law against being friendly. That's all I did." His posture straightened.

Joel took a step closer, his closed hand pounding into the other. "Go."

"My money not good enough? Your drinks are overpriced anyway." Sniffing, he turned in a sulk toward the door. At the exit, he halted. With sloped shoulders he shuffled back to the bar. As the peripheral noise quieted, he grumbled for a third drink.

With a frown Joel watched him. Satisfied he had quieted, the bar owner glanced at the woman who had lowered her head, apparently to stare at her glass of water. "I'll make sure he doesn't bother you."

She answered only with a slight bob.

He wished to see her eyes, but she kept her face down. "Are you all right, Ma'am?"

A muffled response sounded like an "OK."

"I never like it when my patrons look unhappy. It discourages the others." He offered a pronounced shrug she didn't see. "Not partaking? Did he upset you too much? Or did I?" When she looked up, her green eyes melted his brain. "C-Could I g-get you anything?"

"Any what?" Her voice answered from another world.

"Peanuts? A sandwich? A drink?" One hand waved in the general direction of the bar while he drank in her face. Small cheekbones and a petite nose with large viridian orbs all framed by her shoulder-length flaxen locks, which she had freed of baseball cap and the hair-tie she wore when she arrived.

"A drink? Oh, no. I quit. And not hungry at all. I'm just waiting—" She glanced at the carousers. "Their favorite pal, Buds, is taking care of their misery, so I'll just drive them home. Hopefully, they'll let me. They better." The words walked a tightrope between disinterest and depression, but she did not look down again.

He nodded toward the others. The team captain replied with a hearty lifting of his mug. "You usually don't come with them."

"I like to get home to my son." Her voice gained a spark at the mention of a child.

Did that mean she was married? Emotions coursed through Joel. A child deserved the stability of united parents, but disappointment emerged at the thought of a husband. "But, tonight—"

A clipped response slithered from her. "This week he's with his *father*." Her water glass sparkled in the dim bar lights as she twirled the tumbler with her palms. "The house will seem empty without Sean."

"Sean is your son?"

With a slight incline of her head, she answered.

"I'm sorry, Mrs. ...?" He watched her rotate the glass. No wedding ring adorned her significant finger.

On her navy tee, the word Bobcats moved with her sad sigh. "It's Ms Courier, Pat Courier." She reached out to shake hands. "And this is your place?" Her head swiveled toward the bar and tables. "They said you're—Jay—Prout?"

"It's Joel Proust. Guilty as charged." He liked her smile. "Could I get you something besides the H2O? Soda? Juice? We've got the best burger in town. And our nachos are to die for."

She shook her head. "Not ready to expire."

She paused to examine her nearly full glass. "Water's fine. It's about all I drink anymore. Sugar kills. Sweeteners are worse. Coffee—yuck!" Two fingers pantomimed gagging.

Joel chuckled. "Java's a savior. Like it colored with milk." A second smile gave him confidence to take the next step. "May I sit?"

She hid a look of surprise with a cough. "You own the place."

The room quieted, and he looked over at the other patrons, who acted contented. Several played pool, a few watched baseball on the TVs, and some huddled close to a companion sharing drinks and plans. Her teammates talked quietly at tables pushed together in the middle of the room. Happy laughter suggested they had gotten past the agony of defeat and had moved to the land of wait-till-next-year. The four female players were in animated conversations with the men. At the bar Kreegan appeared lost in his drink. "What position?"

He thought he saw mischief dance in her eyes, but it disappeared in a flash.

No hint of risqué thoughts accompanied her monotone reply. "Wherever they need me. Mostly guard the bench. Only play as an emergency sub. Tonight, they needed another female—three are required to play every game. Jeannie got hurt, and Miranda had one of *her* headaches." Pat's eyes displayed doubt. "I played right field, where the fewest balls get hit." Dabs of dirt indicated she had played with effort. "I'm not good. Made an error which let in two runs. We lost by one, so it's my fault." Slumping in her chair, she looked small.

"It's a team game. I'm sure they don't—"

Pat held up an unsteady arm and turned her head away. "They do. I do." She stared intently at the barn-wood on the wall. "I should have never agreed to play. They needed one more girl." Her voice sank, and she glanced quickly over at the Bobcats before swiveling away again. "My best 'friend' asked me to join, said I'd have fun. *Yeah, right.*" Her lips quivered. "I rarely played. Until tonight."

"All teams need back-ups." He gave her his most reassuring smile. "You helped in practice, I'm sure."

In slow motion, she turned and perused his face. He wondered if he was too old for her. With prematurely grey hair and deep-set eyes, he appeared older than his thirty-five years. Based on the average age of her teammates, she had to be in her twenties.

A crash from a few tables away interrupted them and caused winces. A waitress scurried to clean the mess caused by a dropped draft. Joel's educated nose identified it as Michelob, and he rolled his eyes. "Comp that one!" Happily, he saw the barkeep filling a new glass.

Pat's quiet voice brought him back to the conversation. "I got a hit once. Only time I did. The ball skipped between the third baseman and the shortstop. I scored, too when the next player hit a home run."

"See, you contributed." He grinned and appreciated when she matched it. "Didn't you enjoy any of it?"

As she sipped from her water, he waved to the server and called for a refill and another glass. Pat blinked her eyes and took a long moment before answering. "Enjoy? No. But, I needed to be lonely in a crowd. It served a purpose, giving me exercise and some social interaction. It got my mind off other things."

For a few seconds, silence hung between them while Joel in slow motion nodded. "That's sad." The waitress brought a fresh glass and a pitcher. "Thanks." When she left, he poured water into both glasses. "So, all-in-all, it was good?"

"The experience gave me something to talk about with Sean. He plays Little League, and he's pretty good. Like his—" Her face soured. "*Father.*"

"The two of you aren't together?" He regretted the question as soon as it escaped his lips.

In slow motion she shook her head, her eyes downcast and her face seeming more sad than upset.

"He left after Sean came along, because, he couldn't handle the responsibility. Other than child support, he can't. Not the emotional part. I'm shocked he took Sean for a week. Probably wanted to tell people how good of a hitter *my* boy is." Pat wiped her mouth with a napkin. "God, I must look a mess. I need a shower. Sorry." She brushed hair from her face.

"I think you look fine. You just played a game. No need to apologize." He choked back a compliment he feared would be forward.

Her glance dropped again, and then it rose to meet his. She relaxed and leaned forward. "Thanks." Curiosity edged into her voice. "Were you an athlete? You look like you were."

"You flatter me." Joel hoped the interest wasn't feigned. "Played a little baseball for the JV team. Cut from varsity. Good glove, anemic bat." Curve balls had stymied him. "My physicality is limited to long walks with Sagan, my German Shepherd, and avoiding my ex-." He thought he owed an explanation. "She likes to stop in occasionally to remind me why we divorced. Being married to her led to me becoming an alcoholic. Being free of her helped me quit."

Pat arched a brow. "Any children?"

Grief drifted onto his face to etch itself into premature wrinkles. With staff and customers, he had always avoided this topic. For reasons he did not understand, he wanted to share what happened with this woman. "Had." The mental self-flagellation, a daily ritual, kept the memory raw. "We lost her. A terrible accident. My fault."

She leaned toward him, and her hand nudged his. "I'm so sorry. What happened?"

There was too much to tell. "We got surprised by an unexpected storm on Lake Michigan. I couldn't handle our powerboat. Our little girl—" His voice broke. "Sheila." He closed his eyes, seeing and feeling it all again and again. "The waves were too wicked. We—I—failed."

"It was an accident. Not your fault." Pat's hand patted his.

"No. It was."

He gulped at the memory. "I fastened her life-jacket, but, evidently, didn't click it right. It washed ashore days before they recovered her. My fault. All my fault. I was drunk."

"Oh God, Joel. I'm so sorry." Her hand now caressed his, and her voice gained strength. "Please, you have to forgive yourself."

Her words pushed through his walls. This withdrawn non-customer had gained his trust. Was it because he found her attractive? No, more than that. He sensed they had a connection, some shared emptiness. Though the hurt remained, Joel felt strengthened by her.

Friends, parents, his therapist had all told him he must move forward, to pardon himself. But, all that kept him from going to join Sheila, in the unknown whatever, was a promise he'd made her moments before the boating trip.

She had asked him to take care of a tree they had planted. With a deep, abiding love for woods, she had wanted to plant an acorn and watch it grow. Sheila had loved the stories he had told her at bedtime. Stories which told of great adventures all seemed to have begun under the shade of a stately oak. For her, imagination began in nature, and she could never have enough of forests.

He would do everything possible to see their tiny growth flourish in their yard and turn into a hardy adult. A cloud passed over him.

"Joel, are you okay?" Pat's voice lured him back to the table.

He grimaced. "At times, I get lost in what might have been. Feeling sorry for myself does no good." With his tongue, he explored the front of his teeth, remembering how much Sheila had loved his smile. He wondered if he'd forgotten how to.

Pat's hand retreated from him. Instead she again played with her glass, spinning it between her palms. "It's hard. I do understand." Her voice sounded closer.

"What do you mean? How can you?" He wanted her to understand—needed *someone* to.

She leaned her head against the wall, keeping one arm extended to touch her drink. "Life. Living is filled with tragedy." A shadow crossed her face as her breathing slowed.

"Are you missing your son?" That didn't sound right. She said he was with his father.

"Yes, always." Moisture formed in the corners of her green eyes. "But, that's not tragic, only unfortunate."

"What's tragic?"

"Being a bad mother. Not knowing how to model for him."

"I bet you're very good—"

"No, I'm not. Hell, I'm better at softball than parenting." Her skull tapped in a slow, rhythmic knock against the wall.

"Why do you say that?"

After one loud thump, she pulled away from the pounding. "He gets in trouble at school. I had a friend once who told me I spoiled Sean." A wisp of hair caught her lip. She left it there. "And I do, giving him everything he asks for. When I can't, I hate myself. When I do, I hate myself. I'm too lenient. Even though I know what I need to do, I don't do it. That's not right."

Joel reached out to pull the lock from her mouth, but noticed she shuddered when he did. "I'm sorry. Didn't mean to scare you." When she didn't react, he stared at his offending hand and shook his head. "Lots of people spoil their children. He can recover. You can change. The important thing is that he knows he is loved."

In response, she closed her eyes and nibbled on another strand of hair. The gnawing became manic, as if she hoped to bite off split ends or swallow several strands.

Joel had no idea what to say, so he repeated himself. His voice, despite his inner uncertainty, sounded strong. "People spoil kids. He'll be okay. If you love him, you can do better. You will. I believe in you."

Her eyes opened wide, and she nodded as if hearing supporting words for the first time. "I do need to rethink things. Maybe, I can."

A shadow interrupted as Kreegan lurked over them. He swayed and wobbled but had fisted both hands. "I think it's you upsetting the lady. Why don't *you* get out of here?"

"I think I told you—" Joel pushed his chair back, but Pat's voice stopped him.

"*I'll* do it." Her tone erupted as she stood to lean forward, eyes stabbing into the bookkeeper. "*Jerkface*, leave us alone. You stink of alcohol and stupidity. Slimeballs like you need to slither into a hole and wither away. *Stay* the heck away from me!" She slammed her palm on the table, making the waters in both glasses quake.

Joel watched with wide eyes. It did not surprise him to see Kreegan shrink away. Kreegan did not stop until he reached the exit, mumbling incomprehensible complaints, as he sulked out the door. Pat watched him go, not sitting down until the drunk disappeared.

Applause erupted from nearby patrons. Several yelled out support for Pat's outburst. She ignored the show of support as she fixed a gaze on Joel. "Now that idiot is gone." Her demeanor had changed, and her face had become animated, as if the confrontation had liberated her. "I needed to do that."

"Had he bothered you be—"

She shook her head. "Other hims. A whole host of hims. I've needed to stand up for myself for a long time. And couldn't. Before tonight."

"You shocked the whole bar. I'm impressed."

"It's because of you."

"Huh?" Her compliment confused him. He had said nothing important. He'd been amazed at how freely he'd talked to her. Not even during the good days with his wife had he been able to talk as easily. "Why?"

She leaned back, but kept her eyes focused on her table mate. "You told me I could change." She dismissed his effort to protest. "Others have assured me I'd be able to, but I always doubted myself. It seemed different when you said it." Her hand reached forward and touched his fingers after she took a deep breath. "Your words rang true. For the first time in my life, I believed it. And—" again she grew quiet for a long moment, resting her hand over his. "I will. Somehow, at that moment, I knew I could. It won't be easy, but, it's more than possible, it's achievable. You showed me acceptance. That's rare. So, thank you."

"Wow. You're welcome, I guess. Seeing him upset you—" Turning his hand, he squeezed hers. She did not pull back. "You looked so—"

"Vulnerable. I have been."

He nodded. "I'm worried about you."

"Thank you. I need not be. So vulnerable, that is. I need to remember how to be brave. Stand up to Sean, to his father, my folks. Learn to love myself. Maybe, tonight I started." She pulled her hand back and studied unpolished fingernails. "I have a lot to work on. To be who I want to be. It'll take time. A long time."

His hand felt empty without hers connected. "I'd like to help, if I can." Two teammates, both women, approached looking ready to leave. "By listening, talking, or—"

She nodded to her friends, and they stayed back. "I must to do this myself. I need to learn how to be whole. It's for the best."

"Could I, at least, get your number?"

Standing up, Pat shook her head. "I've got to take these drunks home." She nodded in their direction, as they guffawed at something no one else comprehended. "When, and if, a big if, I get my life in order, I know where to find you." Patting his shoulder, she offered a sad shrug. "Maybe, I will." Then, followed by her teammates, she strode out of AMBER DREAMS.

Skye Gazing

"What did you say?" Seeing and hearing the other person stunned him. He assumed his ears deceived him as much as his eyes played tricks on him. When she stepped up to the table and broke his quiet mope, he saw an impossible stick with mauve hair, deep purple eye shadow, and large hoop earrings. A freckled face appeared as bored as he had been—something he had doubted anyone could be. George Henry Thomas Torganovich studied this apparition as he waited for a reply. A tie-died shirt-dress covered her torso above skinny legs as she wavered on three-inch platform shoes. Keeping a shudder from being too obvious, he watched her pick up and study a copy of his book, *The Forgotten*.

Her voice squeaked an answer. "I asked 'Is this any good?'" Her gaze briefly met his, before she read the back cover.

Near the end of the interminable book signing—an aunt and his sister being his only customers in the two-hour snooze-fest—Geo had taken to planning his next non-seller while staring darkly at the table across the store. There, the smiling blonde furiously tried to keep pace with *her horde* of buyers, who crowded between bookshelves, clamoring for autographed copies of her latest vampire romance. That novel, Geo considered a hastily and inexpertly written piece of garbage. "Nothing like that." He drifted a hand in the direction of the top-selling, dwindling stack. "Mine's the *true* story of the last residents of a dying town in the Upper Peninsula. Serious readers who've read it, like it."

"So you're this guy, Geo …?" She paused, taking a moment to re-examine his name, and then looked up at him in curiosity. "Is this a Russian surname?"

Grateful to not hear another butchering of his surname, Geo tugged at his beard. "It's Tor-*gan*-o-vich. It is Russian. And you are?" Wondering why she looked at his book instead of joining all the women across the room, he dared to hope she'd make a purchase. More likely, she waited until the madding crowd for the Dracula-nonsense thinned.

"Skye." With a wavering voice she nodded. She cleared her throat. "My name is Skye. With an 'e.' My parents met on a plane." She pointed up and shrugged. "Weird."

He laughed, questioning if that made her an airhead, but her eyes betrayed a twinkle. "I like it, Skye's a pretty name." He crossed fingers hoping for one legitimate sale. "Do you like history?" Looking as she did, he assumed she must be someone who didn't, rather preferring some quasi-artistic muddle matching whatever designer drugs she used, like the drivel being pushed at the other table. Halting his pity-party, he told himself to appreciate the break in the tedium of watching someone else sell *their* book.

"Master's program in anthropology at RFU. Bachelor's in sociology. This looks interesting." Flipping the book open, she read the first line. "With bodies wasting away, their eyes spoke of days long forgotten." She glanced at him, and her skin lavender in the light. "Good beginning."

"They were fascinating people. I miss them." With his own fractured family, the old folks he'd interviewed for his research had become important to him.

"Have they all died?" When he nodded, her round, moist eyes, pouting lips, and tilting head suggested she shared his pain at their passing, and his loss.

The faces appeared before him, wrinkled, and etched with stories. More than stories. Real lives. Hearts beating to the very end, carrying on a past they could not forget. "A ghost town. I met the last seven residents, and they became like family. Ten years later, only two remained, but both had become senile, had to move to a home. They died; I didn't see them again." His chest felt heavy as he picked up a copy from the table and opened it to pictures in the middle. Never knowing his grandparents, the residents of Griswald became surrogates.

"It took ten years? How'd you afford that long?" Skye leaned toward him with a voice transformed. The earlier limpness replaced by intense interest and vocal fervor.

The Encounters

"It started as an undergrad research paper, and became my Master's thesis. I teach at the Community College and worked on finishing this when I could." Obsessed about it would be more accurate. Sacrificing a social life had been easy, Geo liked alone time, but fine-tuning the manuscript had been more toil than he'd imagined. Giving birth to the final product made it worthwhile. Even if he didn't sell another copy, he had achieved a goal and gotten it published.

Paging through the book, she hummed a tune that tickled his memory. Something popular from high school back in the eighties. The earworm wriggled through his mind.

"Crazy. You knew all these people?" She had turned to the photos. "This guy looks ..." She paused, cocked her head, and suddenly laughed. "Did you like him? Despite the glare, he has the face of someone with reasons to be unhappy."

Of all the folks he talked to, the residents and their relatives, getting Roscoe to answer questions had been the most difficult, and, possibly, the most rewarding. Geo raised a hand to his nose to hide potential tears. "He got hurt in a mining accident, the last of the operations. Crippled him. Walked with a cane, stooped over, and bitter, Roscoe started talking when I'd about given up on him." Geo pulled a tissue from a box on the table and coughed to clear his throat. "I liked him, the most-real one with raw emotions. He told me about how the company pulled out and left them with nothing, especially him. His medical care vanished, and pension voided."

"Pigs!" Her vehemence turned her eyes crimson. "I want a copy. Will you sign it for me?" When he nodded, she took the book to the register.

A real sale! His heart thumped proudly. On her return he smiled broadly at her. "How do you spell your name?"

She rolled her eyes. "S—K—Y—E."

As the speakers announced the imminent closing of the store, he inscribed a short message above his scrawled signature. "Skye, I hope you find this as interesting as I did our chat."

As she read the inscription, she offered a wide smile of appreciation.

He'd sold a book to someone who didn't know him! Not breaking eye contact, he cleared his throat wanting to thank her somehow. "It's time to go. Er, would you like to get a coffee, or a drink next door?" He surprised himself with the question.

She did not fit his criteria for a date. Too thin, too on-the-edge, her appearance screamed of a need for attention, of drama, of involvement with things best left alone.

Maybe, he simply wanted to show gratitude for her buying the book. Maybe, her blue eyes suggested something deep inside he wanted to unearth. Maybe, at the age of thirty-three, he'd been alone too long, and wanted, for a bit longer, to delay going home to an empty apartment.

#

The Oak Woods Restaurant tried mightily to create the ambience of a warm summer day under shade trees. The booths, tables, and high stools ruined the effect, but Geo liked the bartender, who knew how to make a good Bloody Mary with lots of garnish. Skye ordered a Long Island Iced Tea, the specialty of the house.

After discussing his writing life, and her studies, the small talk threatened to die when his tongue surprised him. "Do you have a boyfriend?"

Without a hitch or hint of hesitation, she pointed a slim finger at him. "Hopefully, now."

A miracle happened: Geo had no ready retort, no quick come-back. He sat stunned and swallowed hard. "You barely know me. I don't—"

She looked at her still extended hand and ticked off a list. "Smart, a writer, employed, good-looking without being obnoxious about it."

With little confidence about his looks, he blushed. Short, a bit pudgy, thinning salt-and-pepper hair, women seldom gave a second look. That, and his shyness limited relationships. As he remembered his one long-term commitment—six years of not worrying about the dating game—he regretted not nurturing it. He blamed himself for too much work, and too little paying attention to her, or their coupling.

"Plus, you like history, you asked me here, you're brave enough to shed a tear in front of—"

Damn, she saw that!

"—And, I think you're sexy." Her eyes shimmered a wink.

Stunned and stymied for words, his hand hid his uncertain lips and checked the quality of his breath. With little experience with compliments, he entered virgin territory. "Why, th-thank you. I—"

Skye shrugged, and her lower lip trembled. "If you're not interested, I guess that's okay."

The rare opportunity needed action, and Geo charged forward. "Would you go to dinner with me on Friday?" Even as he asked he wondered why he did so. Was it solely, he hoped not, because she sounded available, and had flattered him?

She scratched the side of her mouth with a naked ring finger. "Mmmm, let me check my calendar." She gazed up and to the left. "I happen to be free that night. Somewhere, other than here, please."

Dating had never been simple for him. The ease made him reassess his impression of her. Beneath the heavy make-up, she had a pleasant smile and good cheekbones. He liked her intelligence, and the freckles on her hands. "I know a place downtown. Great steaks. Sound good?"

"I don't eat red meat."

"The salads are very good there. Are you vegetarian?" That could be a deal breaker. When she wrinkled her nose in response, he focused on her expressive face. Her eyes reminded him of a still pond at sunset.

She sipped her drink. "My grandparents had a farm, and gave me one of their calves, named Artemis. I loved that cow. Silly, I know, but, I can't eat a friend."

Artemis, from *The Three Musketeers*, had been one of his favorite characters when he started reading real literature. He wondered if she named the animal. For some reason, he didn't ask. "I understand. Eating a pet, I wouldn't. Is he still—"

She let out an extended sigh. "Artemis was a she and is long gone. Ever since, I won't eat beef. Not opposed but *can't*." She nibbled her straw and tapped her empty glass with it. "Could I have another?"

"Of course." He waved two fingers at the bartender. "Do you read a much?"

"I read for school. On my own I like real things: history, biographies, memoirs. Books like yours." She shrugged. "Most fiction is air-heady." She twirled a finger at a temple.

"Really?" Geo frowned. He loved good novels and short stories which added layers to life and gave soul to existence. "Some are. Popular, but superficial. Great authors make us look at the world in a variety of ways. Twain, Tolstoy, Hemingway, Fitzgerald. Their books opened up my mind."

"Some do." At first, she looked down, and purple eyeshadow stared at him. Then, her head turned up, revealing sad round eyes. "I like smart novels. But, reality's safer. Tangible. I can lock the past into history, try to steer clear of the worst today offers, and let tomorrow take care of itself. Can't control that."

Geo stoked his beard. It had been the one way his namesake had shown stress during the Civil War, and Geo found it comforting to feel the whiskers warming his chin. "We can't know the future. But planning to face it is smart." The bartender slid their drinks in front of them. Geo waited for him to retreat. "May I ask—if I can be so forward—why do you wear so much make-up, color your hair, and—"

"Why do you have facial hair? You're hiding something, right?" Her smile suggested no offense taken at his questions.

He had to admit she had him there. "Grew it as soon as I could. I look too much like my father without it." In every way possible he had distanced himself from his parents. The pain of the memories of their drunken days still burned. Three contacts a year—phone calls on their birthdays, they never called him, and meeting for dinner around Christmas—was more than too much. A reflection in the mirror of their DNA on his face was not acceptable.

"Makes sense." She nodded and started humming that just-out-of-reach melody.

"You didn't answer my question."

As she continued the tune, she studied her fingers, the nails shiny, but short and unmanicured. The hum sounded louder, more frenetic for a moment, and then she stopped abruptly and gazed away. "Do you recognize the song?"

He shook his head. "Trying to. What is it?"

"*She's Got Betty Davis Eyes.*" She leaned her head on her shoulder staring somewhere far away. "I wish I had them. I would like to be able to do that. Be mysterious, attractive, draw men to me." Her voice became little, a waif lost in a bad dream. "At the bookstore, we connected. We could talk about your book, the people in it. You didn't find me pretty—who could?—but you listened to me. I hide how I look. People notice this," she touched her hair, "and don't see the real me. It's better that way—safer."

A wave of shame shrouded him as he remembered thinking how strange, and not pretty, she was. He had judged her on that and asked her to spend time with him only in gratitude. Yet, he now saw her as complex as he was, with as many layers of cover-up as he had. "We're on for Friday. Let's both be ourselves. I don't know what you'll think of the real me. But—" He drew out the word. "I already like the you I'm talking to."

Gnawing on her index fingernail, she offered an uncertain nod. "Don't shave your beard, okay."

"It's staying. Will you wear a dress? I love your legs." He cocked his head and pouched his lips. Leaning forward, he smiled, and reached out to hold her hand. Her non-Betty Davis eyes smiled at him, and he felt her warmth.

"I will if you wear a tie." When he nodded, her voice lowered, almost to a whisper, and her eyes sparkled. "How about my *hair?*"

He laughed, not remembering ever feeling this comfortable with any woman. A realization occurred. He *did* like her. "Make it any color but bald."

Those Eyes

Those eyes. If not for them, we would have been champions! After three frustrating years of finishing second in the Forest County Travers Invitational, I promised Anna, my sister, the two of us would take home the trophy. Losing this year devastated her, because California beckoned—meaning no more chances to play together in *this* tournament.

We grew up playing tennis. A natural at the game, she glided over the court, and with her talent had inspired me to lift my game. Each of us won the high school districts two years in a row. In our small hometown, coach acclaimed us the two best players he'd ever coached. As young adults we won many mixed doubles regional matches, but we'd never won *this* invitational tournament—and now, never would.

On game, set, and match point, as the ball dropped in front of me, in a micro-second I calculated where and how to hit the winner. Years of practice prepared me for the moment. I'd made similar shots many times before. Either pop it over the net or line it between our opponents, and the elusive laurel would be ours. With excellent vision and lots of practice, I had learned to slow the flight of the ball. This shot was guaranteed. Neither the small crowd watching, nor the bright sun had any effect, and nothing should have distracted me. All I had to do was make the very makeable shot to win the championship.

The woman across from me, a newcomer to the area, had sprinted in desperation to reject any return from the weak lob her partner had hit. For a millisecond, I glanced at her as in her frantic dash forward. When her sunglasses flew off, for the first time I saw those eyes.

But in that moment, something inside of me shifted. Those eyes breached walls and barriers protecting my world. Distracted—enamored—smitten—in that fleeting moment I forgot what needed to be done. As the yellow Spaulding bounced off the clay toward my ready racquet, I flinched. Instead of delivering the game-ender, I dribbled the ball off my racquet into the net, and then drop meekly to my feet.

That mistake cost the point, then the game, and eventually the match.

I blame it on those eyes, which swallowed me whole—along with the ball, the trophy, and life itself. My befuddlement tilted the universe. Her translucent silver-blue orbs glistened in the sunlight like diamonds on a lake. Never had I seen anything like them.

#

The lavish awards banquet in the Travers' mansion hall, with oil paintings and sculptures from famous artists, had a wall of windows facing the bay. From the first time we saw it, Anna and I were awed. It would be hard to get used to being here, surrounded by so much wealth. My sister and I had simpler tastes than the people who lived there. Those people knew power and enjoyed using it.

Invited again as the bridesmaids, we listened to Brannon Claremore and Lantry Kohl as they gave thanks to the Invitational committee, to the Travers family for hosting the event, and to God for inspiring them. They praised our good play, suggesting they'd been lucky to win. Speeches from several Travers extolled all the competitors, and the wealthy patron-family promised to keep the competition going next year.

Throughout the dinner, Lantry and her eyes occupied my mind. Her blonde hair, freed from the ponytail, draped around her tanned shoulders. In a sky-blue dress and impossible heels, she looked stunning.

After the event, the players milled among the hosts. When Anna went to repair the damage from her tears, the vision in azure walked past me chatting with an older woman.

Lantry's words enticed me. "He broke off the engagement. His old girlfriend reappeared, and things happened."

The older woman shook her head. "His loss." A hand tapped the elder's shoulder and she was asked to go see a U. S. Senator who wanted to discuss economics.

Lantry stood alone and my mouth won an argument with my brain. "Congratulations. Fantastic comeback, you played great."

She turned and stepped closer. As she neared, citrus perfume tickled my nostrils. "You had us. I couldn't have reached it in time. What happened?" For a scant moment she tilted her head and the blonde hair swung across her face, showing tennis-racquet earrings matching the color of those eyes. "Your game—" She shook her head, and for a sad second a strand of hair blocked my full view of her face.

My heart raced. After the match when we shook hands, she had said all the right things, but we didn't have a chance to converse. "I came down with something." I felt her scrutiny and loved the examination. I liked that she worried about my well-being.

"Your sister's better player than I am, and you and Brannon are equal. Lucky for us the ball bounced our way." Her voice echoed around me, and I swam in the eyes of the beautiful and gracious winner.

"You deserved it." I bit my lower lip. "I choked."

She stepped closer sending a surge of energy through me. "You okay now? A headache, stomach, what was it?"

I hesitated, but kept my gaze on her, uncertain if I could hit a winner now. "Lantry-itis." It sounded lame, and my cheeks warmed, hoping the chutzpah worked.

"Wha—?" Her face went from a frown to delight.

"When I looked at you—" The reserved part of me told me to stop. My vocal chords laughed at the idea. "The game got overshadowed." I'd either win the point or be shamed. "Forgot about the ball. I would have done better playing blindfolded, might have had a chance that way."

Her gentle laughter danced on my ear hairs. "How about a rematch, on those terms?"

"You played great." That'd be fun, but the championship had been lost. It appeared I hadn't blown my hopes off the court.

She almost never blinked, but now she did. The hypnotic gaze broke, and I saw the woman instead of a vision. She stood next to me, tangible, desirable, and possible.

"I forgot about tennis, because—" I reached out and pulled her right arm toward me and kissed her hand. It felt foolish, and appropriate.

She looked to the side and pulled her hand away slowly. She brought it to her face and sniffed where my lips had touched her skin. "That's sweet." She faced me again. "Did you really forget about the match because of me?"

"My mind filled with you, about wanting—" I teetered on a plank poised high above a precipice. Would she reach out to save me? "Wanting this, time with you."

She pursed her lips and shrugged.

"Not this." I swept my arm around the hall, now being cleaned and cleared by a host of servants as the attendees filtered from the room. "Talking with you, standing next to you filled with hope." I gulped, never having been so forward before, and never having felt like I wanted to chance so much with anyone else.

Roses bloomed on her cheeks and she looked down.

With irregular breathing and heart racing, I pushed words from someplace deep inside into the space between us. "Would you have dinner with me?"

She pointed at the retreating clean-up crew. "Just did." Her Mona Lisa mystified me.

"I mean, maybe, Friday or Saturday. You and me." My mouth hurt from the risk.

"You should have won. You two are more talented."

The lack of an answer scared me. Had she not heard, or did she find the idea so repulsive that she wouldn't deign to honor it with a reply? "Friday work for you?"

"I don't know why concentration deserts sometimes, usually at the worst possible moment." She kept her gaze averted.

"I could pick you up at six, or seven." Wanting to run, to hide under a table, somehow, my feet wouldn't move, and I couldn't stop hoping. I needed to gaze into those eyes again.

Finally, they returned, and she scanned my face. "Would you like a rematch?"

Part of my brain returned from being AWOL, and my body relaxed into a smile. "Before *or* after dinner?"

She smiled. "At the Country Club, Tuesday night."

It would be her turf, her advantage. I knew we would beat them. "What about dinner?"

Her face brightened, and the mystery left. "You and me. If you win," She pointed a finger at me and winked. "You pay. If I do, I will."

Anna used to be the best doubles partner I thought I could have. Now, I have a better one. Blame it on those eyes.

Zina, Aragon

Zina had to hurry. She had only a little time to apply her make-up before rushing to the restaurant. With reservations at six, she and Rob would have time for a leisurely dinner before the movie at nine-fifteen. Ever since he asked her, she'd been looking forward to this. Amazed her he'd approached her, the handsome Rob Quast made many of Zina's friends airheaded. Several would cut off a toe to be with him.

To impress him, she needed to sparkle, to look her best. Smoothing her skin-tight jeans, she hoped he'd appreciate her efforts to please him. Probably not, guys never believed it took so much time to get ready.

In the kitchen she checked her cell, saw no new messages, and put the phone by her purse. Before she unzipped the bag, she heard a whimper.

"Oh no, *Aragon*." The Shih Tzu implored her with his impossible to resist plea. "Do you *really* have to go?" She knew but had hoped the puppy could wait until her housemate got home, when Zina would be staring into Rob's eyes and sipping Sauvignon Blanc. Aragon let out another muffled complaint. He *needed* to go outside. "All right, let's go. But be quick, or I'll be really late."

She grabbed the leash and attached it to his collar. The dog bounded in eager anticipation as Zina thought about, and rejected, the idea of slipping out of the high heels for her sneakers.

Knowing the front yard had far more room than the miniscule patch in back, Zina walked Aragon out the front door. As she took the first of the three steps, large raindrops splashed against her freshly coiffed hair and carefully applied cosmetics. Zina winced. At that moment, Aragon lunged forward. The leash slipped from her hands, and she stumbled forward in a futile attempt to retrieve it.

The next thing she knew she found herself sprawled on the sidewalk with Aragon running away in pursuit of something. The little dog darted into the street, a few feet behind a panicked squirrel. "Aragon, come back!" The growing downpour and the increasing wind overwhelmed the command. "Aragon! Here, boy!"

She scrambled to rise, only to fall back in pain. An ankle screamed injury. Pushing herself to a sitting position, she saw one expensive stiletto off to the side, the other, the one still clinging to a foot, with a broken heel. "Fudge!" She hoped she only had a sprain, but the damn foot throbbed.

As rain slapped against her face, ruining the meticulous effort and the time in front of the mirror. Zina let loose with a string of profanities which would have shocked her Marine father. Now she might miss—or, at best, arrive very late for—her first date with the best-looking guy ever to ask her out. And what if she had to go to emergency? Stupid ankle.

She reached for her one intact shoe. "Damn it!" Her favorite pair—and most expensive—unwearable and ruined.

With careful movements, she pushed herself up, knowing she'd have to change into another outfit.

Her mind ping-ponged between the dog and Rob. If he saw her like this, he'd stalk away. But, what to wear? The short green skirt and flowered blouse? That meant *pantyhose*. And before she could redo her face and find shoes to work with her look, she had to find the errant puppy. "ARAGON!"

Feeling rushed, she discarded the shoes—it would be impossible to walk with one heel and one stub and hobbled to the curb, where, she called for him again. As she scanned the park area, a U-HAUL truck roared past, hit a spreading puddle, and sprayed a cloud of water over her. "Shucks!" She dropped to her knees in the soaking grass, shook an angry but defeated finger in the direction of the disappearing vehicle, and dissolved into tears.

A moment later, she tentatively tested the ankle. It wouldn't take much weight, but she believed it needed only a wrap and not a cast.

Balancing on her left leg, she continued scanning the neighborhood. No sign of the pup. "Aragon. Come home, boy!" The torrent of sky tears weakened her hopes as she realized he had not yet figured out what "home" meant.

Wanting her cell, she remembered it sat on the table next to her purse. Now, unless a miracle happened, Zina would have to ask for a "raincheck"—Rob would probably never want to go out with her after this—and then hobble out to find her two-month old pet.

Probably, all because of a damn squirrel, who dared Aragon to give chase. When the rains came, the pup had set off in gleeful pursuit of the maddening rodent, who undoubtedly with laughing tail swishes and chattering chirps had lured her pup toward the big oak across the street.

With reluctance, Zina accepted she, just like Aragon, had responded without thinking. The foolishness had cost her heels and best outfit. Rushing had doomed the effort. Now with her skin stuck to the textured blouse, her shoes destroyed, and confidence shattered, she wailed for a quick return for the missing Aragon.

After limping inside carrying the damn stilettos—or what was left of them—she retrieved her phone, and, wishing she'd put Rob on speed-dial, punched in his number. Following her frantic explanation, he offered a caustic laugh. "Well, that sucks. Another time, I guess. Maybe, I'll call you, *sometime*." He clicked off.

"Jerk." She sucked in a deep breath and exhaled slowly. "Your loss." She knew he'd never call again, though, despite her anger, she wanted him to. He had great eyes and would be so fine as arm-candy. *Maybe*, she misjudged him? Maybe, he would call, sometime?

A shiver brought her back to her living room standing over the damp puddle on the carpet from her soaked clothing. Her roomie would make a stink about ruined carpet and probably blame Aragon. Poor pooch. "Omigod, I gotta find him." She shook both hands in frustration at her forgetfulness. At that moment she noticed a broken expensive salon-polished nail. "Drat!"

Twenty minutes later, dressed in old jeans, a tee, a windbreaker, and with her ankle wrapped securely, Zina stepped back outdoors, this time in flat shoes. As well as she could, she hurried to the street, checked for speeding trucks, and hustled across to the park. Following the path where she last saw the runaway, she kept calling his name, and scanning the area. A scary thought raced through her mind. What if Aragon got hurt, or killed by a car? What if someone puppy-napped him? So young. So adorable. So friendly. Who wouldn't want the little bugger? "Oh,

Aragon, where are you?

Her mind raced while her footspeed remained cautious. "Don't be gone. I need you." Dismissing thoughts of going back for an umbrella, she hiked further into the park along a shaded trail. "C'mon, boy, here, boy, here!" When she brought him home for the first time, holding and hugging him had helped her recover from the last break-up. Having all but decided on a life of loneliness, Zina discovered that Aragon lifted her spirits and returned smiles to existence. He needed her almost as much as she adored him. Her pet made her happier, more content. She believed it showed in her demeanor, which helped get Rob to ask her out.

If something bad had happened to Aragon, she feared she would spiral downward again. She had to find him! The rains picked up force, and the wind whistled through the wet limbs overhead. Hair blew across her face, and she felt the dampness of the strands attach to her cheeks. She had to squint against the increasing force of the storm. One thing drove her forward, Aragon had to be saved.

Seeing no signs of him, she neared the park restrooms, which could offer temporary shelter from the force of the downpour. As she hurried toward it, Zina slipped on the grass and landed on the lawn ten feet from the brick building. Her whole side wet and miserable, her hopes of finding Aragon drooped, as her ankle questioned the sanity at being out in this weather.

She half-crawled, half stumbled past a curtain of rain cascading off the overhang of the roof. Leaning against the brick wall, she shook her head. "Aragon!" Certain her scream would be lost in nature's assault, but in desperate hope, she repeated it.

"Is this Aragon?" A male voice made her jump.

She turned to see someone holding the pup, wrapped in a blue jacket.

"Aragon!" She took the excited dog into her arms, hugging the young dog close to her chest. Aragon licked her face and nuzzled against her. "Omigod! You're safe."

"His leash got caught. In the chain-link fence." The speaker pointed toward the softball fields. "I would have tried to find who he belonged to, but the rains convinced me to wait." The young man smiled, suggesting what-else-could-I-do?

Hanging tight to her dog, Zina took a moment to look at Aragon's savior. He stood no more than an inch taller than she. With broad shoulders and a gently rounded paunch, he looked thick and strong.

His eyes sparkled even in the shade of the shelter. He reached over to pat the puppy's head. Aragon nuzzled the hand and gave it a lick.

"Thank you for finding him. I love this guy." With her voice shivering in delight, she kissed the fuzzy face. "You worried me so. Taking off after that awful squirrel and—"

"I lost a dog once. It got hit by a car. Worst day of my life." His eyes closed for a moment, and he let out a long sigh. "At times like that we feel guilty, responsible. But, dogs like to chase other animals. Their nature." He shrugged in a happens-to-the-best-of-us way. "Dogs like to chase. It isn't your fault."

"I hope not. Stupid me. Hurrying. Had a big date, so in the rushing around …" Trailing off, she thought she'd be eating her entre about now and feeling the effects of the vino.

"Don't be so hard on yourself. He's okay. You'll be extra careful from now on, I'm certain."

"I will be." She realized Aragon tried to scramble toward the young man. She tilted her head. The fellow understood, taking the animal in his arms, and the pup lavished him with doggy kisses. "He likes you a lot, more than most. I thought he only loved me."

"We got to know each other during the storm." As he spoke, the rain lightened, and the wind abated. "I work with animals."

"Where?" She liked his warm smile.

"At the Clinic. I'm in the Vet School at the university. Usually work with horses and cattle, but some with ones this size." He buried his head in Aragon's wet fur.

"That's great. How'd you decide to do that?" They stood closer now, both showering the happy canine with attention, and Aragon reciprocated with wet tongue and excited saliva. "Isn't that scary, working with big stallions and—bulls?"

"My great-grandfather had a farm. I loved spending time out in the barns." He stood taller and his eyes brightened. "Milking and feeding his Holsteins. Made me want to work with them and be around them. So that's why." With a gentle tug he extracted his jacket from around Aragon and scratched the dog's ears. "By the way, I'm Tom Wherrett. Pleased to meet you, Miss …?"

"Ohhh." She brought a hand to cover her mouth and most of

reddening cheeks. A fear descended over her. She wondered how bad she must appear. In old clothes, with hair not brushed, and face unmade—her earlier efforts by now a muddled mess—she knew she looked like a slob. "I'm Zina. Nice to meet you." She nibbled on a knuckle. "Sorry, I must look awful. In a panic, I went out—"

"It's okay, I'm in wet clothes, too." She tried to interrupt him, but he held up a finger. "You've got a great dog, and that says volumes about what a good person you are. No reason to apologize." As her eyes widened, Aragon gave a happy bark, glancing from one to the other. "Great names: Zina and Aragon. I like both of them. By the way, I think you look fine." His smile widened. "And, you have *beautiful* eyes."

Shocked by the compliments, her gaping mouth received a slurp from the dog, who took turns licking the two faces. "I know it doesn't appear like it, but I do clean up really well. I do."

"I believe you." He nodded. He held his hand out to see if the rain had slowed. "It's stopped. How about, you and me, and Aragon, going to get pizza? The owner's a friend of mine, and he won't mind a Shih Tzu."

"Like this?" Zina had a thousand alibis competing for her tongue but held them under wrap when she heard his reply.

"Like this. Just the way *we* are."

Karaoke Night

Tyche Jensen's mouth gaped as the others nudged her forward. The twenty-three-year-old resisted despite the part of her—the hopeful, do-something-different inner advocate—who wanted to go on the stage. The louder, domineering portions of her brain counterattacked, not wanting the embarrassment and the all-too-likely mockery from emerging into the spotlight. The experienced past screamed, "No," while the dwarf of why-not whispered, "Do it."

Surrounded by heavily perfumed young professionals drinking craft beers and Long Island Iced Teas, Tyche longed to return to the stool she'd been pulled from by her best friend, Mindy, who murmured in her ear. "Go ahead. It'll be fun." Easy enough for Mindy to say, with her magnetic personality and head-turning body. For Tyche, it meant bringing attention to the big ears—never hid enough by her flat hair—the crooked nose—thanks Mom—and for the lack of curves—especially with Mindy standing near with her ideal shape, perfect face, and gorgeous hair. No, Tyche held back.

Being on the platform to sing, even on Karaoke night, would be an exercise in mortification. She'd be a balloon waiting to be popped. No, better to stay in the shadows, believing safety in crowds came from watching others have fun.

Mindy pouted in astonishment at Tyche's resistance. "We agreed. You can't do worse than my screeching. Besides, you love this song."

Mindy *had* sounded like a monkey with its tail caught in a door. But no one complained or laughed at her with her appeal. People in the paneled bar assured her with compliments and cheers. *She* loved the attention, while Tyche dreaded the *comparison*.

The idea to sing came from Mindy and their larger group of friends. Each had gone up and sang their favorite lyrics, belting out slurred words and joyfully missing high notes. Tyche had demurred, but the others, knowing her favorite song, added her to the list anyway, telling her she could go last. Mindy, on one of their two-girl pajama parties filled with laughter and confessions, had heard Tyche sing in the shower, and claimed it sounded good. Tyche knew better. In elementary school she'd been told by the teacher her voice didn't measure up to others. No, this voice needed to be kept unheard, and this song had to stay her private anthem. The fear of ridicule proved a powerful disincentive to be heard by a bar full of guys! No way.

"I can't. Not tonight. Maybe, some other day." Thinking she should have stayed home to watch *The West Wing* or the news, Tyche didn't like the smell of beer or the way guys would ignore her while ogling her friends. Bars like this, with the other patrons displaying drunken self-confidence, left her cold.

"Don't be a chicken!" Mindy's favorite insult, used to cajole, didn't worked as it usually did. Enough previous hurts made Tyche hold back. Accepting her role as the wallflower-friend and dreading being teased, Tyche determined to let others look silly. Imagination—daydreaming of attentive boyfriends who had never appeared in real life, and she, believed, never would—cost less than stepping into the limelight. She knew her position in the social circle: the mousey admiring friend who envied all her gal pals, the safe one with whom others could feel superior.

"Let the next person go. Maybe he's ready." Standing behind them a vaguely familiar-looking guy, who signed up right after Mindy had listed their names, waited for his turn. He reminded Tyche of someone, though she knew he hadn't gone to their high school.

Standing close, she detected his woodsy, fresh scent. Probably an outdoorsman. She wondered if, like she did, he liked to camp. She wondered who he looked like. His eyes did remind her of someone, but she didn't have temerity to look directly at him to determine from where. What if he looked back?

"It's your turn. Go on!" Mindy's voice sounded annoyed, not used to being denied. "C'mon, don't waste *another* chance."

Tyche hoped her friend would give up if she stalled a bit longer. In fact, she wondered if Mindy didn't prefer the advantage of a best friend who couldn't—wouldn't—compete. On her loneliest days, Tyche resented being second—third—but what else could she do?

A hand grasped her elbow. Tyche gasped, and felt herself propelled to the steps. Glancing over her shoulder she noticed the next-in-line guy, of the appealing cologne, who used a firm, but gentle hold to move her forward. The part of her which wanted to sing, and break out of her protective cocoon, didn't resist.

Shocked, and pleased, she found herself on stage with a good-looking young man touching her, even if only on the arm. His proximity excited her. Whatever the cause, he wanted something to do with her—and she wanted to know why, even at the risk of standing mute next to him while he sang.

The music started before they turned to the microphone. He looked at her and winked. "Do this with me." He added a word she rarely heard men say to her. "*Please*."

"With me," and "Please?" This guy acted different. Still, she hesitated. The lights, brighter than she'd anticipated, made her blink even as he seemed to adjust, humming to the opening chords. The screen flashed words, and she heard his tenor begin. A gentle squeeze on her forearm offered encouragement.

The crowd recognized the tune and applauded as the man continued with the lyrics. Her song. One she had sung hundreds of times washing the hurt off, longing for someone.

> I get down on my knees, and I start to pray
> Till the tears run down from my eyes
> Lord—somebody—somebody

His fingers implored her to join in. With a gulp, Tyche meeked out the next line, her trembling voice overshadowed by his.

> Can anybody find me—somebody to love?

She heard Mindy shriek. "Let's hear it!" Looking to the side Tyche saw the guy wink. What the hell?

She raised her voice, bouncing on and off key as though standing in the shower, and followed the prompter. Little mattered. This song had been her anthem for years. Why not let it out? Especially with a live, attractive man standing next to her. One who didn't need to be there. He'd chosen to march her up on stage, knowing the name of the song.

Their voices danced. Recognizable if not melded. Enthusiastic, if not perfect. His arm encircled her waist, pulled her closer. Heads moving in unison, their bodies swayed, and free arms waved. Tyche laughed on line breaks, catching up when the chuckles passed. He smiled at her and nodded, squeezing her gently. His eyes, sparkling in the light, suggested he enjoyed their duet. What a great phrase, "their duet."

> Anybody, anywhere, anybody find me
> somebody to love to love to love!

Relieved to be done, Tyche also sensed disappointment. Finishing meant their brief togetherness would end. He'd undoubtedly wanted to sing and had lost patience waiting for her to take her turn. Still, she would remember those few moments. The smattering of applause mixed with guffaws didn't bother Tyche. She had sung her song, *with a guy*, and she didn't feel like a fool. The achievement of not collapsing or running off made her day.

As she started off stage, the man's hand reached for hers. "Not yet. I sang with you. It's your turn to help me." When she swiveled to look at him, he gazed at her with a certainty that made her step back next to him.

He wanted her to stay! "Another song? My heart nearly stopped with that one." It had for a moment. But then it strengthened and beat stronger. She looked at her friends. Mindy held her hands in front of an opened mouth, her whole frame frozen in mid-applause.

With a confident voice, he reassured Tyche with a squeeze of her hand. "Together, we can. I promise. You'll see."

Standing next to him she shivered, liking something about him—his eyes, his smile—and believing he cared about their singing.

His proximity confused her, and his reassuring hold of her hand thrilled and unnerved her. With an uncertain shrug, she bit a lower lip. The evening had changed, and she didn't understand what it all meant. "This is not easy for me."

He grinned. "I know. Me either."

Wanting to go, something in his eyes slowed her. "The people—being up here. I don't even know what song, or who you are."

With a wave of his hand, he dismissed her concern. He winked and sounded confident. "Wrong, on both counts. Now, it's time to sing. *This time*, we'll do it right."

When the title appeared her jaw dropped, and she turned with a fresh focus to examine his face. "Ryenell?" They'd been classmates back at Trinity Lutheran until seventh grade, when his family, to her relief, moved away. He had tormented her with pranks and teasing above all others, especially after, as sixth graders, they'd been asked to audition for the school concert. Miss Goddard thought their voices might work well together. Instead, they'd butchered it. Eleven years ago, their off-key rendition relegated them to the back of the chorus. Now, he wanted them to sing it again. Why did he pick this song? *The Impossible Dream* had been a hit in the old musical *Man of La Mancha,* long before their time. Why remind her of that awful day?

"Together, we kill it." His voice sounded confident.

She had hated him all through sixth and seventh grade. For good reason. He'd ruined a good pair of her jeans when he slipped melting candy onto her desk seat as she sat down. Even avoiding him as much as possible didn't save her from the practical jokes—lame ones like the whoopee cushion or almost clever times like hiding her bicycle in the gym showers. One day he even sneezed whenever she answered a question or spoke up in class. Another time he faked a note from the cutest guy, the star athlete, in class, making it sound like the jock wanted to date her. She'd been so embarrassed when she started flirting with him. Ryenell even came up with nicknames—like Stickgirl and Touchy Tychee—that bothered her for years. When he left, her life improved enough to allow her to slide into the woodwork. It surprised her when on occasion, when her friends started having boyfriends, she thought of him. Was it because bad attention proved preferable to no attention?

He sang the first line as she continued to stare at him. He'd grown handsome since grade school. Good hair. Broad shoulders. Nice smell. An air of sureness. Too good looking for her. It didn't matter. Probably, he did this as another prank. One last effort to mock her. But his hand still holding hers, didn't feel part of a joke.

The audience disappeared. She stood next to this guy who wanted to sing with her and be next to her. The song suggested dreaming big, and never giving up. Until seventh grade, it had been her favorite song.

On the second line her soprano joined his tenor. She hadn't thought of the lyrics since that day, but she remembered them from their failed audition. No need for the tele-prompter. This time, their voices soared, hit the notes unlike their previous effort years ago.

Remembering how the lines had inspired her, she shivered. She wanted to march where the brave dare not go. Instead, she'd allowed herself to be bordered by fear and doubt. Jailed by insecurity, she'd given up on her dreams. The song suggested life needed to be experienced, not walled off and ignored.

As they finished the final stanza, their voices blended. To Tyche they sounded well-matched. What a strange concept. *Well-matched!* Feeling good. Wanting to be noticed, and not minding the risk of being laughed at. All from a pair of songs: one about a desperate yearning, and one about daring to do and risking failure.

At the steps, Mindy greeted them with wide eyes. Her voice squeaked in disbelief. "Nice job! You two are *good* together."

A smiling Ryenell, their fingers still intertwined, glanced at Tyche. "I knew we would be."

The Encounters

Bench Buns

His spot at the end of the basketball bench offered Doerr Calendar an enjoyable view of the cheerleaders. The other self-proclaimed Bench-Buns focused on the popular pair: the bouncy brunette and the eye-candy blonde, but Doerr preferred the only red-haired girl on the varsity squad. With a slim figure and freckles, Haisley—he thought it a beautiful name—didn't draw the attention of the others. But, he liked the way she moved, and the slightly bored look she revealed between routines. Sitting, instead of playing, left him feeling the same way. It might be common ground—if he ever got up the nerve to talk to her.

During the game, coach wanted him to follow the flow of the play, at any moment to be ready if called to enter the contest. He chuckled at the crazy idea he'd get any minutes. During the contests, cobwebs could have formed around Doerr and the four other bench dwellers. For the first seventeen games Coach had left them glued in place as the top seven led the team to a winning record, while the bench buns atrophied and watched. Unlike his previous year on varsity, this season he hadn't taken a single shot—and never had the opportunity. It hurt because as a senior, he'd been relegated to a spot in the nether regions of Coach's thoughts.

When the team huddled, he listened. Doerr hated to admit his skill level paled compared to the five starters and two regular reserves. He barely had enough talent for last year's losing team lineup, and certainly not for this year's championship squad, which had seven contributors who played far better than Doerr could ever dream of playing.

As he sat and watched, he could hear the crowd cheer the team. The solid support from fans inspired the players, but did little for Doerr, because it interrupted day-dreaming about the ginger beauty he longed to date. It bothered him too that his cousin, Naomi, sat directly behind him. One of his closest relatives and a childhood confidante, she yelled the loudest of anyone in the gymnasium. Every quarter, she encouraged Doerr to keep up the good sitting, or complimented him on his posture.

Most of the time he could ignore her, preferring to focus on his growing infatuation with Haisley. As she chanted one of the typical yells, he sensed she cheered for him, and him alone. When she kicked out her legs in one of her leaping splits, she looked delicious.

During school days he looked for reasons to pass her locker, hoping to catch glimpses of her pulling out books, or chatting with a friend. It happened too rarely. With no common periods—she had sophomore classes—he searched for sights of her in the cafeteria or the hallways. He'd discovered she rode Bus Three, the one going west of town. He used to ride Two, out to the farmlands on the other side of Twin Forks, but now he drove the beat-up old Chevy his parents kept as a second car. Plenty of room to give her rides home, or out to Amen Point to neck and imagine her snuggled next to him, resting her auburn tresses on his shoulder. At the hill, they'd nuzzled on the picnic blanket he'd bring, and saunter to the old cabin in search of more privacy.

Dating her would be wonderful. Haisley danced in his mind and somersaulted in his heart. Not like his occasional dates with Olive, the girl who lived next door. His cousin assured him Olive wanted to him to ask her to the prom. She'd never turned him down when he asked to go out with him, and he knew he could always depend on her. But, he liked Olive, the way one liked a glass of water, thirst quenching and boring. She didn't excite him, not like Haisley.

"Let's go team!" The cheer echoes in his mind as he watched the red-head bounce. Legs, chest, hair, face. All fascinated him. He imagined freeing her from her uniform and fondling her soft rounded breasts. Or would they be firm and full? The fantasy broke when a teammate nudged his side.

"Calendar! Get your head on." Coach beckoned him. "You're in."

Until that moment Doerr hadn't noticed the starting guard limping to the bench. Two of the other guards had foul trouble.

Coach needed him to play at a crucial moment with the team behind by three. "Stick with Number Twelve. Stay on him. Moves to the right every time. Don't let him score!"

"Got it." As Doerr checked in at the scorer's table, he heard his cousin's guffaw behind him. Stripping off the warm-ups for the first time during a contest, he glanced back with an embarrassed shrug. He trotted over to stand next to the player he'd defend, who stood two inches taller, and rippled with muscles and confidence. Between stolen glances at Haisley, Doerr had watched the other team. Number Twelve shot the ball more than the others. Not wanting to be burned, Doerr steeled himself to play tough defense.

Despite the instructions from Coach, Doerr, still thinking of Haisley, got fooled first thing by his man. A quick step later and the team trailed by five. Coach glared at Doerr, who hoped Haisley hadn't noticed.

Naomi pointed at her temple and yelled. "Play smarter."

Twin Forks missed their shot, and Doerr, a step behind, fouled Twelve driving to the basket. Two Free Throws made it a seven-point lead. His chance to wow Haisley would slip away unless he could only make a play.

A teammate scored. Down by five. Moments later, on defense again, Doerr didn't bite on the feint to the left. Instead of being fooled, he leaned one way and, with a quick move, stepped to his own left, took position, and got knocked to the court surface. Lying there, he listened for the whistle. He heard it. Foul on Twelve for a charge—he couldn't help but steal a glance at the cheer squad. Had she seen it? Doerr had caused a turnover!

In the next minute, a teammate hit two foul shots to cut the score to three. On the ensuing play, after the team garnered a rebound, Doerr sprinted down the court to find himself with the ball at the top of the key.

From the corner of his eye he saw Haisley. She cheered and leaped as he launched the shot. The ball arced its way to the hoop. Coach would have told him not to risk it, but scoring could make him a hero as she watched. He elevated with arms extended, he followed the flight of the ball as it hit the backboard, the rim, bounced high, and caught the edge again, ricocheted, rolled around, and dropped off the side. Even as his shoulders sagged, a teammate tapped the ball up and in for two. A whistle sounded. Fouled.

A moment later his teammate had tied the game.

With less than three minutes left in the game, Coach called time out to put the starters back in for the final stretch. As Doerr settled on his spot on the bench, Haisley beamed in his direction.

Several minutes later after the handshakes with the opposing team, Doerr huddled with the team as Coach praised their effort in the comeback win. He even patted Doerr on the back for some clutch defense against Twelve.

Before heading to the locker room, the players took a moment with their families. Doerr's parents never came, so he chatted with Naomi until the cheerleaders headed out of the gym. He trotted after them and called out to Haisley as his thoughts rehearsed opening lines to charm her. "Thanks for cheering." No, too plebian. "I really appreciate—" Too dorky. "You always—"

She turned, and her face brightened.

His heart leaped, even as he cast about for the right words to say. His big chance, and he didn't want to embarrass himself. He repeated her name deciding to go for broke and ask her out. Before the words formed, she looked past him.

"Oh, Naomi, I wanted to talk to you." Haisley extended a hand and touched his cousin—who had followed directly behind him—on the arm. "You look so good tonight. I couldn't take my eyes off you. Will you meet me in the hall after I change?"

While Doerr stood dumbfounded, Naomi winked at Haisley. "Love to. But, never change. Stay as sweet as you are, Babe. Let's get a Coke at Mickey-Dees?"

Stepping closer, they kissed on the lips. "I'll tell my folks." After a lingering embrace, Haisley hurried after the other cheerleaders.

With his mouth hanging open, Doerr watched her go. His mind twisted in the winds of realization as he turned to face Naomi. Pointing a finger between the disappearing Haisley and his cousin, he stuttered. "Y-you t-two?"

Naomi gave a contented sigh. "Thought you knew. Didn't you see her smile at me all game? Haisley's great." She patted her chest. "And she's all mine!"

Quick Impressions

Dolan Watts didn't want to go. The idea repelled him. But, after several disastrous attempts at meeting numerous versions of the "amazing, great girl" various friends suggested would be perfect for him, Dolan became convinced his pals either didn't know him, or believed desperation made anyone acceptable. He had to admit, with his record with women, he needed help. Still, the choices they'd recommended—a cackling airhead, a nose-picking spitter, and a wild-eyed paranoid—had made even holding casual conversations impossible. He asked questions and used active listening, but each of the women left him feeling more alone than before he met them. After those three failed attempts—and after a few futile ventures to bars and clubs looking for potential female companions—he'd agreed to attend a speed-dating event at Twin Forks township hall.

Stepping into the all-purpose room, Dolan saw a giant square of tables with sixteen numbered stations arranged for one-on-one meetings. Four minutes per session meant the whole thing should take a little more than an hour. Posters on easels promoted upcoming local concerts and activities—possible outings for couples wanting to have safe first dates—like the Labor Day picnic at Forest County Park and the Autumn Forks Sing-Along.

Dolan smelled the anxiety rising among the guys gathered at the front of the room, all waiting for the instructions and the starting bell. For the umpteenth time he asked himself why he had agreed to come. Other than being tired of lonely weekends, none of his answers made sense.

Emptiness filled him every time he saw happy, contented couples. Wondering what being in a relationship would feel like reminded him of his insecurity around women. He'd never dated anyone more than three times, always finding some reason not to pursue a longer relationship. Not that the females made much effort either, but he had been the one who stopped calling every time. He always found a reason to assume someone else would be a better fit. They were either too needy, or too greedy, too tall or too short, too fat or too skinny. Deep inside he knew the real reason. He wanted to reject them before they dumped him.

In the bathroom, he used a paper towel to dry his forehead. He'd showered and used deodorant, but feared perspiration would ruin any chance at a good first impression. With several deep breaths, he told himself again, "You going to be fine. Just be yourself. If the right one is here, you'll know. Don't panic. Be cool. Be cool."

As he waited for the ordeal to begin, he observed the female participants. He saw several attractive women, and no ugly ones. One had crooked teeth and large ears but did have great legs. The two big gals had nice smiles. They all appeared presentable, not barf-worthy. He inhaled and exhaled, repeating the positive self-talk in his head.

According to the instructions, at the end of the evening, each person could choose up to five people to be given his/her contact information. At the start, ladies would sit in the inner area of the tables and gentleman, would sit opposite a young lady. The couples would chat until the chime, when they would move to the next spot. During the four minutes, phone numbers and last names should be kept private. Also, the women would wear a number and each male would wear a letter for identification. Dolan hoped his letter, D, stood for debonair and not for doofus or dumb.

The event organizer called all to attention. The last-minute guidelines instructed the men to choose a spot to start and then to wait for the bell. His stomach trembled, making him glad he had not had dinner. The conscious decision not to eat had been part of his hope he might get lucky and go out with someone after the event. Dolan also wanted to avoid hurried runs to the bathroom. *That* would be embarrassing.

The chime sounded, and Dolan gulped as the others tentatively moved toward chairs. Odds had to be more favorable with sixteen possibilities rather than one at a time, right? Dolan doubted it, and considered fleeing, to escape to his solitary world without risking himself, and appearing foolish in front of a whole room full of prospects. But leaving would cement his cowardice, and almost guarantee a life of solitude. With a head full of dread, he found the last remaining spot, seat four—another omen, his least favorite number.

There, he met Nadine, in business attire, who sneered at his navy slacks and a crew-neck red sweater over a striped shirt. Complaining about the unfairness of life, she launched into a tirade about her job and how people always took advantage of her good nature and her femininity. The thin blonde never made eye contact and only brightened when the next chime sounded.

Glad to be done with her he shifted to the next spot where the gal with the pleasant face and an obese body that overwhelmed the seat. Her first comment, "I know I'm fat," initiated several minutes of constant self-loathing while ignoring his attempts to reassure. No diets, she exclaimed, worked, and surgery scared her, but, she whined, what else could she do? She didn't ask him anything about himself.

The next gal, ashen-faced and dressed entirely in grey, scratched her left breast while announcing her ideal date would be going to a professional wrestling match. He gulped and agreed despite hating the soap-opera exhibition of violence. Excited by his lie, she talked about her tremendous love and admiration for Kaiser Kong's patented Kong Krash, in which he launched his three-hundred pounds from the top rope onto his opponent.

Rolling his eyes, he moved to seven. That woman wore a fuzzy sweater covering a petite frame and enough make-up to adorn several circus clowns. But he liked her alert blue eyes and long golden tresses. Possible date material. She asked him his name and snickered at his response—not a feminine laugh, a cruel, belittling chortle. "Dolan, the slow one. Are you slow?" She ignored his effort to reply, and then switched to making comments about his receding hair, his red sweater, and his thin face.

Saved by the bell, he felt relieved to meet triple-chinned LuAnne, the top contender for the least attractive. She winked at him as he sat down, and the eye-motion sent waves of fatty skin ripple across her face. As he introduced himself she grinned, and kept smiling, winking, and laughing at his every comment, even when he talked about losing his mother to cancer. Evidently, she found morbidity very funny. When he asked her about herself, she giggled saying she was an ordinary girl with a big heart and an appetite for love.

He could see she had an appetite. One big enough to swallow him whole and want more. His Honda Civic couldn't have carried LuAnne. It wouldn't get the chance.

In contrast, at nine he discovered a slender person who had short black hair and dark-rimmed glasses. Sitting across from her, he detected the smell of lilacs. He liked that. As he listened to her introduce herself as Carnie, she slouched forward, looking as out-of-place as he did. He had to strain to hear her short answers, most often a mumbled word or two. Rocking forward and back and making only occasional eye contact, she looked even smaller than her petite size. As best as he could understand, she loved collecting hats, drawing dark pictures, and starting fires. He asked what she liked about burning things. For the only time in their segment of time, she smiled. "It's beautiful, the dancing flames—and I like to see things curdle and die."

At ten a broad-shouldered woman greeted him with a firm handshake and an intense visual inspection. "So nice to meet you." She wore an oversized blouse and had short dark hair. "You have a very nice face. And a good body. I like it." She moistened her lips and leered. Dolan thanked her, but when he complimented her green eyes, she frowned. "Not as pretty as yours. You have lovely features, Dolie. Can I call you Dolie?" She didn't wait for a reply. "I like you Dolie. You'd look good in a dress."

He stood, shook his head, and excused himself saying he needed to get a drink of water. He hurried to the fountain, pantomimed taking a pill to buy more time away from her, and wondered if all women acted like the ones he'd met? Seven conversations led to seven disappointments. Not certain which one had been the worst, he hoped number eleven would reverse the course and help him find someone.

Sylvia, sitting at eleven, his lucky number, introduced herself and asked him if he had any cigarettes. When he told her he didn't smoke, she grimaced and shook her head. "Smokers have more fun. People who don't bore me. Well, if you don't have any—do have any pills? You know. I saw you take something over there." She looked hopeful, eyes wide and brows arched. "Your last aspirin, huh? Dang. What good are you? I wanted to have some fun," From then on she droned about how all the men here sounded like prudes.

At the twelfth spot, a musk-scented redhead charmed him with a low sweet voice as she asked about his life, leaning forward with her gaze fixed on him. As he discussed his career, and talked of his goals, she reached out her hand and started petting his. Her tongue caressed her lips, and her fingers tickled the hairs of his arm. When he asked about her job, she made kissing motions, saying she wanted to be a pampered, loving wife taking care—she winked—of her husband as she thrust an index finger in and out of the other cupped hand.

At thirteen Monica, wearing a top decorated with rhinestones announced she loved to listen to others, and then unleashed a string of rapid-fire questions and comments leaving no time for answers. "Do you like cats? I love them. Are you allergic? I could never be with anyone who sneezed a lot." She shook her head at that impossibility. "Square Dancing is wonderful, don't you agree? Can you cook? I can't. You'll need to do all the cooking. Don't you just love shopping? ..." As she continued the barrage until the chime, Dolan merely nodded.

The next person looked safe and acceptable. She wore a flowered dress with a high neckline and long skirt. Announcing herself as a devout church-goer, she quickly asked him if he believed in God. His uncertain response did not please. She launched into a monologue he didn't, couldn't, interrupt. "If you want to be with me, you must be born again. I can help, but you'll need to pray for God's forgiveness, and read the Bible! You know Jesus loves you, don't ..." At the bells he thought those four minutes lasted longer than any hour he'd ever spent.

At fifteen a very tall amazon with long raven-hair, a pleasant face, and beautiful green eyes, looked kind and intelligent. Without hesitation, she said she longed for a man who wouldn't be intimidated by her height. Even as she insisted she didn't mind shorter guys, she kept glancing at a man three spaces behind who towered over everyone else. It bothered Dolan so much that he started to talk gibberish to see if she paid any attention to his words. In reply she complained about the weather.

Mousey Kia, an artist, sat at sixteen. He liked her modest manner, her shy smile, and the way her short brunette hair framed her clean, clear face. It shocked him when she suggested he should become a nude model for her art class at college. When he hesitated at the idea, she held her two index fingers close together and snickered. "Short-coming problems? I won't have that!"

Finding himself near the end with only three more to meet, Dolan chastised himself for attending. It had been a massive waste of time. He laughed to himself. Yeah, what else did he have to do? Watch some idiot show on television—he'd spent hours letting his mind rot in front of the small screen, laughing at the same stale jokes or feeling fake tension at an unreal drama far removed from reality—or sit by the window and watch traffic go by while pretending to do a crossword puzzle he never finished. No, being here at least proved he'd never find anyone, and, based on this example of possibilities, should expect to live as a bachelor for the rest of his days. He decided to finish the ordeal but invested little attention to the three.

At the number one spot, the woman wore a chaste dress with a minimum of make-up, and talked about wanting exactly ten children, no more and certainly no less. After ten, sex should stop.

At the second table the prospect talked about her parents the whole time and the neighbor they wanted her to date—and marry. She thought she might want to do that.

The whole time the woman at the third seat, hummed and clucked, never fully answering anything he asked her. Whenever he said anything, her noise level increased.

The final chime relieved Dolan. Finished at last, he knew he could never get the time back. He could choose five people to share his contact information with, but, out of sixteen, he doubted he could list one. Forcing himself to pick five, he listed six, nine, twelve, thirteen, and sixteen. A few minutes later he received a list who wanted him to have their numbers: three, five, nine, ten, and sixteen. The only matches proved to be Carnie and Kia, the pyromaniac and the size-mocker. Disappointed, he shook his head. No sense in calling either.

Loneliness stared at him. Being used to it, he'd better prepare for a life of it. He had his books (when he could find anything worth finishing), music (so much of it sounded crazy), and puzzles or computer games (many of which gave him headaches). He might get a dog, but he hated the idea of having to clean up after them—and they barked too much. Cats, which would demand less time and attention, made him sneeze. Fish looked creepy and felt slimy, and birds' noises annoyed him. Snakes scared him. Rats, there was no way he would ever own one of those.

With the coming of fall, he could subscribe to Netflix and while away weekend evenings watching all the classic films he kept promising himself he'd rent. No ball and chain for him, no having to fret about buying presents for birthdays and the holidays. Being single freed him from all that. It wouldn't be so bad.

Walking to his car, his cell buzzed, a number he didn't recognize. "Hello." Silence replied, so he repeated the greeting.

"Is it okay I called?" The whispered voice sounded vaguely familiar, but came across filled with anxiety, a feeling he knew well.

"Who is this?" Experiencing a first, a woman calling him, Dolan hoped it wasn't the wrestling fanatic. No, she wouldn't talk in such a low tone. She would blow his eardrum up. Why did he include her to get his number? Number two would have been safer.

This woman's voice had a familiar nervousness to it. "I hated the whole thing tonight, and I think you did—"

"Who are you?"

He heard a sob, and then a click. He hit the return call button. A moment later, he heard a halting, "Hello."

"This is Dolan. You called me, so let's talk. I'm not upset. Please tell me your name."

A little cough replied, followed by an extended sigh. A moment before he clicked the screen to end the call, he heard a trembling voice. "I don't like to watch things curdle up and die. Saying it, I hoped, would make me sound exciting." More silence while he waited. When she began again the words leaked out. "Watching bonfires and fireplaces relaxes me—and comforts me on long lonely nights." She paused. "I'm number nine, Carnie. Tonight, it felt wrong, like I—all of us—on display. Men and women, both. Made me uncomfortable, except—" She stopped, and silence again stretched the distance between them.

She had felt like he did. "Except what?" He had liked her until the "curdling up and dying" thing. Now she had said she didn't mean that.

"Talking to you."

Another pregnant pause produced a shiver, the pleasant happy kind of quivering reserved for special moments of hope. He liked the almost alien feeling. "I liked our time together, too. The best part of the evening." He meant it. Though this part of the evening, he admitted, topped it.

"I had promised," she spoke haltingly, as if waiting for him to reject her, "myself to make one connection tonight. That's why I called. I should have waited, I know, but, when I do, I never do." A sad, mournful laugh ended her words.

"Me, too." He stopped, realizing he always stalled, procrastinating away possibilities and maintaining his very own orgy of self-pity. "I know a place," He bit his tongue and felt the blood trickle from the minute puncture, "with a fireplace, and good coffee."

The sun rose in his world as he heard her reply. "I'd like that."

The Park

Sitting alone at the top of a knoll in the sunny park, Anh watched as children below cavorted on the playground and couples strolled along the pathways overlooking the river. The breeze batted the thin willow branches above her, playing a song she could not recognize. The melody, or the lyrics, made her sad.

The little ones swaying on the swings and climbing on the jungle gym gave her no joy. Worse, the happy pairs holding hands and kissing pained her.

On her vacation days from the hospital, Anh had nowhere to go. No place she wanted to be. No activity enticed her. Staring at everything and nothing from her perch seemed, at the best, tolerable, *and* wrong. As did the world. Understanding of life had deserted her. What had been certain wobbled above an abyss that called to her. One more hurt, one more cut, and she would take the step to the eternal bliss of emptiness and a reprieve from the agony of loss.

Something caught her attention. An angry shriek from the middle of the frolicking children pierced the air. Several adults, including a man in a wheelchair Anh had not before noticed, rushed amidst the boys and girls. One woman picked up a little crying boy and held him close to her. The other parents and guardians called children to their side as the woman hurried off carrying the little one to a nearby bench. There she extracted something from a bag and placed something on the boy's arm. Evidently, Anh assumed, a bandage of some sort. The woman kept talking and stroking the injured child's hair. He kept crying for a long moment, but slowly settled down.

Meanwhile, the caretakers talked to the other children. Minutes later the play resumed, though with less noise, and with greater attention from the grown-ups. The man in the chair hung closer than the others, partly because on the lawn the wheels moved slower than they could walk.

Anh hadn't considered offering her skills to help. The former Anh would have. The current one soon forgot the commotion and resumed her flirtation with misery. The world, even on the bright warm day, oppressed her. The shades of her mind made the blue-sky grey. A germ of a plan grew inside of her. She'd kept some of her husband's sleeping pills. Not enough, but a good start. She'd write a script for the rest. It would be easy. Why not—

A little girl skipped up to the bench. "Hello." With a pleasant voice and happy smile, the child came right up to Anh's spot on the top of the hill. "I'm Vanessa. What's your name?"

Anh trembled an answer. "Anh." She heard an unfamiliar noise coming up the hill. The man in the wheel chair whirred and clicked toward them. "Is that your daddy?"

Vanessa offered a melodic laugh. She turned and waved to the man moving up the incline. "Daddy's at work. That's Papa."

"Does he need help?" Anh wondered if being in a chair might be even worse than her situation. Physically limited, judged by others, and always looking up might trump depression. She doubted it. He looked happy, determined, and strong as he rolled closer.

"No. He wants to do it himself. I asked." The words sounded older than she looked. "He says *he's* got to do it."

It made Anh uncomfortable to watch the man wheel toward them without her speaking to the girl. "How old are you, Vanessa?"

"Seven. My birthday was last week. I got a stuffed horsey, and some games." The little brunette pointed up. "Look, a blue jay. I like them. They're pretty."

Anh watched the bird fly overhead. It landed on a high branch of a maple. "They are. Do you go to school?" She thought herself silly for asking. Of course, all girls Vanessa's age went to school. Anh should have asked what grade she was going into.

"No." As the girl placed a finger on her chin, she paused. "Well, yes. Papa teaches me. It's called home school. But I just stay there, I don't have to go anywhere."

Then, she started to go to meet her grandfather but stopped to add. "Sometimes we go on field trips. To the zoo, or museum. I like stuff like that." With that she skipped to the man in the chair.

"Are you bothering the nice lady?" He perspired, but his breath sounded normal.

Anh and Vanessa both answered.

"Not at all. She's very polite."

And, "No, Poppa. She's nice."

With ease, the man picked up the little girl, set her on his lap and wheeled the last few steps next to where Anh now stood. "I'm sorry. We're headed to take her home. She ran ahead. Didn't mean to disturb you." With brown eyes set deep into a large head, the smile of apology looked sincere.

"On free days, I spend my time watching children play." At times it brought Anh pleasure. "Is the little boy okay? The one who got hurt?"

"He got a scrape and will be fine." The man tickled Vanessa, making her giggle. "It's a beautiful day to meditate and enjoy the park. You come often. I've noticed you before."

Anh felt her face warm. She had come there for days and never noticed anyone in a wheelchair. Over the last few weeks, she had perceived little, other than children running and playing—*and*, happy couples. The boys and girls blurred in her memory. Adults had to have been watching, but in her mind, they could have been giants or dwarves. No recollection of any individuals, only blobs walking in shadows.

She nodded while twisting the ring on her finger. Round and round, not even noticing. It should be ripped off and thrown into the trash, the river, wherever available. Cemented to life, she did not, could not, tear it off. Energy to do so failed her.

The devil, the one she had loved, had given it to her, along with promises of happiness and faithfulness. Maybe, someday, if fate allowed her to survive—a possibility she questioned since the moment she learned of his betrayal—she might feel again. Love, not likely. Believe, no. Care, impossible. But, perhaps to feel the wind make her hair dance, the grass caresses her toes, and the rain hide her tears. Would living for those little joys be enough?

A song from long before she'd been born wormed in an ear. The lyric fit her mood, if not the bright day.

She remembered the title. *Is that all there is?* Someone, Peggy Lee, maybe, had sung it and still got air time on the oldies stations her father had listened to while Anh grew up. Her dad, an American medical officer during the Vietnam War, brought home his nurse-bride in sixty-seven, before things fell apart following the Tet Offensive.

Anh's mother died giving birth to her, the second child, a girl to give balance to the family blessed with an older son. The siblings, bereft of their Asian parent, immersed themselves in American culture. *Metallica, Star Wars*, and American football became passions. Encouraged by her cardiologist father, Anh went to med school, and specialized in carcinogens. At the age of forty-one, her reputation kept her in-demand. Devotion to work kept her too busy to notice the slow death of her husband's interest in maintaining their marriage. When she came home from a late shift to find all his things gone and a note saying he loved another woman, her emotions exploded: first in anger, and then plunging to disbelief and misery.

The last few weeks had been agony. Even her work suffered, and she had at last been convinced to take a few days off to gather herself. Wondering if time away made things worse, Anh found herself in a fog, at this park, the library, the coffee shop. In misery she could not cry, only sit and stare. She needed to walk, run, read, find friends to talk, but did none of that. No reason to do so presented itself.

Vanessa ran up to her to nestle by her lap. "It's pretty here, isn't it?"

She realized she hadn't replied to the man in the wheelchair. "It is. The sun feels good. I like to read up here. Sometimes, I sit and think." Knowing her words misled, she had intended to read, to think, and not merely obsess.

He glanced around her making her very aware she had no book with her. Only a small change-purse, and the personal cloud.

He didn't challenge the lie; instead, he tickled his granddaughter, who giggled and squirmed happily. He smiled at Ahn. "I read a variety of things: history, biography, and novels. I really like Scott Turow and John Irving. You?" The wind tousled his over-the-collar salt and pepper hair. Dressed in a short-sleeve shirt, he looked fresh after his exercise wheeling up the hill.

Anh hadn't cracked a book, or read any articles, since her husband's betrayal. She used to read whenever she could.

With her career she read medical journals and research, but on vacations she often devoured several novels—not the trash so many others read, but classics and literary fiction. "I like Pat Conroy, Wally Lamb, and John Updike. *Prince of Tides* made me so sad."

Vanessa pointed toward the small garden twenty yards away. "Papa, can I go look at the pretty flowers?"

"You have to stay in sight. No running, off. You understand?"

"I do." Her laugh and her excitement lightened Anh's mood. The little girl hurried to the roses, in full bloom and resplendent in the sun.

Anh had chosen the spot partially because she loved the smell. On days like this, the whole top of the hill reminded her of better days. "She's really cute. You sound like a great 'Papa. She said you home school her?" The glorious idea of having enough time to spend with a child to teach them made Anh regret having worked so many hours through the years. Her little Diana, now a college student in East Lansing, had grown up too fast, and Ahn had missed her first step, her first words, and her first date. The Nannies had been there for those. Occasionally Diana's father experienced a few of those landmarks, though he too worked long hours as an executive for a corporation. "Teaching her must take so much time, and energy."

"True on both counts. The thing is, I have time to spare, and being with her may take a lot out of me, but it gives me so much more." His eyes danced between watching Vanessa and looking toward Anh. "Vanessa is precocious and learns easily." He snapped his fingers. "In my situation," he glanced at his legs, "my options are limited. I freelance doing computer jobs out of the home. The income from that and," He tilted his head as if deciding what to say, "the settlement give me a good lifestyle, and time to spend on my only granddaughter."

Anh thought he looked content. She'd forgotten what happiness felt like. Sitting in a chair, unable to walk, to run, yet he appeared strong—he had negotiated the incline with ease. "Settlement? Do you mind...?"

He lifted himself up and lowered himself down in the chair. "Years ago, I was in a car crash ... mostly my fault. The brakes gave out, but if I'd not been drinking, I could have controlled things." He offered a rueful smile. "Took years to recover, even after eight months of therapy. I should have died."

Anh shook her head. "Don't say—"

"My wife didn't make it. Neither did my youngest son. Too many Captain Morgans, and then I took a corner too fast." He bit his lower lip. "Missed their funerals."

Stunned, Anh drooped in her seat. "I'm so sorry for the accident. How terrible."

"This chair reminds me it was no accident." His closed his eyes. A moment later as they opened, moisture cloaked them. "Drinking too much made me a fool behind the wheel. I did it, killed my wife, my son. Because of my stupidity. They didn't deserve to die."

"You have to forgive yourself. Don't—"

"I don't drink anymore. That doesn't bring them back or make anything better." He watched Vanessa follow a butterfly. "Look, don't touch." They saw the girl nod and follow it even closer. "My crime, and it *was* a crime, can never be paid off. So, I do what I can. Connie, my wife, would have wanted me to do good. Take the awful thing I did, and make the world better. At least, do what I can."

Anh's lungs tightened. For a moment, breathing became hard. When the spell broke, she saw he had turned and wheeled to be closer to Vanessa. Anh stood and walked next to him. "I'm sure you do."

Vanessa stopped and waved good-by as the butterfly flitted away.

"I've learned to accept what happened. A lesson. A truly terrible one. There is nothing I can do to undo it, so I need to change myself. For Vanessa." He gulped and turned to Anh. "For my daughter, who thankfully was at a friend's house that night, for all the people who deserve better. And mostly, for me, so I can learn to live again even though it isn't easy."

Vanessa skipped up to them. "Did you see how pretty it was? He flew right by my nose. Did you see?" Without waiting for an answer, she took Anh's hand in hers. "Papa said we could get an ice cream. Do you want to come?"

The tenderness of the touch surprised Anh. The memory of a small hand nestled in hers brought back memories of her own little girl, now grown distant in her late teens' way. Vanessa's innocence suggested promise for the future, for possibilities.

The man cleared his throat and reached to nudge his granddaughter. "Vanessa, we don't know this nice woman very well. Besides, her husband," he glanced at Anh's fingers, "might not want her to go."

Anh twisted the band and shrugged. "He left me. We're divorced. I just haven't—"

The hint of a smile emerged on his clean-shaven face. "That's too bad." His voice belied the words. "My name is Eron. And I'd like it if you joined us. We could talk more."

Anh felt herself blush. On her skin. it would add color, so she didn't mind. She hadn't worn make-up in months. "Are you sure?"

"If you'll let me buy you a sundae, Miss?"

Above them two blue jays perched together on a limb as her inner butterfly smiled. She slipped the ring off her finger and into her coin purse. "I'm Anh. Pleased to meet you, Eron. I'd love a sundae."

Art Perspectives

Rick hadn't even looked at Dia's well-toned legs! Damn. She might as well be invisible to him. Turning down several invitations to dance—they appreciated her legs, *but none of them were Rick*—she assumed those other guys wanted to fill time between fawning over the numerous prettier twenty-somethings. It had been foolish to think she could attract *his* attention—even after two hours of primping for *him*. No fashionable outfit, nor any amount of make-up, could rescue her from plainness.

Suffocating in misery, she needed to leave, get some fresh air, and find refuge from the loneliness of being inconspicuous in a crowd.

First, she needed to retrieve her sweater from the den closet. She slipped into the paneled room lined with books and paintings of local artists. The damn closet creaked as she opened it.

A tenor voice startled her. "A*mazing.*" Someone's hand indicated an oil painting on the wall. "I've been there. It overlooks the Bay. Have you seen this?"

When Dia turned, she faced the back of a young man with bushy brown hair, apparently scrutinizing the landscape. Checking to make sure she had her keys and wallet in her purse, she retrieved the wrap and hoped to not be distracted. "I'm just stepping out."

"The colors are so vivid, so real." He didn't turn to face her but pointed at the scene of the tree-filled knoll above the inlet. "Brilliant."

Caught half-way through the door, she hesitated "Whatever you say."

He persisted with a voice edged with enthusiasm. "Wait, don't you agree? Isn't this just—" he swiveled around to look toward her. "Oh, you're Diane, right?"

She didn't know him, but the voice sounded sincere. He apparently appreciated art, something most didn't. "People think that, but it's Dia. Have we met?"

In the bright room she noticed he had olive skin and sparkling blue eyes. Despite an untucked shirt tail and a loosened tie, his clothes matched and looked clean.

He walked toward her. "No, pleased to meet you, Dia. I'm Chris." After Dia hesitated to shake hands, he reached to take her hand in his. "The host, Guil, told me your name. I assumed Diane had been shortened to Dia. Foolish of me."

She'd often been pointed out as one of the single gals. Most of the other women had dates or husbands. She hated having spent so much time getting ready for someone like Rick; her work kept her happier than any man could. "It's stuffy in there, getting some air."

"To smoke?" His nose wrinkled, and his eyes glazed over.

Her face contorted, answering without words.

He looked pleased. "Me neither."

"Too many people." She shuddered, remembering how alone all those partiers made her feel. "I'm a little claustrophobic." She estimated he carried an excess of twenty pounds, but he did have a pleasant smile, good teeth, and an expressive face. He'd make a good subject for a portrait. "Didn't you come with Shaunna?"

His gaze dropped to the floor. "Sort of, came in a group and I ..." He tugged on an earlobe. "She doesn't see me. All the other guys are riveted to her. I'm good for a ride, that's all."

"That disappoints you." She watched his face turn crimson. How unusual, she thought, a man who wore his emotions on his face. Most wore a constant façade, impossible for her to understand. Hurtful lies came easy for those guys.

She liked the dark blue tie dotted with stars. It looked good with his light blue shirt, grey slacks and navy jacket. The shirt had been pulled loose at the neck. "She's beautiful and all, but ..." He failed to finish the sentence.

Typical! Guys wanted only the best-looking women. *Like Shaunna!* Dia expected to become an old woman with few friends, with only unsold creations to keep her company. She pulled on her sweater. "I need air." She walked through the doorway and out onto the porch.

The Encounters

He followed. "Mind if I join you? It *is* really warm in here." He fingered his tie, loosened it even more, and stood next to her as the door closed behind them.

Dia rolled her eyes. "*Okay*, I guess." She assumed he would moan about Shaunna not noticing him. Why did guys think she wanted to hear about gorgeous girls they wanted and couldn't have? She had no plans to complain about Rick ignoring her.

He let out a long sigh. "It was close in there." The chilly October evening sparkled with stars overhead. "So, do you know her, too?"

With a long face, she looked over at him. "Shaunna, yeah—"

At the top of the stairs, he held out a hand to assist her. "No, the artist. The one who did the painting."

"Oh, I do." Depending on men had gotten her nowhere, so she long ago determined to be as independent as possible. She stepped off the porch, despite her dress shoes, without his guidance.

"Is she here, tonight?" Chris' voice rose as he followed her to the sidewalk.

Dia appreciated his excitement about art. Too often, people, especially *men*, didn't appreciate the creative effort. They didn't understand the time it took to complete a painting. It sounded like he did.

In her two-inch heels they stood the same height. With Rick ignoring her, she wished she'd worn more comfortable flats. "She's not in there now. Why do you want to know?"

Chris shrugged, but his grin suggested he cared. He frowned and shook his head. "Someone who paints like that—" His voice cracked. "Whoever can do something like that must have a beautiful soul." Again, he offered an arm.

Not taking it, Dia laughed—something she hadn't done in weeks. It felt good. "I don't know about the quality of the soul, but I do like her."

He almost sang his words. "Her work spoke to me, the richness. How can I describe it? Like I could have walked into it." He shivered. "Will you point her out if she comes?"

"Why do you assume it's a she?" Hating heels, Dia wobbled, but caught herself with the help of his arm which as if by instinct steadied her at the elbow.

Grateful she hadn't fallen, she thanked him.

"Guil told me." Chris's voice hesitated. "I'd love to meet her."

"What about Shaunna?" Dia hated thinking about her, and hated Rick more for wanting the blonde she-devil. Men had one-track minds. She shifted her purse to her inside shoulder, between Chris and her. Why had she let *a man* she didn't know walk with her. Pigs!

Chris swiveled his head slowly from side-to-side. His chuckle sounded devoid of humor. "A fantasy, too high maintenance."

"Think so?" She despised girls like Shaunna who flaunted their beauty. Dia, with her small bust, large nose, stringy hair, and uneven eyes, long ago decided to concentrate on her art. The earlier primping had been wasted. Rick had been her own foolish fantasy, and a waste of her time. She pulled her sweater tighter around her. Loneliness loomed.

Chris stumbled on an uneven part of the walkway and caught himself before Dia reached out an arm to help him. "Thanks. I'm not her sort of guy. Besides, she's a real cheerleader type, came from money."

The story of her life, she thought, trumped by attractive, perky pom-pommers. "All women want to be treated well." She wondered if, unlike most guys she knew, he'd be a good listener. She doubted it, even though he had large, floppy ears.

He started walking again. "They all deserve that—she would expect far more." No clarification followed.

She paced herself alongside him and murmured in agreement. They fell silent walking past expensive brick homes and well-manicured lawns. The half-moon glistened overhead and, distanced from the party, the air grew still. Other than wishing she had more sensible shoes and a warm jacket, Dia appreciated the quiet briskness. It helped her forget about her former art project partner, Rick, and about that damn Shaunna. Out here, under the stars, they didn't matter, and the future existed again. "Chris, I've got that right, don't I?"

He'd been humming something from Mozart. "You remembered."

She sensed his gaze on her. Not used to men staring at her—Rick never did—she slowed her walk and looked away. Her face felt warm. "So what do you do, school, work, in life?"

He paused and came to a stop. "Senior at RFU, work part-time. You?"

She liked his short answer. Most guys would have gone on and on about everything they did, whether she'd asked or not. "Second year at the Community College. What's you major? Let me guess, American Lit?" She turned toward him.

"Pretty close. History." Chris sneezed, and in a nearby bush, a cat screeched as it raced across a lawn away from them.

Dia started and pointed. "We scared it! I love my Ludwig; he's the best." Every morning her orange tabby woke her with purrs and a paw to her face, announcing breakfast and cuddle time.

"I've had Boone and Crockett since high school." He stared over toward the house where the cat had fled. "Hope that one has a home."

"Cats are cool." Dia looked at Chris and noticed for the first time one thin silver patch of hair behind an ear. "Have you always had grey there?" She pointed, despite feeling sheepish about being forward.

Not seeming to be bothered, he reached to touch the strands. "Got a concussion in elementary when I fell out of a tree. Been like that since."

Dia looked at the tops of the elms and maples lining the street. "I loved to climb as a kid: something about escaping, observing from different perspectives."

"People don't do that much." Chris dropped to the ground and lay flat on his back. He pointed skyward. "Another angle."

She laughed and offered a hand to help him up. "It's a little cool to lie on a lawn, or I'd join you." As she yanked him to his feet, she sighed. "I love going barefoot. When it's warm."

"Hate shoes." He stared at his Brogues and shook his head. "Nothing better than toes on grass—feeling free." They resumed walking. "Besides, my feet sweat."

She looked to the branches overhead. "The best part of summer is finding a good spot and lying under a shade tree to read a novel." Her eyes sparkled, and her step lightened.

With a pleased look, Chris nudged her shoulder. "I work part-time at a bookstore and can get you a discount."

"Really? That'd be great!" Her small purse grew heavy and she shifted it to her right shoulder.

Chris smiled. "Good to have a plan B, mine is a teaching degree."

"Those who can, do. Those that can't, teach." She bit her tongue as the words came out, angry she gave credence to the Oscar Wilde cliché. "I'm sorry. I say stupid things, sometimes. I've had lots of good instructors." She didn't wait for a reply. "What is it you want to do?"

"Research Midwest history." He lowered his voice, sounding embarrassed. "Immigrant patterns in the nineteenth century."

She sang out a quick retort. "I guess you *do* need a teaching certificate!"

The sound of his laugh comingled with hers. The breeze shifted, bringing a whiff of his cologne to her, the woodsy aroma reminiscent of nature walks with her father.

Chris bit his lower lip. "Not a big demand for teachers, *or researchers*. One of my professors has recommended me to the Foundation."

"With the *Travers*?" The locally-run charitable organization financed research and social welfare programs across the country.

"When I get my advanced degrees, I hope to work in their archives, teach at a university, publish my findings, become famous, and enjoy campus life for the rest of my years."

"That sounds nice." The light from the streetlamps created a canopy of shadows and brightness over them. "You'll be an egghead."

His chuckle meant he didn't take the comment as an insult. "Hopefully make some money doing it." He tilted his head. "What about you, what's your—"

"You're looking at an art major."

He slowed his pace again. "Another starving artist?" He nodded. "Is *that* how you met the painter? In a class?"

"We do take the same classes."

Chris stopped and faced her. "That's a tough career, too. Any alternatives?"

"I'm taking some courses in interior decorating."

She liked when he smiled, his whole face glowed.

He took a step forward. "Where are you from? Around here?"

She matched his pace. "The family owned the grain elevator in Twin Forks. You?"

"We had a house in Forest Heights. Grew up there." His voice lost energy as he answered.

"Any brothers or sisters?"

His tone frosted. "Don't care to talk about family. Not tonight." They stopped at a corner, the only busy intersection along their path. "Owned? Past tense? What happened?"

She had memories she wished she could forget. Evidently, so did he. "Death ... Father ..." Each syllable threatened to catch in her throat.

"He had a heart attack." The smell of roses filled her nostrils. Her father's favorite flower.

His fingers brushed hers again. "I'm so sorry."

Dia breathed deeply. The smell grew stronger, reminder not of the garden, but of the funeral and the dozens of rose bouquets surrounding the casket. The two stepped onto the street. "Dad took care of things pretty well for Mom and me."

"That would suck. Losing a parent." His words sounded more than polite, they sounded sincere.

"It does." They walked silently for a few seconds. Partly covered by a thin cloud that had drifted out of the West, the moon gave less light, fitting her mood. After a long pause, she brushed a strand of hair from her face. "I was a Daddy's girl. He understood me."

"Mine definitely doesn't get me. Your mother?"

Dia shook her head. "Thinks I'm wasting my time and should become a nurse." She'd never been so open with a guy before and wondered if she should keep mum.

Chris frowned. He stepped in front of her and put up an open palm to Dia. "You need to follow your dreams or be disappointed."

She straightened the purse strap on her shoulder. "Dad used to tell me that. He believed in me and encouraged my dreams. Even better he always knew how to make me laugh and how to comfort me."

Many nights Dia had dreamed of talking like this with Rick. That fantasy dissipated as they started walking again, and her mind filled with how much she hated her hair, her face, her flatness. All of which had conspired to keep Rick away!

"I wish *I* had one." His halting voice brought her back to their conversation.

"Oh, I'm sorry." She reached out with her elbow to nudge his arm. Their walk continued for a few steps in silence. "You ever believe you'd never be good enough? No matter what, you'd always fall short."

"Yeah, always. Don't you?"

Under a large leaf-less oak, Dia stopped, turned toward him, and explored his face. "It's a sense of emptiness, reaching out and grasping only air."

He looked down, his head bobbing slightly. "Sometimes, I think I could dance on the tables and still be ignored."

Her hands, previously at her side or in the pockets of her sweater, started conducting the breeze. "I could create life and be discounted. It wouldn't be good enough to be recognized."

He rubbed his eye. "Sorry. I—often feel like that." He forced a smile as he watched her hands dance in front of them. "Dia, you're going to do something great."

Her hands dropped. "Huh? How can you say that?" She often fell asleep with the thought of fame whispering in her mind. The negative doubters tried to keep it down, but those hopeful suggestions kept appearing like blossoms in the spring.

He stepped closer. "You're motivated; that's important."

She did not pull back. "That's one of the nicest things anyone's ever said, but why do you think that?"

"I can tell just being with you. I—" He paused, and his mouth gaped.

"Chris, what is it?"

"Is Dia a nickname?"

"Of course."

His hand ran twirled his silver strand. "And you told me you're not Diane or Diana. Right?"

She smiled, shaking her head. As his eyes searched her face, the image of Rick retreated.

Are you—?" He gently lifted her chin. "Are you L. Vincenti?"

She blushed and saw admiration in his eyes.

He slapped his forehead. "Oh, you are Lydia Vincenti, the artist! Dia is short for *Lydia*. I can't believe it took me so long. What a fool I am. Why didn't you tell me?"

She looked down to hide how pleased his admiration pleased her. It also aimed his attention at her best feature, her legs. "Don't like to brag." She had learned her lessons well, the fear of being too prideful. Hide your talents to keep from a big head. Men would never love haughty women. As a result, Dia had trouble separating false pride from self-confidence.

People always treated her differently once they knew she had some talent. All she wanted to do was to paint, to create. Fame meant less to her than finishing her art pieces. But, recognition felt good. She sighed and rubbed her arms in a fresh cool breeze.

"Are you cold? We should head back."

He pulled off his sports coat and gently draped it around her shoulders, ignoring her hesitation to allow him to do so. The warmth from the jacket and his body heat eased the chill.

Several minutes later, he took a deep breath. They watched three cars pass. "Your painting is amazing. I'd love to own something like that."

Her cheeks reddened. This praise seemed more real than the college teachers who always tempered compliments with words about potential. "Thanks, I'm still learning." She pulled his jacket closer. "You'd really want it?"

"I couldn't pay what *it's* worth. I'd love to see your other work. Could I?" His eyes looked hopeful, and his voice sounded earnest.

"They're not all landscapes."

He shrugged. "Do you do assorted styles?"

"Portraits, still-lifes, a little modern." She pointed ahead. "I have some in my car, the white Civic, up ahead."

Rick laughed. "I drive a blue one."

Dia leaned a little closer, telling herself that she did so to help keep him warm with his coat around her shoulders. Their hands brushed, and she fought an inclination to take his in hers.

As she unzipped her purse and pulled the keys from it, across the street, shrieking and laughter interrupted them. They looked up to see Rick and Shaunna stumble to his red Camaro. Leaning against the vehicle the couple necked and fondled as Rick fumbled with the lock. Somehow, in mid hug, the door popped open. Rick and Shaunna staggered, linked at the hips and the lips, before they clambered into the vehicle, with him half guiding, half pushing her inside.

Chris turned away first. "Better to not watch."

Dia found it hard not to stare. "Frigging pigs deserve each other."

"Undoubtedly." Chris reached into Dia's Civic and pulled a large portfolio from the back.

Turning from the annoying view, Dia saw Chris struggle with her art. "Let me get that."

He shook his head. "Got it." The large portfolio didn't weigh much, but with a handle broken, its shape made it hard to extract from the back seat. "Let's take it inside, to the den." With some difficulty he carried the large case into the house, grateful she opened the doors. In the other rooms and the back yard, the party still roared.

While he placed the collection on the desk, she hung his coat on a chair. "Thank you, very gallant of you. I hope you didn't get too cold."

"Extra padding warms me." Patting his stomach, he frowned. "Need to lose this pizza belly."

"You're not fat!" When she offered the well-intentioned lie, she admitted to herself if he lost a few pounds, he'd be healthier, *and* look more handsome.

"You really are amazing." He shook his head, keeping a serious face. "I couldn't tell you were *blind*, what with the great artistry and your ease of walking. Had me fooled."

It took a moment to realize he'd made a joke. "You look fine to me."

Opening the portfolio, she noticed his cheeks redden. Like her, he must not be used to compliments. "Remember, I'm still learning, and these won't compare." She pointed at her landscape on the wall.

He glanced at the painting he'd prized earlier, shook his head, and exhaled. "Damn beautiful. What a great talent, to do something so amazing. And I know the artist!"

She felt her cheeks flush.

For the next twenty minutes they went over a dozen of sketches and oils with her offering short explanations for several, while he murmured admiration and awe at every piece except the one Rick. Passing by that one without comment, he stopped at the portrait of their hostess, saying it captured her soul.

Studying the only modern art painting in the assortment, he saw it had been entitled "Kite Storms." He asked what the swirling colors, blues and blacks with patches of greens and stray yellows, meant. "It screams danger and uncertainty."

She chuckled, and pointed a light blue section, and then at a touch of orange amid the darker colors. "A boy, a kite, and threatening storm clouds. He represents innocence."

He murmured. "Innocence, being frightened, losing faith. I like it."

"My friends think it's too depressing."

"I disagree. The blend of colors—" Chris tapped his nose, "Show the contradictions of life." He patted her on the back. "You've got a gift."

She shivered at his touch. "I've so much to learn."

They quieted as he looked over her work a second time. When he came to the one of Rick, Chris nodded. "You like him a lot, don't you?"

Taken aback, Dia stammered. "I d-don't—"

"Funny, isn't it? I wanted Shaunna. You wanted Rick." Chris bit his lower lip. "Like that little boy with the kite, full of hope, hurt by disappointments." He looked from the painting to Dia. "Like life." His hand cradled hers.

Dia closed her eyes and saw a distant light. She moved toward it. When she opened her eyes, Chris stood closer. "I used to like him, but, it's time to move forward." She stepped forward as her hand took his and squeezed. "It's warm in here, out of the storm."

Peaceful Days

Mort saw the police car in the distance as it headed toward the farmhouse. Their long driveway, the gravel road and the school bus it followed would mean it would take minutes for the officer to arrive. That meant Mort could enjoy several sips of coffee.

The reddish dawn light peered through the double windows of the living room. Another day had begun. Mort Killebrew loved mornings in his farmhouse on Oakmore Road. The world and other people might worry and bustle in the cities and the work places, but peaceful rural Forks Township offered a calm away from that craziness. Since he and his wife, Roella, retired some ten years again, the early morning hours became their sacred time when they had no chores, no appointments, and only an occasional school bus or commuting laborer graveling down their road to disturb them.

Every morning they sat in their ancient La-Z-Boys: his, the corduroyed tan rocker and hers, the sky-blue them. one. Two cups of steaming coffee perched on the antique, maple end table between

Like their bodies, the furniture had aged for decades, and the room, while never quite tidy, always looked welcoming. Plush pillows propped up the too-soft cushion-seats on the sofa they'd had since Roella's final miscarriage forty years before. The lamps, with their dingy shades, had stayed in place stretching back half a century to when the young couple had bought this old place as their first and forever home.

The budget had stretched their resources, but they worked hard, budgeted wisely, and made a good life for themselves. The former pain of panicked payments now resided only as distant memories.

For the last decade, in these chairs, sipping from these favored mugs, they talked, read, did their puzzles, and smiled at one another, content together. Brooking no interruptions, they listened on rare occasions to the *brrrinnnggg* of useless phone calls, many of which they ignored, knowing most to be nothing more than sales pitches they could, should, and would refuse.

With no children, and few neighbors, Mort and Roella had few obligations, and fewer commitments, other than the one they had taken to one another—the only one they cared about as wrinkles and brown spots aged their faces, and as their eyes and ears lessened in dependability. Time became more precious than their adequate savings and modest retirement income. Having one another, they needed little else.

One thing about Roella, Mort appreciated more than all her other attributes. She'd always listened well. In many of the older couples they knew, the wives talked endlessly, while their husbands either remained mute, or grumbled disagreements on sporadic occasions. Roella had the good sense to almost always agree with Mort. He asked her why, and she nodded, "Because for some reason, I love you, you old curmudgeon." It may have been the longest sentence she'd spoken in decades.

Even with dimming vision, he valued how she wanted to look nice for him. A fresh blouse every day—not one of those tee-shirts either, but a real woman's top, with buttons and lace or plaits. He often complimented her shapely legs, which she proudly revealed most days by wearing skirts, a concession to his wishes and her vanity.

He wished she realized how pretty she was. It baffled him why pretty girls like Roella, and so many others, saw only miniscule flaws. A bad paraphrase came to him. They saw only the mote in their own appearance, but not the giant timber in others. He wondered if possibly, the self-deprecation kept her and the others humble and likeable. It had made Roella an almost perfect soulmate.

He stood at the bay window and watched the school bus hurry by. "Old Joe must be running late again. Wonder if the Billings boy dawdled down the lane." Mort laughed for the two of them. Roella never allowed herself the freedom to guffaw or chortle. On her most daring days she offered barely audible twitters or chuckles.

The squad car followed but stopped and turned in.at their drive. "He's coming. "I'll talk to him."

In their marriage, Roella almost always preferred to let him do the talking. She filled in her Biblical role as the helpmate. A good one, too, attentive and supportive.

An excellent cook, she catered to his appetites, making roasts and stews, and her rarely her favored casseroles and pastas, which he had dismissed as mixed up messes. She often told him why she did so. "Food's just not important to me."

She got some things she wanted. Quite a bit, Mort thought. She didn't want to socialize, so they didn't. He wanted to travel and see the world but had sacrificed those longings because Roella loved staying home, and away from anything outside her comfortable space. For her, he accepted a life of watching travel programs on the television, and short trips to Lake Michigan and several nearby county parks. He liked that they each forfeited something for the other. Marriage, he knew, required meeting the other person halfway, even if it meant giving up dreams and entertainments.

"Another beauty of a day." Mort didn't wait for a reply. Roella had usually just nodded and smiled to his reports. "All the beans planted. Awful early. That young guy, Wooden, you know the fellow renting all this land," Wooden had recently taken over the farming the neighboring fields after old man Kressler passed away, "wonder if he'll have the same luck Kressler did?"

The bird feeders needed filling. He'd ignored them the last two days. Keeping the birds coming to their front yard restaurant had been something Roella insisted upon. He understood during the cold months, but in late May they had plenty to eat from the fields and nearby woods. For her though, he'd gather up the energy to go out in a little while to refill the five feeders hanging in the nearby trees. He owed that to her.

He'd need to mow the lawn again. Grateful for the John Deere rider she insisted he buy several years ago, he couldn't imagine using the old walk-behind like he did until he turned sixty-five. It took three hours to mow back then. Now he got done in fifty minutes, even with the touch-up mowing with the Toro under the trees. Roella had often made good suggestions, ones that made life better. No wonder he loved her.

He picked up his mug of coffee—not coffee so much as milk and sugar doctored with a little java—and blew into it to cool it. He didn't like it straight, the way she did.

Never in their years together had she added a drop of cream or a grain of sweetener. She always said she preferred the real thing, not something disguised as dessert. Like her love for him, she implied, she wanted things straightforward and pure.

"When I brought in the paper, I saw a white-tail running near the creek. Unusual. All alone. A hard winter." Shaking his head at the sadness of the attrition of the whitetails, he thanked God that one had survived. He lifted his mug to his lips. The coffee had cooled enough to enjoy. Roella, who liked her coffee to last, hadn't touched hers. She sipped hers all day, reheating half cupfuls in the microwave while he finished his first and second—his only two—before she tasted her first and long before she needed a refill.

They lived life like that. He always wanted to finish tasks and to get things done. Roella wanted to savor experiences, whether work or pleasure. She had always taken time to smell the roses, while he scurried about to make appointments on time or fifteen minutes early. Now, in his senior years, he realized she had the better attitude about things. But he knew he couldn't change a lifetime of anxious worry.

Still holding his cup, he saw the black and white police-sedan turn stop at the end of the sidewalk. Probably their young, former neighbor, Jared, who grew up a couple miles away. "Time has come." He looked over at Roella, sitting in her recliner, with her quiet smile and accepting nature. "They're here."

Mort kicked off his slippers and padded slowly toward the front dor. He pulled on his loafers, they hurt his old dogs, but were quick and easy to put on, and opened the door to stop onto the front porch as Jared headed toward him on the walkway.

"Good morning, Mr. Killebrew." Jared had a strong, resonant voice. "How are things going?"

"Everything is good." Mort wondered if the officer suspected anything. Nothing should seem out of the ordinary. "Something wrong?"

"You haven't been answering your phone. Some of your relatives got worried and called us to check." Jared stopped a few feet from the steps. Likely, he couldn't see inside. "I'm here to see if everything is okay."

Mort paused, knowing he should say something. It would be the right thing to do. "We're fine. Roella needs a couple of cups of coffee to get into gear." He descended the steps to stand next to the officer.

"Same for me. Need at least a couple." Jared nodded. "Roella didn't call her sister last night. Clarissa tried your number, but said she let it ring fifteen times, and never got an answer. She got worried, longest time they missed connecting."

Mort rubbed his chin while cursing mentally. He'd forgotten about that weekly phone conversation. If he had remembered, he would have stayed in the house to reassure Clarissa and kept her content.

A flu virus would have explained it. Instead, he'd been working out behind the barn. "We'd been under the weather a little bit. Rested. Didn't feel like talking. Roella will probably need a few days." He needed two more to tie together some loose ends. Then, everything would be fine.

"Tell your Missus to call her sister. She's worried." The young officer shrugged. "You know about old ladies."

Mort nodded. Roella liked Clarissa, but realized the younger sister liked drama, and stirred things up, never letting a holiday pass without causing some uproar. Roella, who worried about her sister's feelings, often let Clarissa ramble and rant, which left Mrs. Killebrew exhausted, and Mort uneasy as his wife fretted. The two sisters had less in common than most. He chuckled. "Clarissa freaks out. Over the least thing. A sniffle becomes pneumonia. A cough becomes cancer. A missed phone call, an emergency." He titled his head toward the house. "Better get in to warm up her coffee."

"Should I come in to say hi?" Jared took a step closer to the door.

Holding up a reassuring—and a blocking—hand, Mort shook his head. "She'd be embarrassed. Still in her bathrobe, feeling under the weather, No make-up." His shrug suggested common, bonding male understanding of the fragility of females.

Jared matched the shoulder wave. "Anything I can do for you good folks? It must be lonely out here. Need me to look over things?" He offered a small, reluctant smile suggesting willingness to listen, not necessarily do.

"Thank you, but not today." Mort plastered an aura of assurance on his face. "Still able to take care of things. Maybe not much longer, but so far. Things are under control."

He shook the young man's hand and patted him gratefully on the shoulder. "Appreciate you stopping by. Good thing to do. Better to check on people, then not to."

The façade of confidence worked. After more small talk, Jared returned to his squad car. He waved from the road as he pulled away.

Back inside with the front door closed and locked, Mort let out a long breath. "You were right. Nice boy, not too bright."

Leaning against the wall, he closed his eyes for a moment. "Less time than I thought. Clarissa will be calling again. And again." It meant, he knew, everything would not be as complete as he had planned. In the end, though, it wouldn't matter. "We need to finish things sooner than planned.

"I'll be outside. Sip your coffee. When the chores are done, we can start." He bent and kissed her on the forehead. She was cold. Always cold. He went and found a blanket and wrapped it tight around her. "Won't be long."

In the past she would have gone with him, to assist, to talk, to be together. Those days were now only a memory. Only last fall, she had been strong enough to walk out to the barn with him and help him go over the inventory to be auctioned off. The sale hadn't taken place yet, but should happen this summer. He no longer had use for all the tools that had kept the farm going. Work days now meant making it through each day, despite the aches and the hurts. Mort hadn't realized how hard growing older would be. It certainly wasn't for the weak.

With sturdy shoes on and his worn old flannel shirt hanging over his tattered blue jeans, Mort went to the barn again. Things looked ordered. He dragged another bale of straw out behind the building and cut open the twine. With the hay fork, he spread the dusty wheat stalks around the old couch he had earlier placed in the spot. Seven bales. A few more would be enough. Over the next few minutes he hauled three more to add to his creation. He remembered when lifting straw had been easy. Everything seemed harder now.

He looked over area. It looked ready. He had gathered sticks and the branches for several days. The gasoline can stood ready. Roella would be pleased at his preparation and how thorough he'd been. The only problem, besides damned Clarissa, would be getting his soulmate, in her condition, out here.

There was enough gas in the riding mower for the short trip from the barn to the house and back again. Hitching up the trailer, though, took him longer than he thought it would.

Timing, now that he'd decided they had to do it today—all the less-important details had to be scratched with Clarissa making noise—it had to be done before the few neighbors started coming home from work.

With Kressler's house sitting empty, none of the other locals would be home before five. The fields behind the barn had been planted. No one should see it until it would be too late. Things would work.

Back at the house, he wrote out the note and left it on the kitchen table, using his coffee mug as a paperweight.

"Taking a thermos out with us." He smiled at Roella as he added the powder to the coffee. After tightening the cap, he gave the bottle a good shake. She hadn't noticed the taste, so he assumed he wouldn't mind it too much. He carried that and the other supplies to the wagon.

As he stepped back into the house, he felt moisture form in his eyes. He didn't want to cry. "Hell." He let a tear begin its journey. The pathfinder led a squad of drops to the edge of his jaw, and he let them fall to the floor. His hands shook as he recited the Lord's Prayer, knowing, it would not be enough to bring him salvation. He'd been taught to do it, so he did.

With his sleeve he dried his face, still feeling as if ruts had been eaten into his face by the rivulets he had formed. "Now or never."

When he picked her up he knew it would be a struggle, but he carried her slowly, letting the weight be balanced by decades of devotion. The steps at the back of the house almost ruined the effort, but by leaning against the sides of the entranceway, and taking deep breaths, he maneuvered to the propped open door. At the wagon, he half dropped, half placed her into a semi-awkward position. "Sorry, my love." He hated not being more delicate, but he could ask no one for help. This was *his* job.

With his back aching, and his arms sore, he hobbled to the garden tractor's seat. After a stuttering start, the engine roared. Mort kept glancing back at her. He had to stop once to keep her from toppling to the side.

Behind the barn, he stopped. Refusing to drag her to her seat, straining and cursing, he carried her, as he had on their first night together so many years before, to place her on the sofa. A moment later he returned and settled beside her. His hands and the air smelled of gasoline.

He picked up the thermos, opened it, and took a long drink. "Tastes like coffee." He took another draught. "You finished yours yesterday and fell asleep. No pain. Least from the look on your face." He frowned. "We beat cancer. No chemo, no suffering. You didn't want to go through all of that."

He picked up the box of matches. Struck one against the side. He leaned over to light the pyre. "Didn't tell you about it. Didn't want you to worry about me. You would have fretted, babied me. Taking care of me would have worn you out."

It surprised him how quickly the fire grew. It might outrun the poison. Plan B better be used. "Couldn't handle you being alone out here or stuck in some home. Worse, end up living with Clarissa." He shook his head. The heat lapped at his shoes and ankles. His eyes watered and grew dim.

"We belong together." The end happening to them would be nothing compared to what Mort knew would be an eternity of brimstone and agony. "I knew." In the growing smoke, he glared. "About you, and Kressler. Cheating. Betraying me. There's no forgiveness for adultery. Or for murdering you. You won't be able to take up with him in heaven." His skin felt toasty, so he reached down and found the pistol. "He confessed to me and to Jesus. Before I poisoned him, Kressler begged for forgiveness. God is grace, so, your lover's in heaven." He chuckled at his cleverness. "You, my dear, will be with me. Forever. In *hell*." Mort aimed at his mouth and squeezed the trigger as flames encased them in a coffin of blazing vengeance.

The Encounters

Balancing Act

"I don't know *how* you do it?" Meant as a compliment, Mark's words drove home how empty it all left me. "*Three* chicks. One's more than enough for me." Mark knew the truth of it from his own experience. Twice divorced, his classic good looks and athletic build had helped him little in ill-fated marriages. While lacking his external superlatives, I, on-the-other-hand, had maintained one relationship for seven years with a great partner. Gina, my soul-mate, deserted me before her twenty-eighth birthday, surrendering to the lure of the seductive tempter, Cancer.

Since the funeral—an eternity of a year ago—life felt hollow. Filling time with lovers—not certain how I draw them—the chasm within grew deeper with every tryst, widening the distance to any form of happiness.

So, I agreed with Mark. Better to stick to one at a time. But it needed to be the *right* one. Like Gina. And, I had my Gina.

We sat at the Ridgeview Lounge's bar, waiting for our dates. Being a Monday night, the place had open tables. Checking to make sure they hadn't started back from the restrooms, Mark saluted me with his stein of Labatts. "Avery's not due until next week, right?" He didn't know the third one's name.

Avery worked in Hollywood, returning to Michigan once a month to visit ailing parents who lived in Forest Heights. On her trips back, she always carved out a Saturday night for me—telling her folks she needed time to reacquaint with old friends. Tall, blonde, and open to exploration, she was an ideal sex-partner: no strings attached, no commitments, which should mean no jealousy. I hoped she wouldn't be bothered. The others I knew would.

Avery, though, never asked me about other women. She was likely never alone out West because with her looks, she could attract any man—or woman—she wanted. She likely did, too.

Nodding to the bartender, my glass needed filling—Jack on the rocks was my mind-fogger—I chuckled. "The weekend after that. The movie they're shooting has run into some difficulties."

"What sort?" Marc wiped his mouth on his sleeve. His inebriated pretty-boy reflection looked ludicrous in the mirror behind the bar. So, did the bald spot on the bartender.

"Ego. The star wants a wine fountain in his dressing room. Insists on it. The director's having fits. Takes it out on the staff. Pisses Avery off."

"First world problem." He laughed. As my best friend, Mark understood my financial well-being, so his references hit home.

Several years ago, I got a letter asking me to attend the reading of my spinster Aunt Edna's will. As a kid, I spent summers with her at her cabin on Higgins Lake.

For the last few years before her passing, I had visited her regularly. She had encouraged my efforts at journalism—even as my career went nowhere. She introduced me to the editor of the *Ink Scrawls*, a magazine for out-of-the-box thinking. Writing for that helped me survive.

A week after the funeral, her attorney and I met for the reading of the will—no one else attended because no one else was invited—and he told me she left a foundation in my name worth 2.5 million, with strings attached. Flabbergasted, I stuttered out several questions. How in heck did she get that much money? Why didn't she tell anyone she was frigging rich? Why didn't she get a nicer place? Why me? What *strings*?

She had won the lottery, but had kept it secret, not wanting to be flooded with "friends" and "relatives" who never had time for her before. She had no need of the money, being quite content with her two-bedroom cape-cod overlooking the lake.

In her old age, she decided to leave the money to someone who treated her with kindness. Her final decision came down to me or the minister at the local church, but he blew his shot when he committed adultery with an eighteen-year old.

The strings proved tolerable. Every year I would receive $100,000 after taxes, a sum less than the interest on the full amount. At the age of fifty, I would get the full amount.

Despite not having to earn money, I set up a small publishing business to do ghostwriting and newsletters to keep people from knowing my wealth. The damn little place surprisingly makes a profit now, with me spending less than twenty hours a week at work! Financially, life is good.

It was an excellent cover for me with Lowie, my date. She worked as a waitress in Grant Ridge. Short, a little heavy, blonde, she had no idea I'm rich or that I see anyone else. I've convinced her my two-person office—I've hired a part-time secretary—kept me busy fifty-sixty hours a week. I felt guilty about lying, but she bought it without question when I "suggested" long hours.

The third gal, Blair, never asked if I saw other people. Every Friday—and only on Fridays—we spent the night together. Saturday mornings, I left with no need for expectations and no guilt about calling her again until the next weekend. A mousy librarian—short dark hair, glasses, and slight figure, she shocked me with her passion and willingness to please.

Mark pointed toward the far end of the bar. "They're back." Lowie and his date, Morgan, walked toward us. They'd even used that tired old saw about "powdering their noses." I rolled my eyes at that.

"What you boys talking about?" Lowie slid her arm around my waist and kissed me on the cheek. She liked to snuggle, and we usually spent at least two nights, Mondays and Tuesdays—her days off—together at her place. It was rare to go out with her. When we did, it was always a local place, like this, close to her apartment. She liked being a homebody.

"About how lucky we are to have two such hot chicks." Mark kissed Morgan. They twisted into a long grope.

Cupping Lowie's chin, I brought her lips to mine. Raspberry. She preferred fruit-flavored lip glosses. I like it on her. "Want another?" I nodded toward her Long Island Iced Tea.

"Mmmm." She bit my ear. "One more and then let's go home." When she squeezed my thigh, I wanted to go right then.

I snapped my fingers for the bartender indicating the empty glasses. As he came over to fill them, I nuzzled Lowie on the neck. "You smell great." She did, too. More fruit. Apple blossom.

Each of the three had major appeal. Lowie had the extra advantage of having time for me. When I really thought about it, Lowie was the one I cheated, with the other two mere dalliances. A twinge of guilt nibbled on my soul, she deserved better. I should spend more time with her but enjoyed the ego-burst from having three women interested in me. I eased the pang of guilt with a Jack.

The four of us small-talked and drank our final round over the next half hour, but her soft, baby blues glistening in my direction began to gnaw. Where did I get off thinking I could keep this up? I had always hated cheating. Why was it okay now?

Some part of me, from long ago, morals, ethics, commandments told me I had lied, not just left things unmentioned. Had I failed in the eyes of the universal judges, whoever they might be? Those entities laughed at my lame excuses. The downward road to perdition might be smoothed over by good intent, but my slide had deception and getting pleasure as the main lubricants.

To quiet the inner disparaging, I downed one more, and then another when Lowie and Morgan went to the John again—drinks must have run through those ladies. When they went, Mark nodded after them. "She's damn into you. Wish Morgan would be more like that. Still on second base. Maybe tonight?" He fingered his beer. "Don't overdo it, man. Never saw you pour em down like that. What's up?"

"I should fess up." I stared into my newly emptied glass. My normal habit was to never drink too much. It loosened my tongue and made me stupid. I didn't like sounding dumb. Despite my resolve, I raised my arm to call for one more, but Mark pulled it down. "Wha—"

"You want me to drive?" Mark kept his hand on my wrist. "You've had enough."

With reluctance I had to admit he was right, again. Mark knew my frailties too well. He'd watched my descent into malaise and encouraged my crawl out of my current self-delusion. He knew my limit, and I had passed both mine for alcohol and women. I needed to change.

I looked up and saw Morgan headed toward us, with Lowie trailing behind talking to some girl who looked familiar. Where did I meet her? Someone. Recent. Closing and opening my eyes helped not at all. I couldn't place the face.

No matter, the newcomer turned away before they reached our table. Gave me a funny glare. Probably nothing. I blew it off.

Morgan wanted to go, so we slipped our coats on, left a good tip, and headed to our cars. With a smile, I assured Mark I could drive, and we said our goodbyes.

Lowie acted normal until we sat alone in the car. Instead of sliding over to snuggle, she huddled close to the door, and clicked on the seatbelt. When I asked what was wrong, she merely stared ahead. "Let's go." To follow-up inquiries she growled. "Tired."

The chill in the car hung heavy as I drove with extra care. Her mood helped me focus. Luckily, traffic was light, and I managed to stay in my lane. Didn't have to slam on the brakes once.

Stopping in front of her house, I suddenly remembered who that other girl had been: Avery's cousin! She had spotted us necking in a restaurant two week ago. Avery introduced me as her boyfriend. I never thought the cousin would hang out in Grant Ridge. Certainly, the odds had to be long that she'd show up to see Lowie and me together. We hardly ever went out. Guess we never should have.

Lowie had opened her door, but not left the car. With a wicked growl, she growled out her anger. "Who is this *Avery*, chick?"

My mouth gaped, slammed shut, and then made a failed attempt to explain. "She's a fri—"

I never expected the slap, which hit with a force that sent my head sideways. The realization I deserved her wrath hurt more. Tired of hiding behind lies, with apprehension I met her gaze. "Someone I see every few weeks."

Her facial muscles tightened, and her gaze ate into me. "And?"

"She works in Hollywood and flies back to see family once a month."

"So, I've been told. You bed me when you can, and her when *she's* in town?" The question did not wait for an answer. "I'm you're *ordinary* screw, and she's you're *fancy* girlfriend!"

A battalion of lies formed, ready to charge off my tongue. Anything to slow her attack. At least she didn't know about Blair. Part of my brain told me to just shut up. I listened to none of the advice. "There is nothing ordinary abou—"

The slap had been a shock. The spit was more of coffin-nails darting through the car. Most landed on my face. The door slammed before I opened my eyes from the well-aimed barrage. The remnants of it kept me company on the way home.

Back at my place, the answering machine blinked. Blair's voice sounded happy sad. "My ex- wants to get together again. He begged me! I want to try, so, this is good-by. I had fun, but, I can't see you anymore."

My heart ached. I'd counted on seeing her after the evening's debacle.

I expected Avery would call before she flew back. In record time I'd gone from three to none. Mark had been right again.

That night I punched a hole in the wall, swearing I'd never cheat again. Later, while soaking my hand in Epsom salt, my grandmother's solution for bruises, I had time to think. Lowie, Avery, and Blair let me hide from my grief. They could *never* make up for Gina. I had blanketed myself with replacements to deny the hurt, the anger, and the misery of my loss. Until I faced the reality of her not being, *I* could not be me. Instead of attempting to deal with death, I had given birth to a selfish-denier, bereft of feeling and in no way honoring the memory of the woman I loved. Seeking comfort in three others, I had only misused them, *and* abused my character. Gina deserved more. I deserved more.

The best picture of her was in the drawer by my bed. After drying my hand, I went to retrieve it and returned to sit at the table, resting my hand again in the still lukewarm water. Gina's eyes shimmered in the kitchen light. "I don't know how to be."

Her lips moved, and my ears strained to hear, but the words could only be understood if I cleared my thoughts, not an easy task. She wanted to tell me something. Something I needed to hear. With great resolve the room quieted, my pulse slowed, and I concentrated on her.

Closing my eyes, she walked in front of me, placed a hand on my shoulder. The touch sent ripples of happiness through my soul, and I felt her lips kiss my own.

"You're here!" Opening the eyes made her disappear. "Come back!" Shutting them, she returned.

"Only in your mind." I cherished her whispered caress. "Cancer did it. Not you. My death was nobody's fault. Fate. My fate." I had never admitted my real fear. Not deserving her, I had caused the ugliness that killed her.

My guilt was a cancerous thorn ripping through my mind. Her words tried to counter my self-hatred. "Be angry. Cry. Feel the loneliness." Emotions washed over me as I screamed and moaned. She waited.

Time stood still. Minutes flew. Surroundings became unimportant. My eyes stayed closed, at first shedding tears like a cat's fur in spring, and then clamped tight to hold off reality. As I cried and raged, she waited, by my side, her hand clasping my shoulder, an umbilical cord keeping me connected, and alive.

My head dropped to the table top, but still her touch remained. Her voice, patient and loving, cooed in my head. "Give it time. Forgive yourself and forgive *me*." How could I blame her? But I had. For leaving. For not staying. Her next words came as not a request, but an expectation. "And ask for forgiveness—from those women. *Today*."

Not wanting to break the spell, I maintained my blindness with a question. "Will they listen? They must all hate me."

"Do it for you." The statement had the feel of last words.

"Don't leave."

"I have to. You need me to go." One last kiss on the back of my head, and my eyes opened of their own accord. She was gone. Closing my eyes did not bring her back.

The kitchen looked no different. My hand on the table, no longer in the basin, had left an outline of dampness on the wood surface. The light filtering through the window suggested the hint of dawn. The dream, or visitation, had taken me through the darkest part of the night and early morning. I breathed evenly, deeply. Then, before making coffee, I padded to the desk in the living room, sat down and pulled out the stationery, one of the gifts from her. Knowing it might be too soon for the three women, I did it for Gina—and for me. I needed to find my way. With my favorite pen, I began to write. Three letters—three apologies—three *mea culpas*.

Lost Loves

With a dejected stare straight down, Charlie watched the water churn far below along the river channel. Another yard forward would send him to whatever came next, and free him from the lingering fate diagnosed for him. The plunge, which would end on the ragged rocks at the bottom of the ridge, could, also, reunite him with his Ursula, *if* she waited for him in the uncertain afterlife he didn't believe existed.

The low barricade, more decorative than protective, an easy step over for others, would strain his bad leg and aching back. He'd breathed hard reaching the spot. With no one to live for, at that moment he saw no reason not to take these last steps. The nursing home would come soon, unless, he chose this end. Only two more feet—

A voice shattered his last preparations. "Don't."

He turned, sensing a presence. His dead wife, gone for too long, smiled at him. "Ursula."

In disbelief Charlie reached out to hug her, and his hands passed through her torso without contact. "What's happening? Is it really you?"

Her face danced between ages as her form shimmered, translucent in front of him. Young and vibrant for a moment, ecstatic, confident the next, and then wrinkled with years of love. The form kept changing in pattern-less fashion with every blink, every sentence. "You know I'm here only in your mind."

"I don't understand. I can see you, but why can I not touch you?" Maybe, he had stepped forward and crossed over. Instead of Saint Peter, maybe loved ones greeted you? Could this be the never understood spirit world? "Am I—dead, or am I mad?"

"Neither. It's not your time." She shook her head, leaving wisps of face trail behind, before adding a wink, the same as the one she gave him when she chided some lovable errant way. "My sweet, Charlie. No more silly than all your life."

She had often told him how crazy he was. A laugh or a chuckle would always follow. How he missed her gentle nature. Every day he ached at her loss, two years of loneliness. He came here often, among the tombstones, not willing to let her go. Their headstone contained DNA from his kisses. Fresh flowers, even in late autumn with the gray clouds of the day, adorned the slab below her name and the etched dates. "Why haven't you—"

"Usually, Darling, it's not possible. This is special, the only time until ..." Ursula paused and nodded at the blank final date below his name. "This is to help, to tell you that you have more to do. It is important to keep living."

"I miss you. You know I don't have long. I want to be with you." The cancer might slither its way to extinguish his flame, but the other, moving fast, would weaken him, making him little more than a body needing care. Life like that would be—not life. He wanted to decide the time, and not allow the whims of wasting disease to emasculate him.

"What good am I?" None, he believed. Not since she left. "It takes so long to walk. After I go to church, I'm worn out. Decisions take longer than ever. My aches warn me to make good on this visit. It hurt to climb up here to you."

Her haze faded in and out, but her voice remained strong. "You journey is not done. You'll see, my Dearest, you'll see." She often spoke in mysteries, and had kept him guessing, and dazzled, the whole of their forty-seven years together.

"Why can I be with you, today? I've searched every time I visited." He had heard her answer and hadn't liked the loneliness of it.

"I appreciated the flowers, the daily visits. I saw your sweet tears." Her eyes sparkled.

She settled into an age. Sixty, still radiant, still alive, but unaware of the cancer stalking her, she wore a sweater he had bought for her, showing her still seductive shape and matching her blue eyes. The young bride was still present, preserved inside by memories too wonderful to let slip away.

"I need you with me. I need us. It's empty, waiting to die." The pills had been tempting. The gun had been loaded. The rope had been tested. Something—her?—had stayed him.

"Not by your hand. That would ruin it, Love. We can't be together if you choose the time."

"Why?" He had been ready. If not for her calling out to him.

"It would be impossible. There are only a few of us here." With nods she indicated the gravesites all about them. "Most people don't show up. I think they become dust. And most suicides go somewhere—else." Her form shivered. "Everyone who stays has a powerful love, so they wait to be reunited with their forever companion. When it's true love, people wait, alive or dead."

Out of habit he had kept attending church, long after he'd stopped believing. But her presence meant something, something he'd rejected. "So, heaven is real?"

For a rare moment he saw uncertainty on her face. In life she appeared so sure and confident. He loved her for that, and for a thousand other reasons. Why did she have to die? Why couldn't they go together?

"All I can do is to tell you not to make a horrible mistake." Her gaze targeted his soul, beseeching, pleading. "Until the time is right. You can't give in. It would—end us. And that would be terrible."

He gulped, hating the thought. "How?" If being with her required him to believe, he would. If he died today, he assumed, he'd go to hell, away from her, away from happiness. All his adulthood he had questioned his childhood faith. She'd come to save him, to reveal the eternal Truth to him.

"No, you misunderstand, that's not it." Her voice weakened, and her form began to fade. She'd read his mind. Like always, she knew his thoughts before he did.

"Don't go." It had been too little time. "Stay!"

"I can't." Her form regained color, and he could see the crow's feet on her face again. "Those who loved one another can be together after death. Forever, whatever that means. But, if you commit suicide, it would …" Her eyes looked down to the rocky river below. "My wait would be for nothing."

"So, we—" More years without her, brightened only by clinging to this one brief memory.

"Yes." She paused, as her shape brightened, and then dimmed. "It is complicated. There is someone else who needs to talk with you." She turned her neck and nodded toward a small tombstone across the path. "Do you remember her?"

He gasped. Echo Wilkes had been his first love. As a teen, he had dreamed of spending their lives together after months filled with teenage angst, including long talks of her fears and frightful memories. Echo never graduated, died too young, and left him alone. Some nights he still dreamed of her, feeling disloyal to Ursula and their marriage.

"It's okay. I knew about her. And, I like her. She can tell the rest. Good-by, my love."

He sensed a kiss and his lips sought hers, but she was gone. A few feet away a cloud formed into a shape with purple, long hair, dark vibrant eyes, and a perpetual, sad smile. "Echo?"

With less substance than his wife, Echo shimmered and floated a torso without limbs. "You married a good woman."

"How can you be here? I thought suicide meant—some other place?"

"Not always." Her voice required close attention, it being nothing more than whispers carried away with the slightest breeze. "It isn't like people believe. It just is." He hair became a rainbow of colors. "I had to die—for you."

He leaned closer, and she drifted backwards.

He stepped away from the small barrier-fence to close the space between them. The movement had pained him earlier, but now his concentration on the sprite vanished the hurts. "No! What do you mean?" Fifty-eight years ago, she had jumped to her death and left him devastated, with a giant emotional hole to fill. Despite knowing of the abuse from her father, and her mother's unspoken approval of the perversion, Charlie still blamed himself, despite all the reassurances from his parents, therapists, and friends. All the love Charlie had offered had been too little to overcome a childhood filled with a nightmare life.

Yet, he never stopped believing he should have saved her.

"You tried and cared for this doomed girl so much." Her features faded, and she became a floating mist. "I did love you. But, nothing you could do would have changed what needed to happen. I had to jump." Her eyes alone took shape again in the thin cloud. They floated without the form of a head or a body.

"Why?" The pain of losing her haunted his years.

"It changed you for the better." Purple hair gave shape to the eyes-only face. "Because of my death, you learned empathy. Without your growth, you would not have become the caring man you became. You would have been colder, more selfish."

"It's my fault."

The eyes blinked. "No, it was my destiny. Your fate is that someone needs you. In your life as a social worker, you helped many. One more is coming. Live and you will see."

"Who's coming? Jesus?"

A quiver which may have been a laugh—or possibly, a convulsion—came from Echo. "No, not Jesus. A person, someone you know, requires help only you can give. The time will come, soon. Good-bye, forever. I love you." The eyes and the haze vanished, leaving him to stare at grey tombstones and grass.

Charlie shook his head and gnawed a finger. He turned to the low barrier and studied without temptation the distance between himself and the rocks. His head ached in guilt, but someone needed him, sometime, somewhere. It had to be true.

On the slow trudge down the hill the scent of Ursula and a hint of Echo's accompanied him. He did not know if fear had filled his mind, or if he had been visited. For her, and for her, and for whoever else might come, whatever the visions represented, forever-love meant not taking the last step.

First Year

Gasping and wheezing never has impressed anyone. At that moment, with many on the staff seeing my incapacitated state, my frailty became great fodder for breakroom jokes, primarily from a certain PE teacher. It relieved me the students had the day off for the staff's in-service meetings. If the teens had seen my weakness, I would have endured whispered hallway taunts and classroom giggles the rest of the year, if not longer. In that, luck had been my friend.

"You were brave."

Slumped in my seat in a small workroom, the voice surprised me. I'd assumed everyone had left, leaving me to recover in my misery. I turned and saw Gwen Veenstra's smile. We had rarely talked. Despite knowing little about one another, we first-year teachers did have a bond.

I squawked a weak reply. "Not so brave." This came around gasps for air. "It had to be done." I wheezed. "Sorry, it takes me longer to recover —more than others.

The algebra teacher stepped closer. "It's okay. Rest." She stopped a few feet away, looking intelligent with her dark-rimmed glasses, schoolmarm white blouse and blue skirt outfit.

She moved to the other side of the table and placed several stacks of papers on the top. "No one else tried. You did, and *you* saved that poor, little kitty. It looked so scared."

My face warmed. Embarrassment came easily to me in our large high school. Not knowing the tricks of the trade left me open to rookie, mistakes, and I made plenty of them. The students didn't cause nearly as much trouble as the pranksters on the teaching staff, especially Oliver

Van Deusen, nicknamed, Coach VD, an appellation he handled with grace and a glib grin.

His favorite pastime involved playing tricks on the first-years, and especially those teaching social studies, like me. To hate the subject so much he must have had a terrible history teacher when he went to high school several centuries ago.

"I would have been too frightened and couldn't have done it." She moved to the other side of the table, and her eyes sparkled behind the lenses. "It was mean of Ollie and the others, laughing after you retrieved that poor little thing from the ledge." She placed a briefcase onto a chair.

Funny, before that moment I hadn't noticed her high cheekbones or her apple-blossom scent. Frankly, the first two weeks of school I'd been a deer in headlights, trying to survive the social jungle of the teachers' lounge, paying little attention to colleagues' appearances or personalities. Most days, I ate in silence, listening to the experienced ones go on about students or the principal. Their complaints hadn't fit my image of teachers—too many whiners. It made me wonder if I fit in at all.

Being a novice ninth-grade history teacher isn't easy, because most teens don't really want to learn about the distant past. Our job is to motivate and cajole. Humor helps. Caring about the subject is vital. But the most important thing, I believe, is to convince them I care about them. Students usually say they like a subject because of the teacher. That's why when people ask me what I teach, my reply is, "I teach students." After people give me a look, I tell them the subjects I teach.

Growing up, school had been my refuge. Even before the break with my parents, the relationship with my family had been distant. Mother never wanted children, and in many ways often let me know I had been a mistake. Father saw parenting as a duty to be suffered and sought ways to make me into someone as miserable as he. Only in school did I find any nurturing, and only there did I feel free to discover how I felt about life and people. Several teachers told me I had potential, and encouraged me, believed in me.

Miss Veenstra's voice brought me back to this small paneled office with a long table and shelved books. It finally dawned on me I'd been taken to the math workroom for teachers. On the bookcase in the corner Algebra and Geometry texts dominated. She smiled at me. "Someone had to do it. I'm glad you did."

While people pointed at the frightened little feline, which at the end of the day had, somehow, not only gotten into the high school, but had scurried up onto the ledge outside of the second story library, I hurried up the stairs and, with little thought, clambered over the short barrier-wall. The outer ledge provided barely enough room for my size-eleven Reeboks. I clung to the top and crept toward the scaredy-cat at a coward's pace, moving slowly to not frighten the animal, or myself, any more than necessary.

Looking at my colleague, I fingered the life-saving inhaler in my hand, glad to breathe again. "I like cats." I moved the inhaler back to the side pocket of my khakis.

Her smile broadened. "I do, too." She shook her head, and a strand of her shoulder-length, tawny hair fell in front of her glasses. "No one else would risk it. Didn't it scare you to be out there—it couldn't have been easy to bend over on tiptoes with so little room to move?" She nudged the wayward hair back in place, before giving a little shiver.

Fingering the scratches on my hand, complements of the desperate feline, I shrugged. "Getting back challenged me more." The kitten had clung to my chest, digging its razor-like digits through my shirt, leaving little holes in the fabric and pinpricks on my skin, which still burned. Proud to have resisted the urge to wrench the hissing stray away and toss it to the floor twenty feet below, I had kept my balance, if not my breath. The minute someone pulled the animal from me, others helped me over the barrier, and then I began wheezing.

From below Coach—who stood unmoving from the beginning of the incident, other than to suggest the cat should come down the same way it got there—started cackling about how wimpy I looked. He waved a hand in dismissal and walked away. No one challenged his taunt, but several colleagues helped me to a chair in a nearby office.

After using the inhaler, I had thanked those who had watched my collapse and then rest in this little room as they left.

Standing across the table, Gwen smiled and reached out to pat my arm resting on the table.

For the first time, I noticed the Star of David on a gold chain hanging on her neck. Without thinking, a question escaped, unable to be recalled as my brain censor woke. "Are you a *Jew?*" As the words emerged, I cringed at being so forward.

Her hand pulled back, and the warmth from her touch disappeared, not noticed until it went. "What? Ah." She fingered the symbol. "I'm not practicing." Her words froze in the air between us. "It's a gift from my father. The last thing he gave me."

I stood, feeling foolish. "I'm sorry. It was rude to ask after you've been so nice." The apology sounded lame. I bit my lower lip. "Appreciate your staying. No one else did." With no real friends on the staff, it felt good to have someone pay attention.

"Well, it *is* the math office, and I wanted to do some work." Her smile replaced by a frown.

It occurred to me that she had stayed, not to comfort, but to do her corrections. "Oh, yes, I should go." My face felt warm, the urge to leave and hide raced through my mind. "Just didn't know your background. Didn't mean anything by it."

Miss Veenstra settled into a chair in front of a stack of papers. Picking up a pen and the top paper, she started checking math problems. Her voice barely audible in apparent distaste. "I'm used to it."

From studying history, even in the superficial way of an interdisciplinary social science major, I knew all about the depth and vitriolic prejudices against Jewish people. It surprised me that her behavior suggested she still felt the sting of it in the twenty-first century. That nonsense should be behind us.

As I stood, my brain searched for and considered several more appropriate apologies. None would override my mistake. She'd been offended, quickly, but rightly so. Maybe, I wondered, compliments might work. "That is a *pretty* necklace. He—your dad—has good taste."

She looked up for a moment with her voice devoid of any softness. "Thank you." Her focus returned to marking her student's work.

A lump rose in my throat, and I felt ready to bolt for the safety of my Corolla waiting in the parking lot. In the driver's seat, every morning I gave myself a pep talk, beseeching the good Protestant God to help me make it through another day without doing something stupid, or getting fired. Every night I thanked the Divine for one more day despite all my fears and insecurities. So far, despite my backslid faith, I'd survived. "I'm a non-attending, former Episcopalian."

"So, you're *rich*?" Her voice mimicked mine from before. Her eyes fixed on the quiz she corrected. "Another C+." She rubbed her eyes, looking disgusted. "They don't try."

I clutched onto the comment, hoping to reconnect. "It makes me crazy. So early in the year, and some tuned out before the leaves turned color." According to veteran teachers, the gap between the goal-oriented achievers and the attending-because-I-have-to students had grown over the years. "And, not rich. Could be, but disowned."

Her pen stopped moving, and her head tilted to the side making her hair slide in front of a cheek. "What did you do? Must have been bad. Insult *their* heritage?" Despite the harshness of the comment, I detected a hint of interest. She wanted to know something of my life.

"Argued with them. About religion, life style, politics. I voted for Obama. Twice." I saw her nod in approval. "To my parents, I had committed a cardinal sin. We fought about it, and they sent me packing." It had been more than that. Wanting to study education and counseling dismayed them. They had majored in business and thought I should follow their footsteps, and not take some "menial service job."

"I'm sorry." She sounded sincere, and her smile returned. "I guess I was rude, too." Her head righted, and the hair fell into place. "You voted in two elections? You must be older than I thought."

"Twenty-eight. I worked full-time all through college. Took classes in the evenings and on weekends. School took extra years." With a hand on the back of a chair, I asked if I could sit.

She nodded. "You okay?"

I pulled out a chair and sat across from her. "Yes, other than being embarrassed from—" I waved a hand out to the hallway. "And from offending you. I was rude." Feeling the need to talk with someone, I hoped she'd listen, or at least, pretend to converse. The school had assigned a mentor-teacher, but he ignored me, and I needed someone to hear me vent about how my days went.

She shrugged, a visual acceptance of my latest apology. "I voted for him, too." She leaned back in her chair and looked directly at me. "Are you still woozy? It bothered me to see you struggle like that."

I chuckled, glad that I could. "Me too. After rest and quiet, I recover from my 'episodes.' Don't always have to use an inhaler, though I have one." Patting it my pocket, I felt reassured touching it. "Happens rarely. The way the year has started, it could incapacitate me. I love the kids, but all the other stuff gets me down."

She pulled her glasses off and set them next to the stack of papers. Her skin glistened. "The bureaucratic nonsense bothers *me*, too. It gets in the way of working with the students." With a sigh she closed her eyes for a moment. "My sixth hour is my only rowdy class. They're squirrely and so ready to go home." She looked tired, something I experienced as commonplace for any dedicated teacher. "Education classes didn't get me ready for all the nonsense paperwork and the bureaucratic BS. That wears on me."

"I know." She shared my concerns. It pleased me that a pretty "she" had something in common with me. "Teachers needed to be there for the kids, not be burdened with documentation no one ever reads. That crap upsets me. How do you deal with it all?"

She fingered a dangling hoop earring and breathed deep. "I call Mom daily. She calms me down." Her eyes opened wide, and she raised a palm to cover her mouth. "I'm sorry. You and your—"

"No problem. All the conflict left me numb." I smiled and nodded, trying to convince myself more than her. My parents disapproved of my first, my only, girlfriend, because she encouraged me. She grew up on a farm with parents who had only graduated from high school and, most importantly, she grew up Catholic. Resenting their arrogant prejudice and sense of superiority, I argued with them so often it finally resulted in harsh, impossible ultimatums. Being cut-off meant taking eight years for college instead of four, but I persevered, and did it on my own with a little help from a small scholarship. "I haven't talked to my folks since before I graduated." I was too stubborn to make the first call. They'd probably hang up, anyway. "It's good you have a close relationship with your mom. That's the way things should be."

"She helps me every time." She put her glasses back on, returning the librarian look.

Hoping to prolong the conversation, and to avoid counter-questions, I launched a series of my own. "Anything other than Mom? Books, music, games? Pets? Long drives to nowhere to cleanse the soul? Walking a dog? Recreational drugs?" I winked.

She laughed and offered a feigned finger wag of disapproval. Even though we were alone in the room, both of us knew—should know—better than to talk about certain things in school. "Whatever's legal." Her eyes twinkled. "I have two cats, Isosceles and Archimedes."

"Ever the mathematician. Good names." I liked her choices, demonstrating a thinker. "I can't have one, in my apartment. That kitten was cute. Where is …?" I winced, wondering what had become of the little one. The scratches ached.

"The social worker took it. She lives in a big house and has lots of room and a big yard."

"I'm glad." The kitten should be well taken care of. "I read quite a bit: history, biographies, fiction. You?"

She looked at the stack of papers and shook her head. I took that as a sign she was willing to talk. "My preference is for fiction, but the last few years, I don't have time. I used to be a girl with her nose in a book all the time." She sighed. "Now, I don't have much opportunity for anything other student's work or my lesson planner. How about you?"

"After I got my degree, I went into a reading frenzy. A boring way to party, but I liked it." Her beam reminded me of sunshine. Sounds strange, but it's how I remembered feeling with a steady girlfriend. Why'd I let her go? Wanting to forget, the memory replayed. She got a job in Connecticut and wanted me to move there with her. My hesitation doomed us. She could tell security meant more to me than she did. At that time, it did.

Gwen pursed her lips and tilted her head. "I think it's a wonderful way to celebrate." Her face brightened. "Heaven is long, lazy baths with a book and the kitties purring nearby, playing with the bubbles and watching the candlelight flicker. I only get to do it about twice a year, but it happens."

The idea of her stepping out of the water into a warm white towel danced in my head. "Sounds perfect." I gulped. My natural shyness did not lead to easy flirtation. But opportunities like this did not come often. "I like walking in the rain. Quiet summer rains, not downpours."

She murmured agreement.

I paused, wondering if my words sounded hackneyed. "I love swimming, walking along the shoreline, especially at Amen Point."

She laughed. "Is the place real? Sounds unbelievable."

"You haven't been there?" When she shook her head, I went on. "It's great. I've been there several times." I'd spent time researching the history of the place. "Oh, yeah. Immigrants mistakenly landed here in Forest County, believing they'd arrived at the Leelanau Peninsula, and they thanked God by calling the place, Amen." Coming to a New World had to be confusing, and not knowing the layout of the area left them at the drunken skipper's mercy. "Their fraudulent sea captain got away before they discovered the truth. It's a pretty spot, overlooking the Bay." A thought, a bold one for my personality, interrupted, and my mouth cooperated quicker than usual. "Would you like to see it? Maybe after dinner?" I fingered my inhaler, hoping I wouldn't need it. What if she said no?

She looked stunned, her mouth opened and closed, and her eyes disappeared behind their lids.

I had strayed too far, too fast, not listening to my instinctual shyness. My heart beat faster, my mouth dried, and a knee trembled. This question should have come much later, if ever, after several chats, and not in the shadow of my hyper-ventilating fiasco. I dreaded her answer, and prepared an excuse as to why it wouldn't work for me either.

When she opened her eyes, she shook her head. "I can't, tonight. I have these plans."

Appearing nonchalant is never easy, and my face undoubtedly betrayed my weak attempt. Her eyes suggested sympathy. Just what I needed, another person to feel sorry for the guy who can't breathe right.

"Several of us are going to this party at this restaurant, Champps." I had heard nothing about a party. Then she hit me with the worst. "Ollie invited us."

"Coach VD?" He had to be twelve years older than Gwen. The leech undoubtedly lusted after her, as he did with every attractive woman on the staff. I knew he ignored anyone not fitting a certain profile, having heard the librarian, a woman of hefty proportions, complain about his ogling the pretty teachers. The thought of him pawing at Gwen made me want to punch him, before mashing his face into the concrete.

"Yeah, he's a pig. But to shut him up, I agreed." She wrinkled her nose. "We won't stay long, just enough to get him to stop asking."

"Have fun." I hoped she meant what she said. "Be careful with him."

"That's why Janie and Alice are going with me." She held out three fingers. "There's safety in numbers."

Feeling defeated, inside, I sagged. "Better get going, let you get your work done, before your *party*." I stood and turned toward the door as she picked up her pen and nodded at me.

"Wait, I want to give you something." She suddenly stood beside me at the exit to the hall. Without another word, she placed a small note into my hand, before returning to her chair.

Before starting her work, I thought I saw a wink. Looking at the piece of paper, I read a phone number and words which almost made me reach for my inhaler. "I'm free next weekend. Call me. Gwen."

The Encounters

The Fan

Losing sucks. Getting blown out and embarrassed in front of a big, raucous crowd *really* sucks. Even only getting into the game for a minute at the end, the rout dispirited me more than any other loss. The look on coach's and the parents' faces drove the dagger of defeat deeper into each of us. Worse, we knew even our best players could not stick with the other team. The most crushing thought of all was we lost to a rich-kid preppy school. And, when we scrubs finally got to play, down by thirty points and with only 60 seconds left, we got schooled against their third-stringers. Dang. Not even a thousand showers would ever wash away the stink from our futility.

On the walk to the bus, family and a few fans called out support and appreciation for our efforts. It didn't help. Nothing could. We boarded Yellow Number Three—used to be a lucky number for me—with our tails tucked low, our confidence shattered.

My folks didn't make the trip to East Lansing. Less than two hours away, but as Dad often quipped, "Keeler never plays, anyway. No need to spend six hours to watch him keep the bench polished." We sat on chairs, not a damn bench! In truth they rarely came to any of the games, seeing no reason to watch cobwebs form between my sneakers and the court.

Being the last to board, I turned to face Breslin Arena one more time. For a few moments, I had played on the court Tom Izzo's teams made famous. Champions played there. Our coach told us it would be an experience we'd never forget. Years from now, he claimed, we'll think about being here and not the result. I hoped so.

That's when the artist walked up to me. Short and slightly chubby, the girl always wished me luck before games, and made some positive comment afterwards. The others say she has a crush on me. Maybe, but Jocelyn still ruled my heart. It killed me when my girlfriend, the star of my fantasies, dumped me and declared she liked the damn trombone player more than me. His being tall, good looking, and talented evidently drew her away from my average height, modest appearance, and less than star-level athleticism. I hoped she'd realize her mistake and come running back, but deep down knew the impossibility of that scenario. She had made my heart beat faster, but I always believed she seemed less committed to the idea of *us* than I did.

It took a lot of gumption to ask Jocelyn out the first time. When she said yes, I thought life finally made sense. I'd wanted her since freshman year, but always believed her to be out of my reach. That's one of the major reasons I played sports: to get her to notice me. At our small school, the teams needed bodies, and jocks attract girls easier than smart, theater guys like I am. It worked, too, even if I mostly sat on the bench. She liked wearing my Varsity jacket.

Anyway, this artist—I remembered her name was Sparrow, a strange name which fits her—walked up to the bus and handed me a large envelope. She smiled and murmured a compliment about how well I played. Then she hurried back to her dad's Buick. The two of them attended every game—home, away, or neutral court. Her old man starred on our varsity years ago, and, I think, he never got past being a high school hero. It's sad when someone's best days were in high school.

When Sparrow reached the vehicle's door, she swiveled and gave a silly little wave when she saw me still staring after her. Calling out thanks, I hurriedly stuffed the six-by-nine manila into my bag—hoping the other guys hadn't noticed—and climbed onto the yellow mourning chamber.

Choosing the seat across from Miguel, I watched Sparrow get into the passenger seat of the Rivera. My friend chuckled. "You got a groupie." Miguel, one of my buddies and our best player, had several female fans who gathered around him after every game. He's only five-nine, an inch shorter than me, but he has a bright smile and eyes that focus on every girl he's interested in. Jocelyn flirted with him even when we dated. It made me crazy.

The Encounters

I never held it against Miguel. His charm affected all his teammates, too. People said he had charisma. He did.

We became friends in kindergarten and stayed pals ever since. With his scholarship to Ohio Center College next year, and me going to our local community college, we'll not see much of each other after graduation.

"That Sparrow's into you. My man, you should check her out." Miguel had the problem of deciding which girl to pick as his date of the month. With his looks and personality every girl in school hoped he'd ask her out, but he had interest only in the popular, best-looking ones, and none in Sparrow.

"I don't know. She's a little overweight." Not like Jocelyn, who had shapely curves and no sign of flab. Sparrow could stand to lose a few pounds. "Kinda hoping Jocelyn will tire of the damn horn-blower."

"She's done with you, man. Get over it." He leaned back in the seat. "Besides, she's too white-girl for me. I'd want more salsa and less mayonnaise."

Doubting anyone else as good-looking as Jocelyn would ever be interested in someone like me, I shrugged. I liked blonde and curvy. When she and I went out, I walked a little taller, and believed more in possibilities. Life without her became less bright, less interesting.

"Give it up, man." He shook his head, but his voice laughed. "She's uptown; you're country."

"I hate that music, dumb twangy bull—"

"Not Garth Brooks country. Farm boy country." Miguel tugged on an ear lobe. "She wants sports cars and flash, not pick-up trucks and dirt under the nails."

"I shower every day." I glanced at my nails. They looked ragged but clean.

"Look at the friends she hangs with at school. She could fit right in with those rich Academy jocks we played tonight. She wants a guy with money, a good dresser." He shook his head. "You think wearing a tee-shirt and clean jeans is dressing up."

He had me there. Jocelyn had changed over the last year and left me far behind. Miguel understood. Sincerity and intellect didn't matter to someone like Jocelyn, flash did. Despite that, still, I maintained hope she might come back.

Miguel shook his head. "Now, with Sparrow, you'd have the upper hand. She's into you, so you'd call the shots. Not many girls will give you that kind of power. If I was you ..." His dancing eyebrows and chuckle suggested my virgin days could come to end.

Fortunately, he didn't verbalize the rest. He knew the truth. I'd never gotten Jocelyn into bed. I wanted to, and a lot of people assumed I had. But to please her, we decided to wait until after graduation. Then she decided to date music-man. Damn.

A bunch of guys in the last row asked if anyone wanted to play Euchre. Miguel jumped at the chance.

Not interested, I wanted time to think, *and* to look inside the envelope. I didn't want their prying eyes checking it out. With no idea what it might be—probably something to mortify the hell out of me—the coward inside suggested keeping it secret. No sense in letting others see if she'd given me something stupid, or sugary. I waited until the card game got intense, and the teammates closest to me started snoring. I carefully pulled it out of my bag, and gave another look around to make sure no one paid any attention.

I turned on my cell's flashlight and looked at the outside of the envelope. Clear, smooth letters spelled out my name. Keeler Hughes. No hearts or flowers. A good sign that it wouldn't be too embarrassing. Miguel would never let me forget if Sparrow gave me something mushy and super-sweet.

The team kidded one another endlessly. Scoring points mattered more in the locker room than on the court, the more cutting the better. Miguel often did the best in getting someone to turn red. He'd have a field-day if Sparrow gave me anything for him to pester me with for the rest of all time. But Miguel, as usual, ruled in the card game, chattering and bragging—but all in his pleasant how-could-anyone-hate-me mode. Charm oozed from him. Wish he'd pass some on to me.

Getting notes from girls was something with which I had little experience. In fifth grade, Kellianne Morning tossed a tightly folded sheet under my desk. When I opened it, I saw her message, "I like you. You're smart." The words had little flowers drawn around them.

I assumed she only wanted help with her homework. She did and got an "A" on the project we worked on together. I treasured those minutes, spending time with her.

But being too shy to talk about anything other than the assignment, I never asked her to walk her home or go to the movies. Two years later she started dating Lars Jensen, the tallest kid in class, and never gave me another look.

For the second time a girl has given me a handwritten message. Knowing Sparrow as little as I did, I expected it to be some florid sentences telling me how much she liked watching the team, and to not take the loss too hard. Or maybe, she wanted to ask me out, or have a study date. We were in the same econ class, and both of us were in the honor society. Despite that, we've never had a real conversation. Just mumbled exchanges before or after classes or games.

She didn't turn heads, despite having an almost pretty face when she smiled. With an attractive shape, despite the extra pounds, she didn't look gross, and wasn't really fat. Most guys would say she dressed well and looked good in tight jeans. At least, no hair grew in weird places on her face, not like that Kenna Bennings, who in math chomped on gum all hour making her long facial fuzz dance. Yuck! No disgusting habits like Melba Kolter, who snorted instead of talked and cackled instead of laughed. Brrr.

Sparrow wasn't odd, only ordinary. A smart, quiet person who didn't stand out—other than in art class. The staff acclaimed her the best artist in school. Other than that, she appeared to be the epitome of an average high school girl. Usually, except after a game, she kept to herself.

In many ways that's how I acted. Never the center of attention, but a very good student, a mediocre varsity athlete, a supporting actor in our theater productions, and basically a guy who tried to treat other people with kindness and understanding. I don't look bad either, and I hoped my negative habits, chewing my fingernails and not flossing, were innocent and not repulsive.

Looking inside—both myself *and* the envelope—made me nervous. What if she had included something strange like a lock of her hair, or a big heart with our initials drawn on it. Or, a pornographic note with suggestions of doing things even Miguel's active imagination hadn't described. Part of me liked the thought.

With another glance around to confirm no one watched, I pulled out the contents: two sheets of paper. The larger, eight by eleven, appeared to be an intricate colored pencil drawing.

My eyes, my chin, my hair—she had drawn a portrait of me.

Focusing the intense light from my cell onto the picture, something about the image struck me. The person she had drawn had all my features, but had been imbued with a brightness, an attractiveness I never felt. It looked like I wanted to look: confident, sure, even happy.

The eyes shimmered and sparkled. Did I look like that? Did she see me this way? Could I be the individual that stared up at me? I wanted to be that person.

The hair looked so real. As I touched—caressed—her version of my face, I saw even the hint of stubble on the chin, a stray lock—the one I could never get to stay in place—and the crook in my nose all drawn with realism and care. It proved she really liked me, or at least my face.

In the lower-right corner of the sheet, I saw her signature. Not words, but a drawing of a bird in flight. A sparrow, no doubt. It soared upward, as if heading toward the center of the picture—toward me. When I saw that, I shivered, happy she drew it that way.

After staring at—and thinking about—her work for a long time, so long I didn't realize we had pulled into the school parking lot, I carefully inserted the image back into its manila cover, placed it inside my bag. It was then that I remembered there had also been a smaller sheet in the enclosure. I fumbled about, not finding it for a moment, before finally spotting it on the floor.

Reaching for it I heard Miguel yawn. With the card game finished he had returned to the seat across from me. "Lose something?" He pointed at the paper I held in my hand. "You should have played. Lars is a lousy partner, but we still won. I went it alone the last two hands to pull out the last game. The cards were kind." Not waiting for a reply, he put on his coat and picked up his bag.

I glanced at the paper. With a quick flash of light from my phone, I saw what she had written. A phone number and another sparrow, this one with its head cocked, looking straight forward. In my imagination, it winked at me. Putting the slip of paper into a pocket, I sighed.

Tomorrow, a Saturday, I anticipated would be busy, making a phone call, and then, hopefully, if the first call went well, another to make reservations at the Bay View Restaurant. Most of all, I'd work to become the man she had seen inside of me.

Old Woman

I couldn't believe I'd listened to her for more than a minute. But, I did. She had the look of a street person: bedraggled, emaciated, and with stringy hair. Due to her appearance, I leaned away when she approached. My instinct told me to hurry by vagrants like her, yet, something in the timbre of her voice stopped me as she neared.

Her words penetrated the walled defenses of my brain. On the warm, mid-summer afternoon, I turned to her, uncertain of why, but needing to look at this woman whose tone I could not ignore.

She repeated her simple sentence. "I've been waiting to talk to you."

"What?" She undoubtedly wanted money, but I decided to hear her out. In my solitary life, conversations, even with strange street-people, break the monotony of my social non-life. Unmarried, no children and no close friends, my situation often made me long for companionship. But after a couple decades without a partner, I'm resigned to living a quiet life with only my art to keep me going.

Shaking her head, she kept focused on my face. "You aren't deaf, are you? I need you to hear me." Her pupils appeared to be deep blue arrow tips. "Congratulations on your promotion. That's why I'm here."

I knew she lived in bizarre-world. I needed no promotions. As an artist, I worked for myself, and didn't have to worry about pleasing any bosses to earn their approval. Lucky to have received a small inheritance, I could live—if I budgeted—without worrying about brown-nosing idiots.

With a shake of her head, she frowned. "That's surprising. No one has told you. Come with me." She turned and walked to a bus-stop bench along the sidewalk. For reasons beyond my understanding, I followed, barely hearing her mutter about those "not doing their jobs."

Sitting next to her, I noticed she looked younger than the eighty or so I'd guessed a moment before. With no crow's feet or wrinkles—dirt smudges had fooled me—she had a face that might have been attractive if she took the time to bathe. She had a distinctive odor of coffee and flour. Did she work in a bakery?

She crossed her legs, displaying an ankle beneath a long skirt. Her sandals had traveled far, and I remember asking myself, "How do feet look tired? Hers do." Turning sideways I stared at her. "Who are you? Why should I listen?"

"Because, you must." She scratched her nose with gnawed, unpolished fingernails. "No one told you, so I will." Leaning back, she closed her eyes. "You really have no idea what I'm talking about?"

I shuddered. How stupid to talk with a crazy person! But, instead of bolting, I found myself riveted there, as if she had some command over my body. Mixed feeling poured through me. Wanting to run, curious to listen, questioning sanity. Make something of this, I thought. Maybe, use her as the model of a homeless hobo. It might sell.

"It won't sell. No one cares what I look like."

"How the hell did you know that?" The world looked fuzzy and sounded out of tune.

She inhaled and exhaled as if smoking an invisible cigarette. Even closing her eyes on the extended intake, she held her fingers around the non-existent tobacco stick.

The motion unnerved me. Having quit long ago, I could smell the smoke, feel it caress its way down past my throat to tickle my lungs. I wanted one.

"Don't start again. It will kill you." Her eyes sparkled and burned into me. "You would have ignored me if I hadn't stopped you."

Wanting to bark a reply, my words mellowed once released. "What do you want with me? And what do you mean, stopped me?"

Irritation rose and fell at wasting time with her. Daylight hours spent with this mystery woman kept me from working on whatever I'd do next. That worried me. Ideas had been scarce, and I hadn't done anything worthwhile in weeks. Nothing since the series of old barns for the Dairy Company. I like landscapes, farms, sunsets.

My most lucrative commissions are from rich people wanting to be immortalized, or from companies wanting to create a natural aura for their products. Not in desperate need of money meant low motivation, but this dry spell exceeded previous ones. I hungered to create but had found nothing to inspire me.

She held the invisible cigarette in her hand, bringing it to her lips every few moments. Visible smoke escaped her mouth. What I saw couldn't be real. It had to be lack of sleep, and the dearth of new projects. "Seek and you will find. Subjects are all around you. Can't you see? No, because, you act deaf and blind. Listen, look, feel, accept. It will come."

"I need to go. I want—" My legs froze. "What's happening? Have you cast a spell on me?" My voice could move, and the tones jumped from fear to anger and back again. "Let me go!"

"Understanding will set you free." She paused to suck on the air-fag. "As your mentor, there is much to teach you. Today, we'll cover the basics. From then on, it'll be on-the-job-training, with little lessons whenever you truly need to hear my voice. While it won't be easy, you'll learn." With an awkward attempt, she failed to snap her fingers. "I'll be with you—in your head—when you really don't know what to do, which will be less often than you'll think. Panic is normal, but you'll handle it."

My pulse pounded in my wrist, chest, and ankles. "You talk gibberish. What do you want?"

Feeling frantic compared to her composure, I hoped this to be no more than a bad dream. With any luck, I'd wake and forget all about it. As in most nighttime imaginings, the rest of the world had disappeared, leaving me glued in place waiting for her to explain this nonsense.

"Choices decide who we become, and what we achieve." She nodded, her eyes closed as if asleep. But her voice filled my ears and echoed to my core. "Yours have called me here. Congratulations. Thank you."

After so many minutes of nothing making sense—whether from the conviction my imagination ran free, or from the hypnotic tone of her voice—curiosity survived and overcame the anger. Memories of long-ago positive, drug-enhanced hallucinations relaxed me. "What choices? Why can't I move? I don't understand."

Her eyes sprung open, the blue points focused on the invisible smoke. She put the used cig out, grinding it on the slats of the bench, and brushing away ashes not there.

Nicotine-stained fingers reached toward me, and I did not flinch. She ran her hand over my upper arm, a mother reassuring a panicked child. It worked. "You are kind. I have watched and seen. You care. There are many you have helped. It is good."

"What's this all about?" Throughout life, the hurt and the damaged have gained my empathy. Doing what I can, I donate to charity, offer a helping hand whenever possible, and avoid judging people, not knowing the journey they have traveled. This woman might be an exception. She struck me as nuts.

"You rescued a robin, do you remember? Others left it, but you tended to it, and it recovered." Her hands waved in avian flight.

"Felt bad for it." The bird had been lying along the side of the road too long ago to remember the year or even time of day. It must have been spring, because I'd been hiking in the woods. Since my twenties I try to walk five miles a day. On the day she stopped me, I had two more to go. The exercise kept me toned and let me think while enjoying the beauty of nature. I stayed away from cars but had come to the spot to cross the river at a bridge. That's when I saw the robin.

"Janice lived because of you." The words came from all around me, not from her mouth only two feet away.

Janice is a professor at Oregon, but thirty years ago lived in my dorm back at State. Not a pretty girl—she had protruding teeth and a big nose—I liked her intelligence and enthusiasm about learning. We dated a few times, before cancer forced her to interrupt her schooling. Never intending to see her again, I bumped into her one day at a pharmacy. Chatting with her I quietly slipped the condoms back onto the shelf. When she broke down, I decided to walk her home.

In shock at her diagnosis, she told me she'd become depressed, even suicidal. Not knowing what to do, I urged her to never give up, and to keep looking forward. She thanked me and talked about moving to the Pacific coast to see an old boyfriend. I encouraged her. The day before she moved, we made love. Not long after arriving in Portland, she got married and had twin daughters. We talk every few months, even though we haven't seen each other since she left River Forest. I didn't even fly out to see her after her husband died two months ago. I feel bad about that. Having survived cancer, thoughts of overdosing, and years later, losing her spouse, I know she's a strong person. As a pal, I liked her.

"Didn't do anything special." Part of me regrets not going out west to visit the only long-term woman friend I've had. I envy her because she has those two beautiful girls. Seeing their pictures makes me long to have had children—like hers—but I never met anyone to share a life with. Without a real family, life often feels empty.

The old woman broke my reverie with a hacking cough. "You listened. You cared, and your attention saved her. She will always be grateful." The woman nodded as if hammering the point home. "Clara treasures you. So, does Frank."

Witchcraft. She had to be using black magic. I bit the inside of my cheek. "How do you know about them?"

Twice a week I visited the convalescent center where my Uncle lived before he died. Two of the other residents became special to me. Clara even knitted a hat and mittens for me—ones I never wear.

Frank tells stories of the farm in the forties, and of fighting in Korea. His tales make the past come alive. Whenever, I can't visit, I miss them. Of all my acquaintances, I'm closest to them, two septuagenarians in wheelchairs.

"It is a talent, and you are easy to read." She patted my thigh, as though I were a six-year old being praised by grandmother. "There are other examples I have seen, but time is short." Using a well-worn handkerchief, she paused to blow her nose. "Based on a lifetime of kindness and generosity, you have been rewarded. Congratulations."

"How? What? I don't understand." Despite my questions, a sense of contentment had settled over me listening to her speak. Whether crazy or not, she held my attention.

"You've been made an angel. Welcome to TAC, the Terrestrial Angel Corps." Her face brightened, and the arrow tips of her eyes shone with such brightness it made me blink.

I laughed. "Huh? TAC? An angel! You're insane!"

As an atheist I had no patience with such religious gibberish. A backslid Lutheran, I rejected the superstitious dogma of the faithful. The idea of me being an angel—even the idea of the existence of angels—was ludicrous. Still, despite my rejection of her insane talk, a feeling of peace settled over me and challenged my thoughts.

A cloud enveloped us, and all about I saw only mist. In the center of which this strange woman sparkled with energy.

"It doesn't matter what you believe. Your lack of faith is no detriment. Angels come from every faith, or from none. You are now one. Nothing you do will change the fact." Her tone and smile told me she saw a different reality than I did. "There are good angels and bad ones. Christian, Hindu, Buddhist, Muslim, Shinto, Druid, and others. Even Wiccans. You are not the first atheist."

I rolled my eyes. Clearly, she had escaped from bedlam. "And you're an angel, I suppose?"

She nodded, but a touch of doubt crept into her eyes. "You don't know, do you, Martin? I am Michaelina, a long-time angel, almost forty years now. And, no, I am not an escapee from a looney bin."

I laughed. "Where are your wings, your halo? You don't look like one of God's servants." This had to end. She needed a padded cell.

Her hand waved in front of me and I stood on a small rock floating in an expanding universe. Michaelina glided, with no wings, flying of her own accord. She pointed at the vastness before us, and I saw the beauty of the cosmos.

"Angels are mortal, no feathers, no crowns. Beings of earth. They have missions. Some succeed, some fail. A few become evil. Most do not. You are meant to help others."

Still inside of the fantasy, I launched myself from the rock, floated, propelled along next to her. Nothing made sense, and everything did. In my hands a brush appeared and alongside me a pallet filled with favorite hues. While moving I started dabbing the bristles into the colors, and then painted all I saw onto a canvas which had materialized in front of me, creating beauty as I never had before.

Her voice returned me to the bench. "You will make others see the glory of living. With your art, your life, your example. It is your purpose, and why you live, to spread the truth of being." Her eyes laughed, and she leaned back on the bench. "I have chosen well."

Objections funneled their way to the tongue. "But there is no God. Thus, there can be no angels."

"You are wrong. God or not, you are replacing me. My time has come. You are now an Angel, Martin."

To escape the surreal dream, I pinched my arm. The spot hurt and turned red. Could this be hell, stuck with a crazy woman spouting nonsense?

She snapped her fingers, this time successfully, and the cloud surrounding us dissipated. The street traffic stood still in front of our eyes. A robin hung suspended in mid-flight. A squirrel leaped toward a tree, extending in mid-movement frozen front paws stretching to reach the safety of an oak.

With a shake of my head I tried to clear my brain. I must be dreaming, but it felt real. "What's happening?" All remained still.

"We have a few unique talents. My abilities are different than yours. I can enter minds, redirect them, and plant seeds. With effort, and a major expense of energy, some of us can change time, as I have. But it drains me. I am weary."

"Let it go. You look tired." I worried about her. And about my sanity. Had she hypnotized me? It had to be. Time could not stop.

"Not stopped. Life moves forward. Our entities have sped up to a point where all else seems motionless." Michaelina looked smaller than she had, older. Her voice sounded weaker, lower, sadder. "A few more words, and then back to a normal pace.

"There are three things you need to know. One, is you are mortal. Angels live a little longer than ordinary humans. You, I can tell you, have a long time to go." She didn't grace me with a number.

"Two, you can read people. You see people as they are, especially those who hide their true selves." She sighed and lit a second non-cigarette. "This talent helps your art—you can paint the reality you perceive beneath the exterior. Be careful. Many do not want the truth."

She puffed on air. "All of us can change the speed of our movements. But, all has a cost and lessens life, as my demonstration has shortened my stay on earth." She took time, holding the non-smoke in her lungs.

"Your greatest individual skill, which exceeds my ability, is you can heal and comfort people. You are an empath, taking the pain of others onto yourself, relieving them." She flicked unseen ashes onto the ground. "Limit the times you do this, or you will become too weak to continue. If you take care, you might make it to a hundred, giving strength to the weariest until then."

"How old are you?" Of all the questions to ask, why did that one emerge? I wanted to know what had to be done, if I had to travel, seek out the dejected? Could I continue with art? Instead, a foolish inquiry of her age escaped.

"Nothing is expected other than to be who you are. They will come, wherever you are. Your instincts are good, follow them." She sucked again on her cancer-less stick. "Seventy-two. Should have made it to eight-six, but people needed me. Thankfully, I can't get pregnant any more. Never could say no. You will need to learn your limits."

"You have children?" A thought emerged. "Are they—"

She stood, dropped the last of the cigarettes to the floor and stepped on it. "They avoid their crazy old mother. Better luck with yours."

"I don't have any." Wouldn't either—the cure for my prostate cancer had guaranteed that. "You're—"

She held up a hand, and my words stopped. "Get to know them. They will believe. Some children inherit the skills. Yours have."

"What?" Her insanity still shocked me. Until this point she had been uncanny with her comments about my life and thinking.

"You'll see." Her confident smile almost convinced me she could be normal. "When necessary, which will be less than you think, my spirit will return. But you are on the right track, as prepared as anyone."

Before I could reply, she clapped her hands. My eyes blinked, and she vanished. The traffic moved, the squirrel landed on the tree trunk, and the robin continued its flight. Shaking my head, I wondered how such a strange dream could happen while sitting on a bench along a busy street. For a moment I stared at the sidewalk, watching a piece of a sandwich wrapper scuttle along in the wind toward the gutter. As it reached the curb a gust picked it up and sent it floating above the street. I stood, hoping to follow its flight, but it disappeared above the trees.

On the walk home, several ideas for new paintings came to mind, including the old lady's portrait, and another about a scrap of paper soaring above a flock of robins overlooking the city.

#

Two days later the phone rang. With a frown I put down the brush and cleaned my hands before picking up the receiver. My answer sounded more like a bark than a hello.

"Martin, are you okay?" Her voice wiped away the grumpiness at being interrupted.

"Janice! Good to hear from you."

"You sound upset." Her voice had a tremor to it I found unnerving. Always sounding knowledgeable and assured, uncertainty did not fit her.

"Nothing. Just, excited to be getting into the flow of my art again. How about you?' I should have been the one to call her. "And, I am so sorry for your loss. It has to be hard."

She hesitated, which added to my sense of concern. "I'm fine."

"I hope you'll visit soon. It'd be good for you to get away." For years she had promised to return for a vacation. Like my trips west, it had never happened.

"I will." She cleared her throat. "Are you sitting down?"

Her words heightened my worry. I dropped into a chair. "Yes. What's up?" Scenes of disasters flooded my brain. I feared terrible news about her well-being, or her family's. Had cancer returned? Had she been fired? Had her husband cheated? Were her daughters ill or injured?

"Martin, I need to tell you something about the twins. You remember them?"

"Of course. Are Tricia and Teresa okay?" While never having met them she had sent pictures of them through the years. I felt like I did know them. "Did they get hurt? Is it one of them pregnant?" Visions of horrible accidents and mangled bodies coursed through my consciousness.

Her long pause worried me, but before I repeated the question she answered. "I should have told you this years ago but didn't want to upset my husband. But, now with him passed, I can tell you."

My thoughts jumbled. What could it be? Had he abused them? Did one of them have a terrible disease? Were they in some sort of financial trouble? "Janice, tell me. What are you talking about?"

"I hid the truth from him, From you. From Tricia and Teresa." She faltered, and I feared she might disconnect.

"Tell me!"

Her voice trembled. "They're fine. *Your* daughters, the twins, are both fine."

Aisle Encounter

The arm brushing past broke his concentration. Sitting on the carpeted floor of the store's history section, he hadn't sensed someone peering over his shoulder at the bookshelves. Her fragrance—a vaguely familiar, floral scent—escaped his notice until the arm passed close to his nostrils, and then reminded him of college days. The lack of awareness, he thought, proved more evidence of his aging.

Gustavus Adolphus Rundstrom—Tav to everyone who knew him—didn't feel old, but everyday life reminded him. The once-easy process of lowering himself to the floor of the shop he used to own proved daunting. He always liked to examine the books as a customer might, but over the last few years the bends and twinges of his long, lean body resulted in winces and creaks. At the age of sixty-seven, sitting on the floor challenged him—an obstacle course in maneuvering joints and muscles past the hazards and pits of pains, arthritis, and inflammations. Navigating this unwished-for-adventure, he journeyed alone into senior-world with little enthusiasm, but with gritty determination to "not go gently into the night."

The historian in him wanted to see what lay around the next corner of life. But he needed to be alert and aware. Lack of acuity bothered more than the aches.

In response to the contact, he murmured. "Oh, I'm sorry. Here, let me move." It would not be easy—requiring him to shift on the floor, *if* he could.

"You're fine. I didn't mean to startle you." The melodic voice, like the perfume, reminded of his past.

Searching his memory, another task that took longer, he turned, hoping the face would help him remember.

"Omigod! Tav?" Her short hair, still deep brown and not grey, framed an unwrinkled face. The smile, which had charmed his best friend years ago, still brightened her appearance. Even using a scent similar to the one from their college years, she had changed little, carrying their common age better than he did. She could pass for 40.

"Carlotta?" His eyes widened at her return, and his voice emitted an old man squawk. "I never thought I'd see you again." He tried to disguise the agony of scrambling to his feet. The symphony of sounds his body made, the new soundtrack of his life, echoed in his mind. He hoped she couldn't hear it. With an unintended grunt and the assistance of her hand, he made it up.

"It's so good to see you! You're here? I heard you sold this place." She nudged his arm, a habit going back to college. "And how is Ilene?"

His happy mood morphed into grief. "Died three years ago. Cancer."

She gasped. "I'm so sorry." Her hand stroked his arm, and her eyes grew moist. "I didn't know."

"The only good thing is, it didn't linger. Didn't give us time to fret." The reasons to own the store had expired along with her. He needed someone to love, and to love him. Since selling he had gone from active manager to morose retiree. Ilene had always handled the finances, while he dealt with the customers. Together, they had made the enterprise successful. If he managed it alone, he worried it would wither and die like so many other independents.

The new owners impressed him, they brought the necessary energy and innovation. Because of them, WORDS AND PAGES might survive.

"You two built this place. It has to be hard for you." Her touch lingered on his forearm.

He missed intimacy. Marrying Ilene had been the best thing he had ever done. She completed him and filled the holes inside as no one else could ever do. Meeting at State, they had coupled after a first date.

Their social group approved from the very beginning. Ilene and Tav soon became best friends with Carlotta and Roger, the "It" couple of their class. On graduation day, Ilene and Tav married at a quiet ceremony at the University's Beal Gardens with Carlotta as Matron of Honor. She claimed she lost a like-sister and gained two best friends.

Over the next ten years the two couples lived next to one another in Forest Heights, partied, went on vacations together, and shared in each other's triumphs and travails.

"Miss her so much. Keep taking it a day at a time." Shaking his head, he'd always thought he would go first. Now he needed someone, or life would continue to feel empty.

He also had believed he'd never see Carlotta again. Why had she returned after so many years? Shortly after she and her husband had moved so suddenly, they had divorced in California. Neither kept in touch, leaving Ilene and Tav feeling betrayed and deserted.

The sudden departure and the splintering of what appeared to be a happy marriage shocked and surprised Tav and Ilene. Without their best friends around, they threw themselves into their business, nurturing it and building it into the largest independent bookstore in the state. "The emptiness inside doesn't get filled, though."

"I know it hurts. You two had forty-three years. A long time. I'm impressed." She pushed the book she had selected back onto the shelf. Ilene had said she always had been tidy. "It's good to see you. You're looking well."

"And you. Pretty. Nice dress." He admired the flowered blue pattern—and the still definite curves and shapely legs, but he doubted they could talk about anything real. She had always been more into small talk and gossip than they'd been. "Wondered what became of you."

She tilted her head and smiled. "Thanks for the compliments. How about a coffee? I saw chairs in the café. We can catch up."

Moments later they sat across from each other at a bistro table. Opening a packet of Stevia to add to his decaf, he watched as she carefully sipped a steaming cappuccino. Never much of a coffee drinker, he wanted to avoid the hyped feeling a regular brew would give. "It's good to see you, but I am surprised you're back in *Michigan*." Very astonished, having heard nothing in decades. She hadn't returned for weddings or funerals in the last thirty years.

She lowered her eyes. "I should have called, wanted to many times." She shrugged as she had many times in earlier years, her way of asking for forgiveness without apologizing. "Two reasons. I came back to see my Aunt Jessica. She's ninety-two, and in failing health. Haven't visited her since I left." She sighed. "She's at a nursing home here in town."

Tav never remembered Carlotta talking about an aunt, or any other relative. Her family had sounded cold, and distant. "That's very good of you. And the second reason is ...?" His voice trailed off, waiting for her to continue.

"I wanted her to know how much I love her. I never told her." She stared into her drink, stirred it with the spoon she had kept in the cup even when she drank. "The other reason is I miss having friends. I made a lot of bad choices in my life. Leaving everyone here is one of many I wish I could undo. People like you, and Ilene. You two knew how to be good neighbors." She shook her head. "Good friends. Little of that out on the coast. People are always on the make. You never know who to trust. Out there, I forgot how to be human, and want the feeling back."

Tav leaned forward. Her openness suggested he could be as well.

"We pondered why you didn't answer our letters. You replied once, and then nothing. Did we hurt you somehow?"

She nibbled her lip. "No, never. Not you. I changed. Got caught up in a lifestyle. The Midwest seemed so old-fashioned, and dull. Like an idiot, I thought people back here didn't know how to be." She stirred the liquid at a languid pace. Her eyes appeared focused on the slow eddy. "Truth is I got lost in the hectic world out there. I put important things out of mind and concentrated on money, style, and the superficial. I stopped being real."

Tav had been in LA once. The glitz had been impressive, but unsatisfying. Conversations inevitably turned to people and away from ideas. He thought Carlotta would fit in well, but he never wanted to go back. "So, will you be staying long?"

Still agitating the contents of the cup, she tugged on an earring. "I want to. If ..."

He waited, but she merely stared into the cappuccino. "If what?" One of the things he had liked about her as a neighbor had been she had never hesitated to tell them what she thought. The woman sitting across from him acted uncertain, tentative. He sipped his java as he examined her face and saw deep regret.

With a reluctant sigh, she blew on her drink. "It impressed me how you forgave her." Carlotta glanced at him for a moment, before refocusing on her drink. "You kept loving her, despite what happened. I could never do that."

Shocked by her statement, he swallowed hard, and almost spit out his coffee. "Wh-what? Forgive her? For what?"

"*You* know. What happened."

Tav wondered if the woman had gone senile, remembering things which never happened. Her words made no sense. Ilene always thought Carlotta had been wound too tight trying to live up to the image she'd tried to establish. No one could have been that perfect during college: top grades, active social life, and leadership roles on campus. "We forgave each other. People who love each other do that. We wanted a good marriage. She managed better than I did. Like when I forgot—"

"Omigod! You don't know?" Her eyes widened, and she leaned back in her chair. "She never told you?"

"Told me?" He assumed she must be talking about some silly, long-forgotten miscue. "What are you talking about?"

"It's nothing." Her face grew ashen. "I should leave."

Tav place an arm over hers to keep her from standing. "What do you mean? Explain yourself."

Her gaze darted about the room, finally returning to stare down at her tanned hands and manicured nails. "This is a mistake. My tongue got the best of me. Please don't ask." She shrank in front of him, curling back into herself, something he had never seen her do before. "Please, let go of my arm. You're hurting me."

He lessened the pressure but maintained the contact. He would not allow her to leave without finishing what she started. Long ago, Carlotta and Roger had talked with them about everything. She could be like that again. "I need to know what you mean."

"You never figured it out? Why I left so suddenly. Without telling anyone? Roger called it one big mistake, but I knew the temptation would be too much. I had to leave, and Roger had to go as well." Her eyes filled with moisture and her arm trembled in his light grasp.

His voice steeled, and he kept his focus fixed on her. "Go on."

"They said they loved each other. I found out by accident." Her voice wavered, and a tear strolled down a cheek. "I recognized her scent on his jacket. It lingered too long to be from a casual hug. The way he evaded my questions confirmed it. He admitted it that night." She shook her head as if deeply hurt by the memory.

"Who are you talking about?" Why couldn't she tell him?

My husband, and your ..." Her whole body trembled.

"Ilene? Roger? I don't believe it." Tav's mind raced. He had seen no signs of betrayal. He remembered working long evenings as they built the customer base. Ilene did the accounting at home. Nothing ever seemed out of place when he returned, tired and exhausted from hob-knobbing with clientele and staff. Some days each had been too tired for love-making, but throughout their years, Ilene had kept him satisfied and happy.

"He said they didn't want to hurt you. When we left, I assumed you knew. And that's why he moved with me. Because he couldn't stay here and face you." She shook her head and dabbed at her face with a napkin, smearing makeup.

Tav said nothing about it, allowing the splotch to mar her face.

She shuddered across from him. "I can't believe you never found out. But, I guess, I should have known. Ilene could always keep a secret."

His stomach spun, and his throat throbbed. The room rotated around him, and he hoped he wouldn't vomit, unless it could blot out somehow this unwelcome news. At Ilene's funeral he had felt disoriented, but at this moment he felt both empty and full of pain. A scream erupted in his mind, but his voice froze in the air between them. "How long did he screw *my* wife?"

"Only a few times. I stopped it. I never forgave him, or her." She bit off the last three words. "I haven't been happy since. It's why my second and third marriages didn't work. Never trusted any man. Not after the bastard cheated on me with my best friend."

He glared at Carlotta. Feeling betrayed, he hated the messenger. Did she come back to tell him this? Had Ilene have other lovers? Doubt and anger spiraled through his memories, obscuring the image of his wife, and of himself. "How else did she lie? What other secrets did she have?" When Carlotta didn't respond he slammed a fist onto the table, and their cups jumped, spilling liquid onto the white surface. "What secrets?"

Several patrons stared at them, and Carlotta sat back, a look of fear blanketing her. "Nothing major." As he leaned toward her with venom in his eyes, she shuddered. "Before you married her, she and I made out a few times. Experimenting. She liked it more than I did."

He rotated his hands in front of her, demanding more.

"She had an abortion, before she met you." Her hands trembled.

"What?" His fingers curled and dug into her arm.

"When she realized the two of you couldn't have children, she told me she regretted not having the baby." Tears journeyed to her chin as her voice quivered. "Nothing else. That's all I know. Please, don't hurt me."

He released her arm. A guttural word escaped from his lips as he pushed his chair back and stood. "Sorry." He turned and walked away.

"I thought you knew. I didn't mean to—"

The rest of her sentence erased as he threw the exit door open and stormed outside. With no idea of where to go or what to think, he strode along the sidewalk. Nothing made sense. He brushed past pedestrians, not caring about being rude. Before long he found himself at the downtown park, near the waterfront, where he stared at the fast-flowing stream in the Forest River. To the waves, he screamed expletives.

Tav had always trusted others. Too easily Ilene had told him. At times, he'd been hurt, but always before he'd bounced back and returned to his easy-going nature. People in general had good hearts with Ilene being the epitome of kindness.

His head throbbed, and he rubbed his temples. It didn't help. When his back twitched, he knew he needed to rest. When it acted up, only sitting relieved the discomfort, until with time—ten, fifteen minutes of being still—he could move more easily again. He found an empty bench a few feet from the railing. He sat, fists pounding down on the seat on each side of him.

Keeping even-headed had been his mantra. During crises, the smart ones never panicked or allowed their emotions to control their behavior. He'd been challenged before, but never in the past had his emotions been so ripped raw, making him border on a full-force explosion. Life meant little without his illusion of a happy, *faithful* marriage.

Wanting revenge, he saw no way to take it. The bastard Roger had died long ago. Ilene, the liar, existed only in an urn on the mantle.

When Tav let out another shriek, birds flew from the branches overhead. The sun itself hid behind a cloud.

The water of the deep river called to him. It offered to embrace him, envelope him in forgetfulness. No more worries or agonies. No more revelations. No more lonely nights. He closed his eyes. Feeling alone, he doubted he would be missed.

As he prepared to find a way to clamber over the fence, his thoughts slowed. The clouds drifted, and the earth's star reappeared. The birds chirped again yards over his balding head. Lessons his father had taught him told the importance of learning from the past, not being controlled by it. Her betrayal had happened long ago. After it, she had stayed with him. When Roger had left, she had not followed. Why?

In answer, his mind fell through time to the moments before she died. Ilene had clasped his hand and sighed. Her words at the end kept him from despair during many days and long, restless nights. What she had said helped him even now. "Through everything, the good, the bad, the best and the worst, I loved you. Always remember, I loved you." Her eyes filled with the mists of affection, pain, and life. Seconds later they closed for the last and final time.

A shrill bark startled him. At his feet a puppy appeared. Tail wagging, the small dog with big eyes offered a come-play-with-me-bark and bounced up and down at Tav's feet. He reached down, scratched it between the ears, and let the dog lick his hand. Tav held hands up, palms to the puppy. "Sorry, no treats." He laughed despite his mood. "You are a cute one, aren't you?"

A young man ran toward them and slowed in front of Tav. "There you are, Parsnip." Out of breath and with a relieved smile, he shook his head as he scooped up the puppy. "Thanks for slowing him down. For a little fellow, he can move pretty quick." He offered the pet a small biscuit, which quickly disappeared. Parsnip licked his lips thanking the jogger with a low happy bark. "He likes you. Doesn't stop for just anybody. There's a couple more at the shelter, including one from his litter. Each is just as adorable as mine."

Tav tilted his head. A dog would change things. After giving the number, the young man and Parsnip headed in the direction he'd come.

On the other side of the river, Tav saw a young couple stroll across the River Forest campus. They held hands and snuggled as they moved in slow motion along a path. Overhead, he saw billowing clouds coast gently away across a deep blue sky.

In the drifting formations he imagined he saw a star—Ilene had loved studying the nighttime sky. To the left he made out the shape of a tree—the first time they had made love it had been under a giant oak. On its trunk, she'd drawn an elongated heart with their initials scrawled in the interior.

In another cloud formation far out over the Bay, he imagined a puppy face, with tongue lolling. A huge burden shifted from his shoulders as he remembered the reality Ilene *had* stayed with him. With his finger, he traced a heart and their initials in the air above his head.

Tav thought about Carlotta's comment about forgiving Ilene. But she didn't need forgiveness. *He* needed to give it. To Ilene. For himself.

Tav pulled out his cell and dialed the phone number. A puppy needed him.

Two Men

    We used to meet every Tuesday and Thursday at the top of a knoll in the park. A bench there overlooked the empty playground filled with quiet during the schoolyear while kids attended classes. The peacefulness and the natural setting helped us relax and feel at ease, even though we never talked much anymore. We sat, grunted, and quipped—only on rare occasions did actual sentences happen.
    On that first day of October, winds blew across the browning grass below us. Eli cleared his throat and pointed. A little boy, too young to be by himself, toddled along the sidewalk toward the swings, teeter-totter, and slide. After a moment, far behind him and trying to catch up, an emaciated young woman stumbled as she struggled across the lawn against the blustery breeze.
    While I grumbled, certain she should keep a closer eye on the child, Eli shook his head and snorted. "I hope that's his sister. Not the Mom. Too young. She'll fly away if the gusts pick up anymore." He popped his dentures, balanced them on his lips, and dropped them back into place, a truly sickening sight. My eardrums ached as he yelled into the wind. "Watch the boy!"
    Of course, the two down below could not hear. He wasted his breath a lot. Something I never do. Eli muttered and spat. "He's a chunk. Should be safe, but her—I don't know."
    Eli's spittle landed close to my left foot. Convinced he had the manners of someone who'd been feral from birth, I glared at him. "You're disgusting!" Rebukes never phased him, and served only to satisfy me, giving me an out if anyone else heard and dared to complain

about his repulsive and annoying habits.

Once again, I wondered why I spent time with the geezer. He'd never been likeable and had gotten less so with age. But we had history, having worked together for over thirty years at our shop, repairing auto engines. Through perseverance and an ample portion of good fortune, we had made a go of **Fixin Brothers**—keeping the name and never correcting the false impression it gave that we shared DNA.

Watching the boy play while his companion sat on a swing, I remembered the reasons I put up with this grumpy old man. We had sold our business three years ago when I got arthritis at the tender age of 64, and Eli turned 68. It proved to be bad timing. Three months later, my wife died, leaving me with no talent for taking care of myself.

Eli and his Ellen kept me from starving or going mad over the next few months. Ellen, who somehow has always tolerated her uncouth husband, invited me for meals and holidays. It made up for both couples having no children in the area. Mine live in New York and North Carolina. Their only son moved to California. It's lonely without family around.

I think Ellen liked having me around to keep Eli from annoying her too much. She shooed us to the garage shortly after every meal, demanding some peace. In his retirement, Eli started a handyman shop, and he used to fix up old lawnmowers and snow-blowers. I helped him sometimes, but he had to give up doing any work after his stroke earlier this year, leaving him with nothing to do but remember better days and stare at tools he would never use again. It's hard having nothing to do.

Often I went to the library to look at magazines, or to one of the museums around town. On occasion I explored the zoo exhibits. Most days, I walked at the mall, to watch people, and feel lonely in a crowd. At least Eli is another human I can say I know.

Down below the laughing little boy ran back and forth between the slide and the jungle gym. The woman—she did look more like a girl— kept glancing around. When she noticed the top of the knoll, I waved. She didn't return the gesture, but looked away quickly, as if people scared her. She had the haunted look of one who didn't know what tragedy would happen next.

After a while, I got up and walked the area and decided to stroll to the cemetery on the other side of the hill.

Having tombstones so close to a park struck me as weird, but I guess it made sense, both green places where people go to get away from day-to-day life and its troubles.

Sauntering by the markers, I avoided my wife's. Too painful to look at. Better to hang onto the memories of her when she lived. She understood me, catered to me, and made existing worthwhile. With her gone, nothing made sense anymore. I'm sure she's in heaven. Sad thing is, I probably won't join her there, not that I deserve to. What we had together is all I'll ever have, and that's yesterday now.

Even as a kid, I didn't mind graveyards. My mother took me with her to plant flowers over my grandparents' last resting places. I never knew them. She talked about how much she missed seeing her folks, and now she's buried next to them back in Midland, where I grew up. Hope they all made it to the same place.

It was peaceful in settings like that, the bodies never much different than my friend up above, not great conversationalists, but consistent in their solitude. They never moved. *He* did, on occasion. I looked up and noticed he'd gone from the bench. Probably had to take a whiz in the bushes. Hope no one saw him, or he might be arrested for public indecency. I understood though, the older a man gets, the more often he passes water. Damn coffee. It used to run through me quicker than a bunny running from a dog. Luckily, I don't have that problem anymore.

Despite ancient ears, I heard a scream. Careful at my age, I took a long time to scale the slope to our perch. More yelling, sounded like "staying home." Goosebumps covered my skin. Something bad had happened, and I hoped Eli had been able to help whoever needed it. My mind filled with worry about the girl and the boy.

As I reached our perch, I looked down at the playground, and saw no one. Glancing to the parking lot I noticed a car that hadn't been there before. A bearded man in a plaid shirt shoved the young woman into the back seat of a sedan that might be a Buick. All the new models and makes confuse me. He slammed the passenger door shut and screamed. "Never leave home without my permission. You belong to me!" Of course, he didn't say it without more colorful language, something I try not to do.

A face—the woman's I assumed—appeared in the window, looking panicked and afraid. The boy appeared next to her, his face crunched into a ball of fear before the car squealed away. At that distance I didn't try to read the plate as the car sped away. I hoped the bully wouldn't beat them, heck, I feared he might kill them.

Not carrying a cell had major disadvantages. No quick way to call the cops. Eli never had one either, part of our retirement plans to escape responsibilities. We'd have to get back to his place, three blocks away, to make a call. By then I knew the trail would be even colder.

Another problem, Eli had disappeared. Worried he had hobbled down the hill to try to intervene, I scanned the playground and parking lot below. The fool couldn't be seen. I wondered if he had been dragged to the car with the boy and the female. How stupid, if he tried to play hero, as if he could have done anything.

Without a cane, walking very far would have been unthinkable for Eli. Still, he made it to the hilltop twice a week. He said he needed to move or go crazy staying at home. Sometimes, I worried he'd start his car with the garage door closed. As one gets older, I know from personal experience, there is less and less reason to live.

With no sign of him at his outdoor bush-bathroom, I started down toward the playground, looking for any evidence of him. He would not have run off—couldn't move that fast.

Behind the slide I found him, moaning, bleeding, frightened. I called his name. Got no response. Kneeling beside him, I checked his pulse. It slowed, hesitated, and stopped.

With eyes closed, I started to sob. Not with tears, but with loneliness at another loss. Likely, my friend had tried to help the boy and his waif-mother and had collapsed during the scuffle. And the bastard had gotten away.

A hand on my shoulder startled me. I opened my eyes and saw Eli's corpse lying in front of me. I turned to look up.

Eli smiled down at me. "Glad to see you're here. It's been a long time. But we don't have time to waste, we need to get moving, if we're going to save her and the boy."

Standing, I stared from the body on the ground to the man next to me. "What the—?"

He shrugged. "Heart attack, I guess. Went fast. Like you did. The young punk hit me, and—I don't remember—just out."

It didn't make sense.

The Encounters

What kind of gibberish had he spouted? "How—I don't—what's happening?" Eli appeared younger, stronger, more confident. But his body lay next to me! Had I fallen asleep up at the bench, or been hit over the head? "You're dead!"

"So are you. Don't you remember? Car accident. DOA." He paused to look at his feet. I hadn't noticed until then that they floated above the ground. "I hope Ellen will be okay. Maybe, be a relief. Be done with the pain-in-the-ass husband I've been."

My feet hovered as well. No wonder walking hadn't slowed me as much as it had him. "I didn't know I—is this a dream?"

"All I know is we need to save the woman and the kid. It's my reason to be here. Otherwise I'd be ..." He glanced up, and then down, shrugging as if uncertain of the direction he'd be going.

"What's *my* purpose?" If I had passed away, I should have known, shouldn't I? The possibility of not being alive confused me. I'd talked with Eli, or had I? He had grunted and complained, not conversed. And my aches and pains—gone and had been for weeks.

"When did I ...?"

His head spun—a complete 360! I copied the move and did it! Hoping being dead meant I could do other amazing feats, I leaped up, and shot to the tree tops. When I looked down, Eli laughed and ascended in slow motion to join me by an empty nest on a high bough. "I wonder what else—"

"A lot. Think about the guy, the kid and the woman. Maybe we can see them."

Doors opened. Curtains pulled back. The city lay before me, and I saw the truth. I had moved on to another existence. "I can! The East side. Cumberland Village. Mobile home court. Let's go!"

Time meant nothing to our spirits, nor did space. As I spoke we arrived and looked down at the car. The tormenter stood outside the door of the car and wrenched it open. He yanked the woman from the backseat and threw her to the pavement. "Enid, you're gonna be sorry. Running off. Never again." The boy whimpered in the interior.

Together, without a spoken word we swooped down toward him, and flew right through him. He screamed. "What's happening?" He looked around, and then glared inside. "Got some bad stuff. Get inside, Brucie! You too, whore, or I'll hurt the boy."

With a whimper she reached for the child. Together they scrambled to their feet, and hurried toward a dilapidated mobile home. Several women on porches nearby screamed. One pulled out a phone.

I darted back toward him, slowed when I entered his being, I stopped by an eardrum. I screamed, and he collapsed. Eli hovered by the woman, put his head into hers. Her eyes opened wide, and she pulled the boy closer to her. They ran into the home.

Inside of the abuser's mind, I shrieked harsh invectives. He twisted his neck, searching for his attacker, and could see no one. He yelled and thrashed about. A siren sounded in the distance, music to my ghostly verbal assault. His head pounded as I slammed my fist into his brain. He shouted obscenities and swung at the air. I didn't stop until after the police pulled up. They drew their weapons. I floated out, and saw the bully fall to the asphalt, whimpering nonsense words and swearing.

Eli joined me. "She's safe and is talking about what he did. He'll be locked up." He smiled. "That's why you stayed. For this. We did good." Mist formed between us and inside of me. I no longer felt my body as I heard, for the last time, Eli speak. "Now, it's time to leave, my friend. Time for us to go."

Last Visit

August 2000

The realization this might be our last week together frightened me. Much of life revolved around my besties, Margo and Ariel. Soon, the three of us will be off to different colleges. I never thought I could deal with life without them by my side.

While Margo and I have been friends the longest, I always knew Fate had big plans for her, and she would leave me far behind. She's off to the University of Michigan, joining other leader-types filled with good brains and gifted by families free with money, and, occasionally, love. *She said* she worries about the pressure, but she'll handle it with her natural aplomb. I wish I had an iota of her chutzpah.

Ariel and I are different. We get good grades, are kind people, and have potential. But, unlike our larger than life friend, we do not stand out or get people's attention.

One noticeable difference from Margo is we do not make clothes sparkle. Outfits always hang on Ariel's tiny frame she wears dark colors. I, with my solid build and a face fine for radio, qualify to be the poster child for dowdiness.

I wear something other than jeans and a tee only on for church and for dress-up Wednesdays—Margo's idea. She convinced most girls to participate and even got some of the guys to wear button-downs and ties. She helped me find fashionable tops and skirts at **Once Again**, a resale shop. From softball and running cross country, legs are my best—my only—attractive feature.

Ariel is going to an art school in Chicago. Beginning in ninth grade, she became my other best friend. As a fellow artist, she is way better than I am. She does mostly fantasy drawing—I have a unicorn she drew tacked up on my bedroom wall, the only decoration created by someone I know. Little, mousy, and paranoid, Ariel is only at ease sketching or painting, and she is *brilliant.*

I talked to her first. Being friends with Margo had cured me of shyness, so when I saw this lonely, out-of-place new girl sitting in the bleachers while I ran the track, I wanted to know where she came from, and what kept her busy in what looked like a sketchbook.

When I finished my mile, I jogged over to her and introduced myself. I think she almost fainted at my approach, but she meekly greeted me. When I asked what she was drawing, she showed me. My jaw dropped to realize she'd sketched the athletic fields with players replaced by mythical creatures. The school building stood in the distance, transformed into a gothic creation with gargoyles and turrets. Unicorns and elves and a host of other life forms dotted the campus.

"Damn, you're good!"

Her cheeks turned red. "Don't say that."

"But you are!" People who denied their talents, whether from humility or hoping for more compliments, often annoyed me. From this girl, it sounded different.

She shook her head. "That word. Don't use it."

It took a moment to understand "damn" had offended her. Margo and I, two good church-going girls, used far worse when we talked, even if our parents never knew. "Sorry, won't use it again." That proved to be a lie, but an unintended one. "You do amazing work. Looks like those things could jump out at me. And you did it in pencil!"

She looked down at her chewed fingernails. "Don't want to haul oils and all the materials out here. Too bulky and might lose things."

Wanting to draw in the late afternoon sunlight made sense. It also made sense to avoid being burdened with too many supplies. "Love to see your other work."

She put her pencil into her purse, before opening the sketchbook to previous pages, with each illustration as impressive as the first. There were several self-portraits, capturing the soul of her eyes, and giving her a surreal aura. Then several still-life drawings which looked like photos.

On the next pages, a snarling cougar looked ready to leap off the page and lash out, a German Shepherd ran through a flowered meadow, a cackling witch soared on her broom amid clouds, and a decrepit mansion crumbled engulfed in a haze. When I praised her work, the artist shrugged as if she'd drawn stick figures.

I let out a low whistle. "These are the fu—darn good!" I pointed to a scrawl in the lower right of one sheet displaying a Medusa towering over a blindfolded Greek. "Is that your name?"

With a slight nod, she fingered her signature. "AB, for Ariel Banks."

I told her my name, Esther Theisen, and appreciated the grin she offered in response. "You must be new around, haven't seen you before." At our school, Margo knew everyone, and, therefore, so did I.

"Transferred yesterday, from Christian. I don't know anyone here."

About to ask her why she left River Forest Christian, I heard a shrill whistle and turned to see Coach Nostrum glaring up at me with a finger beckoning for me to hurry to our post-practice meeting.

"We'll talk more, gotta go." I bounced down the steps to listen to another tirade from the coach. She's made me a better athlete, but her breath does reek.

Over the next weeks, Ariel and I talked every day. She told me I'd been the friendliest person she met. At least until being introduced to Margo. Ever since the day we met, we'd been tight, Ariel and I sticking together while Margo made the rounds with her large circle of followers and pals.

I learned Ariel's old school enforced stricter and harsher discipline than I had imagined. With a Dad who's a preacher, I thought I had it tough with family and church expectations. At River Forest Christian the rules included restrictions against creative expression and artistic efforts. Ariel hated the censorship. At our school she felt liberated, but worried about being considered an outsider, even in art class. Not knowing anyone other than a next-door, drop-out, stoner-guy, she welcomed my friendship, and Margo's. We helped her be accepted by the others.

During one of my sleepovers at Ariel's house, she and I sipped hot cocoa on a cold November night. After a joint—pure church-school Ariel could always score some pot from her neighbor—dressed in nightgowns and tucked under a quilt her grandmother made, I asked about how she could be okay with smoking dope.

With a pleasant chuckle, she examined the jay between her fingers. "There is nothing in the Bible against marijuana. Jesus turned water into wine, so I think of this stuff as my wine." With squinting eyes, Ariel inhaled the sweet smoke and held it for ten seconds before exhaling in slow motion. "Better than wine."

I loved our times together, when we laughed and joked, daydreamed and hoped, and shared our deepest secrets and biggest fears.

S love of learning and an interest in the arts gave us a lot in common. Unlike many teens, we read for fun, had philosophical conversations, and thought about more than gossip or how to have fun. Some people told us we're too smart for our own good, but we took it as a compliment and not the insult they intended. Intelligence is attractive, at least to us. And, we keep confidences well. Something most people don't.

Not that I have a lot to keep hidden. With my folks so busy at the church, and my sisters shining stars, my darkest anxiety had always been being ignored. Ariel understands. Been there.

She listened in silence to my complaints about all the attention my sisters, Becca, the athlete of the family, and Miriam, the pretty one, get. Every few moments, Ariel patted my back or squeezed my arm. Her empathy made things easy to share. As I finished, she let out a long sigh.

"My biggest concern's different." She gnawed on a thumb with more intensity than usual, suggesting some terrible worry sat on the end of her tongue. "You can't tell anyone, not even Margo. Promise?" She looked small and vulnerable, like a little child scared of the dark.

"I won't tell anyone. I promise." Margo and I loved each other, but with her so busy, I didn't think I could ever find the time to have talks like this with her. Not anymore, at least. She's almost too popular.

Ariel's voice, dim and hazy, sounded like it came from inside a wall. "It would kill me if you told." She searched and studied my face. "I trust you in everything, but no one else must ever know."

I nodded and felt my eyes water in support of whatever deep secret she prepared to honor me with. Her belief warmed me.

"I think Mother suspects, but she's never asked." Ariel sniffed and seemed to pull even deeper into herself. Her eyes reminded me of melting ice-sculptures. Next to her I felt the quilt pulled taut against her, making her look like a head emerging from a many-colored cocoon.

My voice squeaked, much higher than my usual alto. "What is it?"

"I don't think about it often, but …" She turned her head toward the desk, away from me, whimpering like a hungry and lost puppy.

A fear rose from my stomach and stifled my words, turning them into a frog's croak. "T-tell me." Had she committed some ghastly crime? Was she pregnant? Did she see ghosts and spirits?

The room grew colder and the light flickered, at least, in my mind. The screaming question I wanted her to answer swallowed by Ariel's silence. I heard the ticking of her bedside clock, an old-fashioned alarm she favored over the digital ones everyone else had. To me it sounded like a countdown to an explosion.

When she began, I heard the words through what must have been clenched teeth. She had not turned back to face me. "I'm going to hell." She gulped. "I'm glad my brother got killed in Iraq. He deserved to die."

"Wha—?" Those words, monosyllabic and far away, released from deep in her vault, created shock and disbelief.

"Starting when I was nine and he was sixteen, he—" Her voice cracked. "—made my life totally miserable. For a while, just pawing at me and using his fingers. Before long he—" Her body quivered, and the mattress shook. "—did it."

My mouth fell open and a gagging gasp erupted. "He fu—he—"

A sickly nod confirmed the answer. "Many times. He twisted my arm, pulled my hair, punched me, threatened more if I said anything about it to mom, or to anyone. He scared me. I never told."

"Damn, Ariel, that is so sick." I reached out and hugged her from behind. "He was such a monster. How could—"

"He went into the army at eighteen. I prayed for him to die. Every day I asked God to sentence him to hell, to be killed so he could burn forever. When he did die, it made me happy." Her voice chilled me. I never thought good Christians prayed for people to be killed. "God answered my prayers." She shook my arms loose and leaned away, hunching into a tiny quaking hill. "I pretended I missed him, for mom's sake. Inside, I gave thanks every day. Free at last from the fear he'd come back and take up again. I'll burn in hell, but it's worth it."

"He did *deserve* to die." Reduced to patting and rubbing her back, I tried to imagine how she felt, and knew she did what she had to do. To carry such a weight alone for years had to be horrible. "It wasn't your fault! The bastard. No one should have to live through what you did."

With another sniffle she turned and sobbed into my arms. I cried, too. The tears dampened our nightgowns, tracing rivulets between the flowered patterns. We stayed clenched together for long minutes before she pulled back and wiped the smears of moisture from her face, and then reached out to dry mine.

As she dried my face, it felt like a connection that had been missing in my life. Her touch felt electric. "Thank you for telling me. It had to be—I don't think I could have handled such a thing. You are so brave."

Her tears slowed when she forced a smile. "Thank you. You're a good listener. *I* am so lucky to have you as a friend."

"The fact that you shared what happened means a lot to me." I leaned closer to her. "I don't think I'll ever trust anyone as much as I do you. Some guy would up and leave. My sisters would give advice instead of listening. With you, I can be open, to get really, like intimate."

"Me too. After Joel, what he did, I'm—"

"Scared and scarred." I finished for her. We both shivered as she nodded. "My parents love each other, I think, but sometimes it seems like nothing more than a business relationship."

Ariel's face darkened, her words almost inaudible. "Men are a-holes."

"Not Reverend-Dad. He's a good one" To calm myself I played with my ponytail—always loved it dancing on my neck. That didn't lift the sadness. "Guys at school are jerks. I don't understand them." As I brought my hand down from my hair, it brushed against her small left breast. Embarrassed, I mumbled an apology.

I sighed. I rubbed the offending hand over my eyes. I sensed her gaze on me. A strange, unwelcome thought had popped into my mind and I felt guilt even allowing it into my consciousness. Good girls didn't think like that. The daughter of a minister must not.

I heard her voice, soft, yet penetrating. "What are you thinking?"

Did she know? I wrapped my arms around my torso. We had talked about so much. This could change things forever. That frightened me.

She waited as the thought flashed through my head. At the age of sixteen, Ariel, and I understood the need to experiment, to explore stuff, to figure out who we'd become. We'd gotten drunk together, taught each other how to dance, do make-up, and helped each other with homework or family chores.

Margo and I had tried recreational drugs—it shocked me when Ariel joined us. At her old school, many of the "religious" kids claimed since there were no commandments against weed, or acid, or coke, it was okay. She, like Margo and me, had decided after several scary times to stick to pot and booze.

We three friends had talked about everything, except the things bouncing around my brain. I felt as close to these two as to anyone, but Margo always had a guy. The latest one wrestled as a heavyweight for the varsity. Ariel and I had no beaus present or likely. Maybe ...

Time seemed to cement itself at 11:19. I heard Billy Joel in the background slow and then fade out of consciousness. Ariel's eyes seemed focused on me. Nothing moved other than my stomach, rolling in protest at what I considered.

My voice quavered and squeaked. "Ever think about ..." I turned and looked at her as my head felt like an explosion gone wrong. I saw my hand wave a trembling finger between us.

Her mouth dropped open. A shadow passed over her and she looked away for a moment. "No." Her voice became a breathy whisper. "Maybe." She turned to face me. "Do you want—?"

"I don't know. Do you?" I didn't, and I did. With no idea what I wanted, I knew I wanted our closeness to last.

Her frown made her look thoughtful in a pretty sort of way. "Lots of creative types are, like, in Hollywood, sports, the music world."

"Billie Jean King, Martina Navratilova." Tennis was my favorite sport. I took a deep breath and liked the scent of apple blossoms on Ariel. She always smelled good.

Her small shoulders shrugged. Her left hand reached out tentatively and petted my right breast through the fabric, pulling back almost immediately. Part of me froze—was it repulsive to her? Part shivered with delight at the human touch. I gulped.

She reached out to stroke my hair in a soft, easy caress. The light touch stirred feelings I did not understand.

Not wanting to be passive, I reached out and pulled her face toward me. With closed her eyes her head rotated in a slow seductive roll as she moaned. She appeared pleased and her mouth parted, looking warm, inviting, and close. I leaned forward and kissed her lightly on the lips.

For a moment, we both gazed at one another, and then she cupped my face with her hands to guide my head toward hers. Our lipsticks linked, and our mouths merged. For a moment, the universe stopped. Then, caught between curiosity and fear, I took the next step, thrusting my tongue forward.

It ended as quickly as it happened. The two of us rolled on the bed in laughter, and I sensed a shared relief at surviving the experiment.

When the hilarity slowed, we rested for a moment before sharing a platonic and friendly hug.

"Well, that's not me!" Ariel's eyes dampened, and her body relaxed.

"Me either. No way!" When our tongues had danced, my mind had recoiled in revulsion. While her breath smelled of mint, the reality of girl-on-girl left me feeling nothing. Billie Jean might enjoy it; I did not. What was that line? I remembered. "Not that there's anything wrong with it." Another one jumped into my head. "Some of my best friends are." Not mine, but that idea fit. My laughing lessened to an occasional giggle as I glanced at her.

She held one hand over her mouth to hold in guffaws and the other on her stomach. It made her look a little bigger than normal. She took several deep breaths, giggled, took a few more breaths, and finally shuddered to silence. A minute later, lying flat, she looked at the ceiling. "Promise, we won't let this change what we have." Her hand reached out and squeezed mine.

"I can't imagine a future without you close." I really meant it. "No matter what happens, let's always be friends."

"You got that." Her voice went from certainty to dreamy. "If I ever get married, you know, and have kids—God, can you imagine me with kids? We have to live next door to each other, so we can watch them grow up, have Dews together, still talk. I want that."

"Wish we'd be going to the same college. We have to visit often." With a voice edged with fear, I wanted to have someone know me wherever I went. "You're like a sister to me."

Her voice lowered to the whisper of someone awed by an idea, "Sisters, I like that. Family. Sibs. Friends."

I thought she might spit on her hand and shake mine. Instead she jumped up and went to her drawing board and started sketching something. I got up and stood behind her.

She drew two hawks soaring together over a lake. It was a rough sketch—ten times better than any finished drawing I could do—but it captured a sense of hope and freedom. The illustration showed their eyes alert and their wings flapping in unison, two friends linked forever.

Country Living

Living in the country did have certain advantages. Quiet. Fall foliage. Fresh air. Lack of Witnesses.

Muriel smiled at the thought. While the design had taken time to conceive, it now had few flaws. Perfect plans being no more than myth, the low risks and the ease of implementation made her idea a winner. Killing—no, facilitating, orchestrating—needed forethought, and she had taken her time with her scheme.

She wanted to ease the passageway to wherever Gordan would end up. Murdering too often involved blood, weapons, and overlooked evidence. This death—no more than an encouraged accident—would save her all the fuss. In truth, the whole effort had nothing to do with crime. Of several ways it could happen, she had settled on this as the first real possibility. This pre-planned fall gave hope of success.

Events should happen as she intended. She had him to thank for being so predictable and, therefore, so willing to cooperate with the plan. Thoughtful, as always. Helping around the house, opening doors for her, and cooking at least twice a week. These kindnesses had been part of the reasons she married him. That, and the well-endowed bank account and the farm: two thousand acres, worth far more money. In other areas he had been at best adequate, so the estate needed to make up for all his *shortcomings*.

On her drive into town she allowed herself the relief of expressing her complaints. No one could hear her, and the car would never talk. "We've just been married too long. Forty-three years! There are only so many times one can listen to that awful honking cough or watch the fingering of your ear." The thought of it made her shudder.

With a firm grip on the steering wheel, she muttered. "Would it have killed you," Muriel smiled at the thought, "to take me out to a nice restaurant sometime? A little fine dining? Why, I'd even have dressed up for that." She gave herself a moment to picture the scene: linen tablecloths, cloth napkins, candlelight, music, and food prepared by real chefs! And Champagne! To taste good wine, without the screw-tops of his staple Lambrusco, would be divine. God knew, he had enough money to pamper her and end their plebian life, but he had no interest to—and worse, wouldn't.

"No, you always wanted me to cook. I got so sick of making you meals. Cleaning up." Her once beautiful hands looked wrinkled and old. She did make a good pot-roast. But twice a month, too often! "At least once in while you made chili. Not too bad for an old fart. Your grilled steaks or salmon tasted okay, too. But NOTHING else." Her loud voice made her hearing aids squeal. "Now, see what you made me do?"

She yearned to be free.

Knowing things had to change, she'd considered several alternatives. Poison would have been good, except too detectable. An accident with guns much too messy and would require her to buy bullets. He hadn't hunted in years. Farm accidents happened often, but in retirement he no longer did anything dangerous with machinery other than to keep the gas generator in good condition. They needed it if the power went out—a too common experience at this farmhouse surrounded by fields open to the West winds—and he'd been suggesting she learn how to start it up, in case, he said, anything like a broken leg or illness ever happened to him. His instructions detailed the order to start it. He even insisted she memorize precise guidelines on the way to do it. Such a Boy Scout!

Grateful for the knowledge on the steps to take to keep warm, she knew powering the generator up would happen soon enough—forecasters predicted an unusually frigid November. She'd want to stay toasty during the chilling Michigan winters, at least until January.

Once he rested in the ground, and the attorneys cleared the money, she'd be moving South, probably that town on the Atlantic coast—he'd been too parsimonious to buy the place she'd eyed there—to live year-round. Warm weather and the sun, spectacular views and a servant or two, would fill her winters for the rest of her life. Muriel would finally be rewarded all the years of putting up with his stinginess.

The Encounters

The plan should work. Probably *had* worked, she knew as she walked into the grocery store. His stubbornness, her best ally, would push him to take up the challenge. She had played on his pride about keeping things in good condition. Telling him at *his* age he needed to take it easy and to not do anything *risky* while she went into town guaranteed he would make the repairs while she had a locked-in alibi. Within the hour she would see the results. Hopefully, he would be *finished*.

The third-floor balcony needed repair, so he would walk out carrying the tools. Undoubtedly, he'd believe with his prescription he wouldn't suffer from the vertigo which had handicapped him. Unfortunately for Gordon, she had switched the pills for a placebo. She had carefully disposed of the actual pills at fast food trash bins. As further insurance she had doctored his favorite tea, which he always drank at lunchtime, with a disorienting concoction she knew to be undetectable. Not even to make him question his ability, but enough to induce the dizziness sure to hit him when he looked down from three stories up.

Weather had aged the railing and flooring of the terrace, her favorite refuge where he rarely went. With a little help from her, the planks would be weak and with the unevenness of the porch, he'd need to reach for the support of the spindles, which she had earlier, with some difficulty, managed to loosen.

Walking down the aisles, Muriel sighed numerous times. She tried calling him several times, making sure to do so in front of customers and employees. To the manager she fretted about how her husband had become forgetful, and how he always forgot his medications.

During checkout, Muriel made sure to mention how worried she was about Gordan. "He tries to do things he can't do anymore. I hate to leave him alone, but he needed some things from town." She shook her head.

The cashier, Judy, patted Muriel's arm. "You might have to put him in a home." She shook her head. "You poor thing. It must be hard."

Muriel nodded. "I love him so. It would kill me if anything happened. I'll call again as soon as I get to the car." Judy thought she should.

Muriel fretted to Judy about how awful it would be if Gordan got injured. Against her wishes, she repeated, he often worked without her around. He always said he didn't want her hovering about while he did his maintenance projects. He'd even been talking about fixing the roof over the porch.

"I hope he's okay. He won't let me help him." Muriel had scripted her concerns, having practiced in the car. She even had rehearsed the worried hand in front of her mouth, and the little shiver of worry. "He's getting too old to clamber around up high. Don't want him to get hurt." She saw Judy's concern, and knew the performance had been well-received. "I'm going to hurry home."

Judy wished her well.

On the drive, anticipation ate at Muriel. What if the fall had resulted only in a broken leg? If left a vegetable, the money would soon be gone. The plan had to have worked. Or, she would have to add the poison to his drink, and hope no one suspected anything suspicious.

As she pulled up the driveway she saw success! Gordon lay dead, his head smashed on the rock garden she had asked him to move to the spot only weeks ago. Too much blood, but not as bad as a bullet through the heart. She double checked his pulse. Gone. Adios. Her smile betrayed not by guilt but by the task of cleaning it all up. She knew she wouldn't have to do it. After the removal of the body, one of the neighbors would clean the area. Or she'd hire it done. She had the money now.

#

"Any of us would have helped. No reason for not calling a neighbor." The seventy-year old farmer shook his head while forking baked beans into his mouth.

"Sure is. All of us would have come over. Wouldn't take long." The younger man sipped his coffee. He always enjoyed these church meals after a funeral and had filled his plate a second time. "At least all the crops got harvested. A damn shame, but an okay time for a funeral."

"The Lions don't look so good this year. Sure wish they had better defense." The older man used his napkin to wipe his face.

"Maud's potato salad isn't as good as it used to be, but I liked the coleslaw." The farmers stared at a pretty woman walking by. They both thought she looked too pretty to be the preacher's wife.

"He always took care about doing things, kept everything in good condition." The elderly man cut into the ham on his plate and took a big bite. "Food sure is good." He spooned gelatin into his mouth. "Can't believe such a terrible thing could happen."

His friend paused to belch. "He was always so careful."

"Not the last time." Despite the dark occasion, the senior chuckled.

"Surprising thing is Gordon never told her about that damn well. He always left detailed instructions on how to do anything. Must not have for the generator."

The other man shook his head. "Why she stood over those rickety boards is beyond me." With a burp, he leaned back in his chair. "Can't even start the generator up from that side. Lucky, she didn't blow herself up. Guess, not so lucky, she drowned. Don't know which is worse."

"Got to hope the fall killed her pretty quick. Only suffer a bit." The older neighbor snapped his weathered fingers, still pliable after a long life of hard-work. "Being stuck down there would have been mighty lonely. No one close to hear her screams."

The other one patted his stomach and offered a satisfied yawn. "Might snag another piece of cake. No sense in letting it go to waste."

"It'd be a shame." He got up to look over the dessert table a second time. "I'll bring you the cake. Get me some more coffee."

Back at the table the two men each took a bite of the chocolate double layer cake. The older one spoke first. "Probably not thinking right, having just lost her husband. Depressed. Not thinking right. Makes a woman mighty down, to lose her man."

"Such rickety boards, too. Can't imagine why he had those things there. Oh well." The neighbor nodded. "Funny, both went in accidents. Two funerals in less than a month. At least, they're together again."

The Bridge

As a breeze teased their hair and the rippling stream sang love songs below, they surveyed the vista from their vantage point on the bridge. The valley's verdant farms and vibrant forests stretched to the west beneath the cerulean sky dotted with puffs of ebony.

The span, an arched wooden walkway, connected two grassy knolls over Lincoln Creek on the perimeter of Travers Park, the largest nature-preserve in the county. The knotty-pine structure, a popular spot for lovers, had been recently rebuilt after the original one had all but decayed and fallen into the stream.

One hour earlier they met during a workshop at a teacher's conference on the campus of River Forest University. When Saige challenged a facilitator's method—who harshly insisted no questions be asked until the end of the session *if* time allowed—she had simply stood up and walked out of the room.

Luke nodded. In his classroom, queries flowed freely, and he saw them as a sign of interest and learning. He had been drumming fingers at the didactic style of the instructor, who called his session, "Encouraging Independence." The contradiction of it had made Luke temper his growing irritation with an ironic smile.

Hearing several gasps and a smattering of support for her protest, he followed the rebel teacher into the hallway, and saw her disappear outdoors. She moved fast.

Outside, in the coolness of late April sunny afternoon, she leaned against a silver maple, holding a pen, mimicking puffing on a cigarette.

"Good job!" He waved.

She started when she heard him call out to her. Instinctively, she took a quick, tobacco-free puff. "What?"

"Hello. I said you did good in there." He stood several feet from her, just inside the perimeter of the shade. "That's probably the healthiest thing you can smoke."

She held up her hand and looked at the ballpoint between her first two fingers. "This is one of the times I wished I'd never quit. Still fiend for them, especially after listening to brain-dead lectures like that idiot." She jerked her head in the direction of Astrand Hall.

"I thought you deserved a standing ovation." He clapped his hands together. "But no one else did, so I left."

She cocked her head and examined the complimenter, who had dark glasses, sandy hair flopping over his ears, and an easy smile. "When he said thinking without knowledge is useless, that put it over the top for me. Thinking makes us seek information and stretches our minds. He wants robots to download his brain into."

Luke's laugh built up inside of him and emerged full and hearty. Seeing her frown turn into a grin of agreement, he relaxed. Maybe, she could be friendly. "Teachers like him make people hate school. He thought we thirsted for *his* wisdom, to fill the emptiness of our little heads."

"That's right." She chuckled. "I'm Saige Wilcart, and I teach over at Lincoln Springs Alternative. When my kids ask questions, even trying to bird-walk, I know I have their interest."

He nodded, impressed by the fire in her voice. "I agree. The same things happen in my classroom."

"It gives me a chance to redirect and show how much of life is connected." She pounded a fist into her other hand. "They get it, because they're smart kids."

"With at-risk kids. Whew. Tough crowd!" In the stories Luke had heard about the program, and small high school sounded like a hangout with no serious learning. According to his fellow teachers, the awful kids at LSA ran wild and terrorized the staff.

"Somedays. Not usually." Her eyes sparkled, as if thinking of pleasant memories. "I like them. They're challenged by obstacles, crazy families, and poor choices. Not bad kids at all."

"Really? I've heard—"

The Encounters

She stepped forward and stood her tallest at his comments. A voice filled with determined pride sliced through the air. "They are treated like throwaways. Their old schools didn't give them what they needed. At LSA we believe 'if a student can't learn the way we teach, why don't we teach the way they learn.' It works. They become good students."

He leaned away from her glare. "Didn't mean to offend you. People refer to your school as a—"

"Stoner High. Loserville. Hideaway for bad kids, trouble-makers, losers, druggies, delinquents. Heard it all." Her chin raised, and her eyes burned lasers at him. "They're kids. And I'm proud of them. All they need is another chance. That's what we give them. We think of it as family. They want to learn, and they *do*, once they feel safe and see we want to work with them."

"I—I'm sorry. I only ..." He looked down, feeling his face warm. Admiring the vehemence for her school, he wished he shared similar excitement about his. "Forgive me. I spoke from ignorance. I just heard—"

She shook her head, and her voice ground with irritation. "People who don't know much about us think we let our students do anything, that the inmates run the jail. They think we're a joke. They couldn't be more wrong, because, our school is filled with intelligent, caring teachers and students who earn the credits they receive." Her tone softened. "I love teaching there."

Luke thought about the teachers he worked with every day. Most of them complained about the school and their classes. Many of them sounded unhappy and discontented, not loving their profession at all. He never wanted to lose his spark, but saw few of the older ones still eager to teach. Would that happen to him?

"You're right about the things people say. Your students are being labeled and ignored. They deserve education as much as anyone." He understood that knowing nothing about her school other than gossip, he had judged the place. "Please, accept my apology for my assumptions."

She tapped a foot, and crossed her arms, the fake cigarette forgotten. "Maybe. It'd help if I knew your name."

He slapped his thigh and shook his head. "Another sorry." He held out his hand offering to shake. "My name is Luke Zeier."

Shaking his hand, she smiled. "Nice to meet you, Luke."

"I teach history at Richmond High. Third year there. See lots of kids who fall through the cracks. They could use a friendlier place like yours." He hoped she forgave him. Her green eyes sparkled, and her long reddish locks draped over her shoulders. In blue capris and a loose fitting white blouse, he thought she looked at ease, despite her anger at the presenter's message, and the foolish attitudes of people about alternative education.

Nodding toward him, she took up the pretend cigarette again. "I quit when I graduated. A present to myself, and to not be a bad example—to kids. Most of them smoke like fiends. When I get stressed, the urge is powerful. Pretending helps, and the breathing is easier now."

Scratching his chin, he raised an eyebrow. "I see. It would frustrate me. I gave them up when Aunt Hennie—I loved that lady—died because of them." He fingered a ring he wore on a chain around his neck. "This is hers. She gave it me and made me promise to stop the Marlboros. I wear it in memory of her, and to remember what she asked me to do. It'd be a sin to start again."

She closed her eyes and shook her head. "I kno-ooow." When she opened her eyes, she looked at her hand, slipped the pen into a pocket, pretended to drop an air-fag, and stomped it out with a sandaled foot.

Luke gave her a thumb's up. "I haven't smoked one since she died. Never will."

"That is so good for your health." She sighed and shook her head. "I should never have started. Not indulging saves me money, my clothes don't stink, and no more burn-holes in my shirts. But still …"

As an easy silence enclosed them, Luke studied her. So many of the women he met had an uncertainty about them, as if they questioned whether they'd be discovered as incompetent or ugly on the inside. This reluctant ex-smoker had an aura of confidence which overrode any regret at giving up her habit. He liked the way she met his gaze. "The session will go another twenty minutes or so. You want to go for a walk? It's a beautiful area."

She cocked her head and looked over at him. "Thanks for apologizing. Not many men know how to do that."

Luke hoped his face didn't turn red. "How about that walk?"

"I'd like that." She stepped next to him. "Help get my mind off that a-hole in there."

Several trails wound through the hilly park, passing over the creek and bordered by the river. Shaded by large oaks, the longer path, which in the fall often lay littered with acorns and leaves, and was populated only by birds, squirrels and a few runners. Luke had trained there often and knew the terrain well. But, sensitive to her unfamiliarity with him, he chose the more open way along the river on a path that would lead them to the bridge with its view.

"So, what do you teach?" He asked, thinking it an innocent opening.

Her expression clouded. "Students. I teach students. About life. How to get along. How to become successful." She glowered at him. "The subjects I teach are math, mostly algebra and geometry. At *our* school, we believe education is more than standardized tests."

He gulped at offending her sensibilities again. Something, above and beyond the conference presenter's arrogance or Luke's own comments, must be bothering her. People who snarled with little provocation usually had some big disturbance in their life. He wondered if she had relationship issues, or if someone had died. "I do, too. In my classes, I want my students to think both logically and creatively. The tests *are* a nuisance and overemphasized. We have a lot of good teachers, and lots of teens who are invested in learning. I'm sure you do, too."

She shrugged and held her hands up between them. "Sorry, I get defensive. It irritates me so much that some people look down on our school and our staff. Do you know that a couple of elementary teachers thought I didn't have a teaching certificate?" She grunted. "And I have two degrees in education! Honors college. And yet they think because I teach 'those kids' anyone can teach our kids with no credentials."

"That's so terribly wrong. People make foolish assumptions. Even me. I have to work on not doing it." A robin flew in front of them, and he pointed at it. "First one of spring is flying. Mom always said that meant it would be a good year."

"Robins are a good sign; *however,* we see them." She stopped to look up into one of the tall willows along the banks. "I rescued a robin once and set it free when it recovered. According to research I did, most rescued birds don't make it through their first year. Winters are tough for them. But, a few live as long as 14 years." In a gesture of prayer, she brought her palms together." I always wanted to believe the one I helped made it."

"I hope so, too." They started walking again. With quick glances at her, he saw she wore little make-up—and didn't need it with her smooth unblemished skin—and her verdant eyes appeared to search for the details in their surroundings. He nodded when she pointed at a turtle sunning itself on a log along the bank. "Good catch. I love it here. Ran along this path in high school."

"Cross country? You grew up around here?"

"Yes, to both. Four letters, all as a harrier for Twin Forks." He didn't mention winning one meet at this park, his only win ever, aided by his love and understanding for these trails. "Where are you from?"

"Alpena. Came here my last two years of college, and then got the job at LSA. I've never been at this park before, even though I keep thinking I should check it out."

"Magnificent views, great walking areas, excellent beach, and good boating. But, I don't swim well, so I never do much here now other than hike the woods."

"No more running?" She glanced at him with sad eyes.

"Screwed up my leg in an accident during college. Every time I run, it starts to ache, and I don't want to deal with the pain. This pace is fine." He rubbed his kneecap. "A little ice tonight and I'll be ready for another few miles tomorrow."

"What happened?"

"I used to drink. Thought I could handle it. Please, never drink and drive." Since surviving the collision with the pole, he had sworn off alcohol and drugs. "Arthritis reminds me every day. Some life lessons come hard. Fortunately, I didn't hit anyone—just an unmovable object. My car did worse than I did."

"Thank God." She stopped and stood in front of him. "The kids have stories like that. Most have big mistakes in their lives. But they're not as lucky as you. At their ages, their 'accidents' and 'screw-ups' follow them. Torment them." Her hands danced in front of her torso to emphasize her words. "They need understanding. That's what our school does. Gives them an opportunity to start fresh, with no one judging them for their past mistakes." Pumping both fists, she shuddered. "Everyone needs someone to believe in them." She closed her eyes as she leaned against a maple tree a few feet from the bridge. "My students need that and if we don't do it, no one will."

Nodding, he cleared his throat. "It's good they have you—and the program." Luke tapped his chest. "At my school, too many teens go incognito, or hide behind masks of anger or apathy. We—I—see them every day, and we mostly let them alone." Their eyes met, and he sensed he had her full attention. "Many of our students go through the motions of learning; a few excel. And the lost ones, flail against the system, or fade into the hallways. Either way, we don't have time for them. They're too much trouble."

She walked onto the bridge, and he followed. At the middle of the span she turned and faced him. They stood a yard apart. "Do you understand? They're hurting, damaged. And you see how no one steps up to ask what's wrong?"

He stepped closer and nodded. "They get lost in the size of our school. Because of the having well over thirty in each class, we're stretched too thin to individualize or intervene with every troubled one."

"Unless they're good football players."

Starting to defend himself, he stopped with his retort frozen on his tongue. Last December the star of the basketball team had received special tutoring and extra time to redo several projects. No other students got that much extra attention. He doubted if a reserve player would have been treated as well.

She focused on his eyes. "You know I'm right. The jocks, and maybe the popular kids from 'good families, are exceptions, aren't they?" Her face contorted, as if ready to scream, or cry. "How are the outsiders, the rebels, the misfits treated? Not the same?"

Luke thought of one sophomore, a girl with short, chopped hair dyed some ghastly color. She drew bizarre pictures and grunted indecipherable answers when questioned. Reading one of her essays, he'd been struck by her deep understanding of the causes for the Revolutionary War. He wanted to talk to her about it, but she never came back to class. Later that week he heard she'd been suspended for getting caught with a baggie of weed. The police had been called, and she ended up on probation and transferred to the alternative school.

Sighing, he looked over the railing at the peaceful waters flowing toward the river some thousand yards ahead. "We push them out the doors, and hope—someone else will work with them." He gulped, hating to admit this. "Those kids *are* tossed away."

Her barely audible reply sounded far away. "I was."

"How—?" His eyes searched for an explanation, but she shook her head with lips tightly clenched. Whatever had happened to her, she would not share—yet.

With a lowered voice, he wanted to sound as compassionate as she needed. "It is wrong to treat those kids differently. We should do better, and the district should support your program better. People—like me—take teachers like you for granted. I'll do better."

Swaying at the apex of the bridge, she reached out to hold the barrier. "We all need to." She looked down into the stream. "Too many people think we enable these kids, supporting their poor choices. We don't. Every day we teach values and promote smarter choices." She took in a deep breath. When she exhaled, she involuntarily whistled. "But sometimes, we just buy them time. Keep them in the system. That's all some of them need—to outgrow the stupid mistakes of being a teenager. Why don't people see that?"

He gently patted her shoulder, and she turned to face him. It surprised him when she reached up to take his hand. He liked the touch. "You helped me see that. I know you help them. You make a difference."

Saige looked down at their hands linked together. "At a conference once, a motivational speaker, Larry Bell, told us something that troubled me. 'Remember, on your very worst day, you are somebody's best hope.' It scared me." She shook her head. "To think I, with all my issues and insecurities, could give hope to at-risk youth." She squeezed his hand.

He pulled her closer. "He was right. These kids need adults to care, someone to be there. You help them. I'm proud of you."

She looked up with her eyes moist and shining. "Let's walk more together."

"I'd like that." Their fingers interlocked. "I'd like that a lot."

Best Seller

After his first drink, a weary Tristan Walker leaned back in the reclining seat, relishing the plushness and the luxury of First-Class flying. Being pampered like this could become habit-forming. This flight relaxed him far more than the way he used to travel, cramped between large people in the cabin section. Almost always they smelled two-days shy of a shower.

Seeing the slightly-less-attractive flight attendant approach, he hoped for another Seven and Seven. That would help him nap and recover from the lengthy book tour on the coast.

"Excuse me, Mr. Walker. I hope you're comfortable." Gazing into her light-blue eyes, he reevaluated. The two servers looked equally gorgeous, each beautiful in her own way. He liked this one's soft, suggestive voice: a flirtation of tone. Her name tag read Susan. "Someone in Economy recognized you in the boarding area, and the word spread. At least three passengers, the ones reading one of your books, would love to meet *you*." She accentuated her request with a coquettish smile, and a warm shoulder squeeze. "They hoped you'd be kind enough to autograph their copies." The closer she leaned, the better she looked. "I'd *love* one too."

Fame's largest drawback—unexpected attention—also served as a major perk to Tristan's ego. "Which one?"

"I bought *The Dead Oak* at the airport after seeing you on Jimmy Fallon." Her proximity allowed him to drink in her rose perfume. "After your interview, I knew I *had* to read it." A strand of hair fell across her forehead as she bent toward him. With slow, sensuous motions she brushed it back. "You made it sound—" Her breath warmed his cheeks. "—so *intimate*."

Basking in her proximity, he thought she'd look even better without the stewardess uniform. It relieved him she hadn't seen him on with Stephen Colbert. Tristan had tripped stepping up onto the raised seating area, and Colbert later referred to him as Tripstan. "Of course, I'd be happy to sign. Maybe, Susan, after another one of these?" He tapped his empty glass.

With a radiant smile, she took it from him, her fingers lingering longer than necessary on his hand. "Of course, Mr. Walker. I'll get that for *you* right away."

Watching her sway down the aisle, he decided he liked the brunette as well as the other one, the blonde he'd preferred earlier. Susan's perfectly rounded derriere swayed beneath the navy-blue skirt. With a lustful shudder, he imagined Susan would be happy and willing to show special appreciation for an autograph.

In the last few months, his life had changed. All types of women showed more interest than did before his being acclaimed by the *USA Today* as one of America's best storytellers. The extra sales generated substantial income, but the increased notoriety brought him much desired female attention. He liked being *the* pursued.

He rolled his eyes. Long ago he had promised himself he would not let the notoriety turn him into a vain leech. Despite the flattery and the recognition, he knew he wouldn't seek her out at the airport. For all the lascivious thoughts and covetous imaginations, Tristan believed in monogamy. He had been cheated on, and it hurt too damn much to bed strangers, not when Shea still occupied his mind. Shea, his one-true-love, if such a fairytale possibility existed, had done the cheating. It had torn him apart, and all her apologies had fallen short of salving the hurt. Devastated by her straying, he blamed himself for holding her at a distance until that night when everything changed.

In the wreckage of her car, gifts had been found—ones she had gotten for him, complete with the long letter pledging eternal love, swearing to never drink again, and begging him to put her transgressions behind them. She even wore the diamond, the one she had awed over in the jewelry store, the one he had been planning to buy before he discovered her betrayal. In the long note, she explained she'd emptied her bank account to buy it—and to wear it—as proof of her enduring and forever after faithful love for him.

Before that horrible night, he had wanted to accept her previous apologies, but his stubbornness dared to test her—to *make* her prove her remorse. A half year had passed since the funeral, and still thoughts of Shea kept him from dating. No one would ever match Shea, nor the posthumous image he had constructed of her.

Susan returned and winked as she handed him a filled glass of the carbonated drink. "I'll get my copy of the book, and then, if you think it's okay, we'll let the others up, one at a time. They—we—appreciate it—appreciate *you*."

After a quick nod, he took a sip. For all his recent fame, he still preferred a Seven and Seven on the rocks. Shea, who favored martinis, had kidded him for liking such a simple, soda-based drink. But, the smooth intoxicant symbolized quieter times, before all the attention showered on him began to fulfill his excessive adolescent dreams.

The sweet beverage reminded him, he had explained to Shea, of stealing his father's favorite cocktail, under the less-than-watchful eyes of the old man. He remembered the loneliness, the lack of friends, and the cash-depleted family savings, which made his teenage years miserable. Many times his father berated his only son, telling him he'd never amount to anything. Tristan's major sin appeared to be keeping his nose constantly in "useless" novels and classics. Partly to say, "Screw you to his old man, Tristan had adopted the drink as his own.

The old lush had loved to throw barbs at his ex-wife, and at the son—their only child, who looked so much like her. Tristan and his mother shared green eyes and high foreheads, ski-slope noses and dark, wavy hair and smiles—and had laughs that sounded similar. Mr. Alfred Walker didn't like his son, though he had insisted on and won full custody to spite his cheating wife, hoping through the son to make her miserable.

It worked only to make Tristan hate him.

His mother never contacted either the son or ex-husband. Evidently, she had remarried and had a new family somewhere out East. Not even a damn birthday card came from her.

The one good thing about the divorce: it gave Tristan time to write. Holed away in his closet-sized room, he created characters and scenes for the stories he hoped to finish. When money didn't allow him to go to college, he clerked at the local bookstore, took notes, read, and watched the normal and the strange customers who filtered through the shop.

Shea had been the most interesting one.

Wanting to free his mind of the haunting memory of his family and the loss of Shea, he recalled his career as a writer. The first manuscript had been a true disaster, ending up hidden in his computer files to hopefully never sully his reputation. He had trashed his second after the sixth rewrite, even deleting any evidence of it from his hard-drive. Too stubborn to give up his dreams, he kept writing. With his third effort, *Empty Tomorrows*, he broke through some internalized wall of doubt, published it on Amazon, and found modest success selling some five thousand copies in the first two years.

An actual publishing company marketed his next novel, *The Dead Oak*, about a teenager and his alcoholic mother. Earning excellent reviews, it became a big money-maker, and soon would be in movie production with Ben-frigging-Affleck signed to star in the screenplay Tristan wrote. The following work, *Alone in the Family,* about a lonely man whose wife and children ignore him, had joined *The Dead Oak* on the bestseller lists and had resurrected the sales for his first novel.

Far better-off financially than he ever thought he could be, he wanted to be careful with the windfall. He would buy that white Lexus he'd been eying, but doubted he'd buy a house. The condo fit him and didn't require much time or effort for upkeep.

Tristan chastised himself—he should be thrilled with life. Money, praise, attention. He had everything, didn't he? What else did he want?

Shea. He wanted Shea, or someone like Shea. A woman who didn't pay attention to his fame, or to his growing bank account, but who listened and who challenged him, daring to not always agree. With penetrating hazel eyes, Shea had looked deep into his soul without pulling back and had loved life with a passion. He doubted he'd ever find anyone like her.

For the next half hour, for distraction's sake he accepted the price of notoriety, chatting with readers. Susan took a moment to again tell him how she really enjoyed the opening pages, which she'd read during a short break before take-off. Her eye dances convinced him all he had to do was ask and she'd willingly hook-up with him after her shift ended at the River Forest Airport.

Next, a retired financial adviser liked the tension of Tristan's novel, and looked forward to reading his other works.

Then, he met a social worker in awe of his description of alcoholism, saying his words captured the horrible reality of the disease. She'd read his last two books, but had his first novel with her, having bought it after reading the others.

When the third didn't come forward, Tristan asked Susan why.

"She's not into autographs, I guess." Susan shrugged, suggesting he shouldn't worry about it.

Having enjoyed the fawning far more than he'd anticipated, Tristan wanted it to continue. "Is it okay if I go find her? I'd like to meet her."

Susan hesitated, then nodded. "She's back in Cabin. I know the other passengers would love to see an actual celebrity." She placed her hand on his arm, but her tone had an edge. "It's fine. I'll point her out to you."

Together they navigated the wide aisle of First Class, with Susan touching him the whole time. At the divider, she nudged the curtain open, and whispered, leaning close to his ear. "Seven rows, on the right, sitting alone, by the window." Susan's breath tickled his ear and tempted his resolve. Once again making him wonder if he should revise his policy on one-night stands.

Stepping though the entry, Tristan counted rows. Seven was a lucky number for him. His seventh birthday had been the last happy time with both parents. He'd scored a total of seven points as a high school basketball player, remarkable because as a substitute he played in only seven games. Two of his books had made it to Number Seven on the best-seller lists, before the announcement of the movie deal. He liked Seven and Sevens. It was a good omen.

Several people called out as he approached his reluctant reader. He waved to the well-wishers as he moved to her row. She appeared to be in a bubble, unaware of the clouds outside the window, or that he stood next to the empty seat beside her. Immersed in *his* book—pride swelled in him—she had auburn hair tied into a pony tail and wore a long jade dress with short sleeves.

When he cleared his throat, she glanced toward the shadow of him in the aisle and held up a finger as she finished a paragraph. She used a Sierra Club bookmark featuring a howling wolf to mark her page. After closing the novel, she at last looked up. Her eyes, which matched the color of her outfit, were two emeralds shining with challenge. Like his, *and* like his mother's.

"May I help you?" She had a confident voice, one not meek or doubtful. "Do you need something?" Freckles dotted her face and she tilted her head making her red locks swing.

Uncertainty flooded over him. Having planned to graciously offer to sign her book, he sensed she had no interest in marring the novel with ink-scrawls, especially when doing so cut into her reading time. "I'm sorry. You see—" He pointed awkwardly at the novel in her lap.

She stared at him, and then at the book. Turning it over, she fingered the outline of the photograph. Turning her gaze back to him, she nodded. "Oh, of course, Mr. Walker. Pleased to meet you." Her casual tone showed no awe at his presence. "Someone said you were on board."

As they shook hands, she offered the empty seat to him.

Settling into it, he pointed at the white clouds outside the window. "I love the view. It's so beautiful out there. Magical landscapes." When his arm brushed hers, his skin tingled, and a warm energy spread through his body.

She nodded. "When I look outside or read, I'm in another world, filled with imagination, alive with fascinating people, unusual happenings, and enchanted worlds." She fingered the book in her lap. "Good writing takes me to interesting places and exciting adventures. I *love* to read."

He felt a glorious shiver run through him. For incomprehensible reasons her opinion mattered more than it had a moment earlier. He wanted *her* to love *his* writing. "So, do you like it?"

The seconds she said nothing agonized him. The pause meant she had to consider the question. He held his breath, fearing what she would say.

She held the book in both her hands and tilted it toward her chin, "I'm not done with it yet. Your characters are alive and believable. That's important."

Her pause filled the air between them and built a tall wall of "but." She coughed. "Are you recovered yet?"

The inquiry confused him. What did being "recovered yet" mean? From the writing? From the creative process? From the publicity tour? From the celebrity? From Shea? No, she didn't know about Shea. "I don't understand."

She pulled the book close to her chest, drawing his attention to the shapeliness of her form.

Glancing quickly away, he hoped she hadn't noticed. "There is pain in everyone's life. Most of us bury it, keep it hidden, and only let it out on lonely nights when we cry, or drink. Sing sad songs, or clean like a maniac. Some lash out at others. You write. Your story comes from a deep hurt."

It had been a hard book to complete. None of the critics had come as close to that truth as much as this attractive woman—who didn't want an autograph—had. "It never goes away. Writing about it helped a bit, but some things …"

She nodded, let his sentence go unfinished, and pressed the book tighter against her, arms wrapped around it. He liked seeing his words nestled so close to her heart, *and* to her breasts, held in a tight embrace.

"You should keep writing." She nodded, as if seeing his journey, and understanding the hurt within him. "It will help. Much as we would like to, we can't change the past, only learn how to live with it. And grow from it."

He leaned back in the seat, stared at the ceiling, and then turned to face her. Eyes like hers, he could appreciate forever. "Hi. I'm Tristan, and I'm very pleased to meet you, Miss …?"

The Encounters

New Girl

Several gasps interrupted the taking of attendance as the new student handed the teacher her hall pass. Mr. Vickerson, a man who hated interruptions, read the note with a glower. "Welcome to class, Miss Gibbs. Take a seat." With a crooked finger he pointed to a desk in the middle of the first row, the least preferred spot, closest to the him, and his often-disapproving eyes.

As the newcomer moved quietly to take her seat, Mr. Vickerson glared around the classroom. "Students, I want you all to greet Corinna Gibbs, whose family this week moved to Twin Forks. I believe you father has a job at the lumber yard?" A few students offered hellos.

Her voice no more than a whisper, she clutched a notebook tightly to herself, her shoulders scrunched as if trying to make herself smaller. "Yes, sir. He's the new accountant."

Sitting in the second row by the window, Henry Walther noticed his classmates looked shocked at the appearance of the new girl. Her deep brown skin made her, likely, the first Negro ever in the school. He looked around at the other members of the government class. Several bit their lips, a few glared, and some just stared. Loggs shook his head and mouthed the word, "Nigger." Several of his friends nodded.

After roll call ended, without addressing the undercurrent of rumbling, Mr. Vickerson launched into his lecture. "The 1964 election will be a referendum on President Kennedy's performance. Most expect him to win, but ..." At the mention of the President's name, Mr. Vickerson's face contorted into distaste. "There are still doubts about the 1960 election and questionable results from Illinois and Texas."

The teacher sniffed. "While he has initiated many liberal programs, his effective leadership in still in question. World tensions are high, and there is much dissension domestically." He turned and used the chalkboard to list some of the issues facing the country.

"There are concerns about the rising inflation, the threat of how to contain Godless Communism, worries about Red Menace in Cuba, the Berlin Wall, the need to catch up to the Soviet Union in the race to be first to the moon."

Henry thought it odd no mention had been made of the new Civil Rights law or the recent race riots in Birmingham, Alabama. Did the presence of a Negro in class make that too awkward?

Vickerson jotted several names on the board. "Nelson Rockefeller, Barry Goldwater, and Henry Cabot Lodge are the three most likely Republican candidates, though Governors Bill Scranton and our own George Romney are other possibilities." He turned to look around at his students. "We here in Michigan have never had a President, and I think a first termer like Mr. Romney will not be foolish enough to run."

Henry soon tuned out. He daily read newspapers and listened to the news. Mr. Vickerson, even though a teacher, probably knew less about politics than Henry, who had worked on his father's two doomed campaigns to be elected to the state House of Representatives. The town hadn't voted for a Democrat since the thirties, and that wouldn't likely change for decades.

In the school many students considered Henry too smart for his own good. A serious thinker, he found most classes simplistic and boring. Henry hated the rigidity of the school curriculum, which taught the basics well, but did little to challenge brighter students.

Every classroom looked the same with the desks lined in proper rows surrounded by concrete walls with small bookcases holding textbooks and a few reference materials. The American flag and posters about the class served as the only decorations. In this room several aged posters diagrammed Checks and Balances, the Separation of Powers, and the Three Branches. Colorful maps of the United States and of Michigan brightened the room only a bit.

At least from his seat, Henry could look out across the parking lot to the woods, where he could watch the birds and the squirrels. With luck, a stray white-tail deer might appear.

The Encounters

While the lecture droned on, Henry studied the new girl. She looked uncomfortable. It made sense. Being an outsider in school would be challenging for anyone, let alone for a petite black girl in a field of white faces. She hunched over her notebook, scribbling notes and trying hard to ignore the eyes staring at her.

Henry looked away, ashamed if he had been rude. Why did others resent her? She looked pretty in her checkered blue and white dress. Her hair shimmered, and her glasses gave a studious look. And, he had noticed her shapely legs.

It relieved him when after twenty minutes Vickerson finished and assigned them to start reading Chapter Two. For homework they should answer the review questions at the end. A fast reader, Henry intended to finish during class, which would give him time for reading during study hall. After school he hoped to explore the river next to the family farm.

When he finished with time to spare, he saw a motion behind Corinna. Someone had tossed a folded piece of paper next to Corinna's seat. Sitting with her book closed, evidently finished as well, she leaned to pick it up. Without looking at the message, she slid it into her purse.

When the bell rang most of students rushed to the door while Henry sat and watched Corinna wait quietly until the room emptied. Even Vickerson hurried from the room, undoubtedly to go to the can or to puff on his beloved Marlboros. Henry got up and walked to where she still sat. "Are you okay? Vickerson didn't make it easy on your first day."

She peered over her glasses and used a finger to push them up tight against her face. "I thought everyone had left."

"Nope, not me. I'm Henry Walther. Very pleased to meet you, Corinna." He extended a hand.

Accepting the offered limb, she tilted her head and squinted up at him. Her eyes radiated wary gratitude. "You must be the only one."

He glanced around the room. "Less than three-hundred kids in the whole school. They want to be with their friends, not hang around a classroom." As an apology for the others, he shrugged. "Where are you from? We don't get new students here, we lose them. Their fathers take factory jobs, or their family moves away. Our town doesn't attract many newcomers."

"Dad got a good offer. We moved from Cincinnati. My school there had over two thousand students." She gathered her bag and supplies.

"Welcome to Nowheresville, USA." He grinned. "Twin Fork's not too bad—just not much to do. I hope you like it here." He saw her checking to see if the piece of paper was still inside the purse. He bit his lip. "Throw it away."

"What?"

With a wave of his hand he pointed at her hands. "Not something, I'm sure, you should read. Some people don't like anyone new."

He knew if Loggs threw it, she shouldn't look at it. The class bully, Loggs enjoyed intimidating others. Henry fought him back in seventh grade, and held his own, resulting in an end to his being a target.

"Especially if they're colored?" Her eyes narrowed, to belie the calm quiet of her tone. She pulled the sheet out and unfolded it to see the word, "Nigger." She crumpled the sheet. "At least he spelled it right. And he didn't light it on fire."

Henry winced. The bombings and lynches in the South screamed across the headlines. The violence down there and racist remarks from his classmates made Henry wonder if things could ever get better. Despite the protests and the power of Martin Luther King's speeches, little had changed. "Whoever wrote that is a fool and a—"

"Bigot." Her finishing the sentence led to his regretful nod. "Mom didn't want us to move here. But we're here. Better get to the next class." Hands trembling, her facial muscles tightened. "Where is—"

"You probably have geometry with me. Near the stairs. If it's okay, I'll walk with you."

"How did you know what class I had?"

"Small school. College-prep Juniors have government, geometry, English, and chemistry before lunch. In the afternoon, it's study hall and electives, like Spanish, shop, or art." They walked together toward the doorway, where she paused to let him go in front of her. "No. Ladies first." He thought her ebony skin darkened for a moment. He hadn't thought Negroes could blush.

"Thank you." She hurried to enter the busy hallway. In a small voice, she glanced at chattering students leaning against lockers or milling about near the water fountain. "People won't like seeing you with me."

Henry stopped and touched her lightly on her hand. He saw her eyes widen as she pulled her arm tight to her torso. "A couple maybe. Be their problem, not mine."

The Encounters

Henry talked as they walked toward the math room. "It's the third day so you haven't missed much, except in this class. Mr. Remington moves fast. We have a quiz next week over the first two chapters. He pushed it."

For the first time since he met her, she chuckled. "I'll be okay. I'm pretty good at math."

"Really?" Most girls didn't do well in the advanced math classes.

"At my old school, I had honors geometry last year, but the counselor here didn't want to put me in a senior class. He said it would be good for me to review. Probably thought I didn't learn as much as here." She rolled her eyes. "There's nothing else I can take this hour."

Ignoring glares from several students, he pointed to the classroom door. "Right up here."

"Thanks. That's close."

"Geometry's my weakest class." Henry brightened. "Maybe you could help me some. Those proofs kill me."

In the classroom, she stopped to introduce herself to Mr. Remington. Henry waited for her, and when she finished with the teacher, she walked closest to the window, the desk he often chose. He sat next to her.

After the lesson on the board, Remington assigned twenty problems. Before Henry got halfway through the work, she had finished. As she her closed the book, Mr. Remington asked why she'd stopped. He told her to come to his desk, so he could check her answers.

Hoping to finish before the bell, Henry only glanced up front occasionally. Mr. Remington appeared to be quizzing Corinna. She didn't return to her desk until the bell. Henry saw Remington do something out of character for the serious-minded instructor. He smiled at a student, at Corinna. She must have impressed him.

In the hallway, despite it not being crowded, several students jostled her. When Henry moved to her other side to run interference against the rudeness, with a sad smile, she nudged his arm. "I have to get used to it, stand up for myself, and be strong."

Their lockers were in the short hallway where the next class was. They saw notes taped to the front of both. His read, "Nigger-lover." The one she found had a drawing of a stick figure—hanging from a crudely drawn tree. Crumpling it, she caught her breath.

Having seen it, his voice boomed loud, causing several students turn to stare. "*Darn them.* I'm going to get whoever—"

"No." Corinna scowled at him. "It won't do any good. I—we—must be better than that. They're scared of change. People fear what they don't understand." Her voice calmed, and her eyes became intense candles flaming with determination. "Dr. King preaches nonviolence. I need to stand strong, and not give in to the tempter of vengeance. I need to do that, too. Love conquers hate."

She glanced around and saw the others had looked away. "I believe in the Dream."

His fists clenched, but he nodded. "We should report it."

She shook her head. "The principal won't do anything. They never do. It will just make me more of a target."

Frustration bubbled in his mouth. "We can't let them get away with this nonsense. It will get worse. You might get hurt!"

At the bell, they scurried to the next classroom, Corinna whispered. "I know. So could you."

#

In the lunchroom, Henry invited Martha, his sophomore cousin, to sit with Corinna and him. She agreed. Henry listened as Martha and Corinna chatted about being the new girl in school—Martha and her family had moved back to Twin Forks during the summer. While they talked, Henry surveyed the cafeteria. Teenager gossip and laughter dwarfed the ugly stares. After surprised glances and a few angry glares in Corinna's direction, most of the kids fell into their normal routine. Being only the first week of classes, many students enjoyed being back in the social whirlwind lunchtime provided. Spending the day with friends made listening to their teachers more tolerable.

Cleaning their trays after eating, Corinne tapped the trash bin when Henry kept looking all around. She cleared her throat. "Let's not search for trouble. If it finds me, I'll deal with it. You can't protect me all the time, and I know you want to, but I'll be okay. Remember, I believe in non-violence." They heard Martha call her name. She turned to join her new friend, calling over her shoulder to Henry. "See you in study hall."

Over the next week, Henry and his cousin chatted with Corinne at lunch every day. On the second Thursday, Martha greeted Corinne at her locker. "How'd it go?"

With a worried frown, Corinne shook her head. "Henry got in trouble. He's with the principal."

"Oh, no!" Martha stared at Henry's locker. "What happened?"

Most students scurried, either to the buses or to extra-curricular activities. "In study hall Loggs sneezed the word 'Nigger,' loud enough for even Miss Donner to hear." Corinne shook her head. "Henry accosted him before she said anything, and Miss Donner wouldn't listen to any explanation."

"That's awful."

Corinne pulled a light jacket from her locker. "I told him not to react. There are bullies everywhere." She shook her head. "And most teachers look the other way."

"How do you do it? I'm scared, and I just met you. They judge you because your skin isn't the same color." Martha tapped her cheek. "It's stupid and wrong. I think you look—you're pretty."

"For a colored girl?" Corinne bit her lower lip and looked away.

"I didn't say that. Or mean that. I wish I had your figure."

Corinne exhaled. "I do get sensitive. Especially, after a day like today." They walked toward the exit. Corinne carried only the literature book and her purse. Corinne nodded toward the texts pressed against Martha's chest. "Lots of boys will be in envy of those books." Henry's cousin replied with a sad laugh. "No one so far." When Martha's purse slipped from her shoulder to the crook of her elbow, Corinne reached over to push it back up. "Thank you." At the front exit, Martha paused at the door. "You're nice. What bus do you ride?"

"I live in town. I walk. It's not far."

"I've got to run. Our driver, Pence, is funny, pulls out early."

"Hurry. I'm fine." Corinne waved good-bye. She turned and looked toward the office some twenty yards away. Next to it, the awards case called to her. Hoping Henry would be released soon, she studied the trophies. None of them sat in the case proclaiming any championships for girls. At her old high school, she had run track. She shook her head in disappointment. This school only offered cheerleading as an athletic possibility for her.

Henry's voice broke her regret. "Mr. Johnson wants to add one for football. And, he thinks Loggs is the best player in school." As she turned to face him, his eyes darkened. "It didn't matter what Loggs said, or what he does—he's a star." As he reached her, his fists opened, and he reached out to touch her hand.

She pulled back. "Don't. I can't."

He reacted as if slapped, dropping his hand and staring. "Can't what?"

"I'm a colored girl. You—you're—"

"A teenage boy, who thinks you're really pretty, and smart. And I like you. It's like that song by Doris Troy, *Just One Look*. The moment I saw you—"

"Hush." She glanced around with fearful eyes. "How do you know that song? That's our music."

"I heard it at the college, a mixer." He smiled sheepishly. "My cousin goes there, that's how I heard it. I liked it."

Her eyes widened. "Well, no matter what, don't even think like that. They won't let it." She shuddered. "You better catch your bus."

Shrugging, he walked toward the exit, slowing to wait for her. "Too late, won't make it."

"Why not?"

"Pence never waits. I'll call my mom." He opened the door for her. "We can talk while I walk you home."

She swung her book to clutch it tight against her upper torso. "Henry, where are your books? You have homework."

He gave an embarrassed laugh. "You do like me enough to care about my classes." He looked up as if thanking God. "Still at study hall. I'll get them tomorrow."

"But, your assign—"

"I'll get caught up." His eyes studied her face. "Your eyes are so full of light, of life." She frowned at him before he continued. "You said you live only a few blocks away." Walking toward Main Street, he kept his eyes on her features. "We could be Romeo and Juliet, challenged by the hate of their clans, destined to be forever linked."

"You're crazy." She didn't laugh, and her words snapped from her tongue. "More like, forever lynched. Remember, they both died." With a grimace, she shook her head. "Do you know how upset people will get? Maybe you can handle that. But, I can't do that to my family. People throw rocks, destroy property, hurt the innocent."

She stopped at an intersection and waited for the light to stop the minimal traffic. "It happens. I've seen it. No, I will not be part of causing harm to my family. We live here. I need to graduate. I don't want you, or anyone, to get hurt."

When she sniffled, he pulled out a white handkerchief to offer her. The gesture brought a smile to her face as she accepted the cloth. "Thank you. I'll wash it and bring it tomorrow."

A big Pontiac cruised by, the windows down, and someone inside yelled out at them. "Monkey girl go back to the zoo!"

Henry raised an arm to give a middle-finger salute. "Damn them." The license plate blurred as the car sped away. "A fifty-five Star Chief. I didn't recognize them or it. Probably someone from Berrington." He guided them onto the street, careful not to touch her. "Most of us aren't like them, or like Loggs. I'm sorry they did that. It's why I'm with you. Otherwise, they might have stopped."

She walked faster, surprising him at the pace. He kept watch for other offensive traffic, and to make sure the Pontiac didn't return.

"Henry?"

"What?" They reached the sidewalk, where she stopped. She pointed at Smith Street. "I live down a block. It's best if you don't go."

"Why?" The song lyrics fit his feelings about her. "Just one look, that's all it took." She must like him too--she had waited for him after school. It meant she cared.

Her voice became a sharp-edged sword. "Because smart colored girls don't hang out white boys. Because, I don't want to be used."

"I would never do that." It bothered him that she thought he would. "There's nothing wrong about walking together. We could even get a soda or fries if you like." He wanted to spend more time with her.

Her lower lip trembled. "We must never do that."

"I don't see why not. Boy. Girl. A sunny autumn day. We could—"

She shook her head. "No, no, no!" Waving away his protests, she faced him with sad eyes. "If we dated, and then broke up, I know what people will say about me. Life would get uglier." Her hand raised to block a reply. "It will make people angry. Now, only a few hate me because of color. It'd open Pandora's box." She reached to hold his wrist down. "It's going to be hard for me to be accepted here. Please, just be my friend. People won't like it, but that won't be too bad. We can only friends. Don't make it worse for me." Her lower lip trembled. "Please. This is important."

Henry sensed the shadow of history pass. "Progress happens through challenges, not from things being easy. Problems make people think."

"My life is difficult enough." Her eyes grew large. "Every moment in school is frightening. Being the only one who looks different is scary." She stood facing him with her hands clenched. "The glares and the stares, the 'accidental' bumps in the hallway, the fingers pointed. The assumptions. Teachers think I must be slow, because of my skin color!"

"I know that—"

"No, you don't. You're a guy, ready to fight to protect the poor little damsel." Her voice rose, and a bit of spittle glistened on her lips. "In this town, in the middle of a sea of condescension and pity, if I'm not strong, I will drown while you sympathize and watch from the safety of being white. And, Henry, I will be strong!"

"Okay. I know you will." He felt hurt.

"Why are you so different from—everyone else? White people. The other students? The teachers? Everyone?"

"Because ..." He knew she deserved an answer. "My mother's best friend from college is a black woman. They still write one another."

Her mouth gaped. "That is rare!"

"Our families get together every few years, and I got to know her son. We became buddies. Knowing them taught me skin color shouldn't matter." He shook his head. "Black, white, yellow, red, whatever. It doesn't make sense to me why people act like they do. I don't think we're different inside."

She smiled. "I agree, but most people don't see it that way."

"Isn't that their problem?" he growled. "They're fools."

"Yes. But the Klan hates and kills people like me, and whites who work with us." She sighed. "They want an all-white America."

"How about a fair one!"

"I'd like that. But it's a long way off."

He had not considered the consequences. As a guy, he could be brave and combative. She didn't have that advantage. The riots in Birmingham following a KKK bombing of a black church filled the evening reports. Racial divide threatened to tear the country apart.

He looked down and saw a gulf between them. His face rose in synchronization with his voice. "I believe you." With a sad hand he wiped away dampness glistening on his upper cheek. "Through whatever comes, let's be friends." His voice broke. "I won't do anything to make it worse for you. But, I'd still like to walk with you."

"Thank you." Her eyes looked hopeful, and she laughed. "No need, I'll be okay. There's not much traffic. I'll make it."
"You sure?"
"I am."
"Okay, but, will you help me with geometry?"
Her eyes rolled as she chuckled. "Of course. That's what friends do."

Quiet Rietta

Rietta came back. After the first two sessions, Remy had expected the shy woman to disappear from the Saturday morning enrichment class he taught. The other students had all responded with smiles and enthusiasm to his warm banter and easy manner. Only Rietta had stayed inside her shell, barely looking up from her constant writing—did she also record his jesting and anecdotes? After each class she had hurried out the door, avoiding the pleasant small talk Remy and the others shared. He assumed the wicked weather would keep her away, but surprisingly, she sat in her corner, pen in hand ready to scribble as he talked. Her presence impressed him.

Forty minutes earlier, thickening clouds had darkened the Western sky. Thunder boomed, and flashes of lightning blazed in the heavens. The forecast, Remy learned later—he paid little attention to such things—had been too optimistic: the storm would not wait until late afternoon. As he locked his bike at the rack, the first drops splashed onto the pavement, and he wished he'd driven his old Ciera to the community center instead of pedaling the seven miles. This promised to be a lengthy downpour and he had no wish to be drenched on the way home. Hopefully, one of the other instructors would offer a ride.

Inside he admired the liquid rain-art on the windowpanes and watched as early students scurried from their cars to the safety of the building and their various classes. He sauntered to the all-purpose room, ran copies of his handout, chatted amicably with the secretary, and sipped the weak coffee that never needed the creamer he always added to the robust brewed he favored.

Returning to his spartan classroom, with no decorations or posters on the wall, the space being used for a variety of purposes, Remy arranged his materials on the desk and took several deep breaths. Teaching students for the township required far lower expectations than at the university. Most of these adult students wanted only the basics of how economics worked, and he struggled to keep it simple after a decade of teaching college-level classes.

Greeting them as they trooped to their seats, Remy did a quick count. All twelve had made it, including the mousey one, who again looked ready to fade into a shadow. During the class most of the others asked questions, many simplistic or ridiculous. (What is profit? What's important in a market economy? To pay off the debt, why don't we print more money?) With her usual doggedness, Rietta listened and scribbled.

For the day's session, Remy used a brief lecture and a short video to illustrate his points on the circulation of money in society. Since the housing crisis and the onset of the Great Recession of 2008, Remy had noticed students had an increased interest in learning about the economy. That made teaching at the center more gratifying.

After his presentation, the students then filled out worksheets—in the enrichment program, the instructors gave time in class to complete assignments—about what they had learned. With no tests, exams, or papers, the question-and-answer format gave the students and Remy a chance to check their progress. Students had to take responsibility for learning. Since most of them only hoped to not sound stupid when talking with their friends, Remy felt certain, if they paid attention, they would hold their own in conversations about the market economy, business, and sales.

At the end of the hour, the rain gave no sign of letting up, and the students returning to their cars and onward to other commitments. With several classes still in session, Remy waited in the lounge to ask the flirtatious yoga instructor for a ride. She'd likely offer far more than a lift, and he planned to lie by saying he needed to do lesson plans.
As he sipped his coffee, he detected a whiff of orange blossoms. "Excuse me, Professor Bavarsky." With blinking brown eyes and trembling hands, the quiet, shy student stood next to him. "Cou- could I as-ask a que-question?" In powder-blue blouse and navy

capris, she looked small holding her still-damp jacket and an oversized purse.

"Of course. Rietta, right?"

When she nodded, he continued. "Please take a seat." He stood and pulled out a chair for her.

Biting her lip, she sat on the edge of the cushion, as if expecting someone to challenge her for being there.

"Can I get you some coffee?"

She hesitated, glanced around the room, and murmured agreement.

At the counter, Remy poured the hot liquid into a Styrofoam cup, picked up several sweeteners, a packet of non-dairy creamer, and a stir stick. Back at the table he placed the items in front of her. "I didn't know if you take it black or sweetened." He watched her add half a packet of sugar. "It's good to stay dry in here. Pretty nasty storm, isn't it?"

She nodded, and then blew into the steaming drink. Putting the cup down without taking a sip, she coughed into the inside of an elbow. Her eyelids fluttered. "I, I—there's something—" She took a deep breath and then pushed words out. "My sister and I own a flower and gift shop."

Remy had wondered what the young woman did. During the first class when everyone introduced themselves, others talked about family or a job. The only thing she said was her name, Rietta. He thought she sounded frightened of the world. "What's the name, and, where is it?"

When her lips moved, he could hear nothing. Remy shook his head. "I didn't get that."

Her cheeks reddened, and words replied in a timid whisper. "HERS AND HERS. In downtown Berrington." She lowered her eyes to gaze at the purse in her lap. "I live in an apartment above the store."

"Sounds practical." On the enrollment form for the class she'd printed her full name: Henrietta Theresa Navarre. He remembered it because he'd never known a Henrietta before. It being so old-fashioned, it made sense for her to shorten it to Rietta. "I think I've been there several years ago. Before the divorce, I bought my wife candles and cards there."

"I'm sorry, 'bout your marriage." Her attempt to smile turned her expression into a grimace.

"It's been a few years. Hardest on the kids." At the time Jared and Melodee acted unbothered. Both recent college grads, they had moved East—Jared to New York City where he tried to make it as an actor, and

Melodee at Cornell working on a graduate degree—and Remy rarely saw either one. Maybe, he could fly out for the holidays.

He longed for the robust Arabica he drank at home. The translucent liquid in his cup tasted like darkened water. "How can I help you?"

Outside, the winds howled, and the sound of pelting rain lashed against the roof and windows of the building.

"I hate loud storms." Rietta shivered.

Remy bobbed his head. "Me, too. But, we're safe here." He wanted to sound convincing, but the force of the gale left him uncertain.

"With the slowdown, we're not making any profit. If we sell, I don't know what I'll do. Hermione has a husband who works and earns enough for them." With narrowed eyes, she forced words out. "We need marketing help, advertising ideas—some way to attract more customers."

"I'm hardly a marketing—" He noticed her stutter was gone.

"I understand. It's just you sound so smart about money, I thought talking with you could help." Her soulful brown eyes looked fully open for the first time since he'd met her. "You probably don't remember me, but we've met before you taught this class."

"When?" He studied her face. She didn't act like the shy young girl from a few minutes earlier.

"You came to our school to talk about attending college. You went to Michigan State, but you shared a lot about student life and why or why not we should go to college." She wrinkled her nose. "I was only in sixth grade, but I liked how well you treated us, even though a couple of kids acted bratty. They embarrassed me."

Remy remembered. It was twenty-seven years ago, and that day convinced him to work with older students rather than junior high ones. "I did my best." He chuckled. "You had some mischievous friends."

"We did." Her smile brightened her face, and she appeared at ease. "The representatives, from the other schools, didn't listen like you did. They acted stuck up. We, all of us, liked you."

"Well, thank you." For the first time he realized she must be older than he had imagined. With her sparkling eyes, she looked appealing. "Did you go to college?"

"Got my Associate's degree. But, Hermione insisted I help her keep the store. We inherited it from our folks—" Her eyes misted.

"I'm so sorry for your loss. Losing your parents is hard." He told himself to think of her only as a student, and not an appealing woman.

"Thank you. It is." She stared at her fingernails.

After a moment she continued. "She can talk me into anything. Or always could. Despite that, the fact is I know more about the business than she does." Her forehead tightened as if deep in thought. "If we sell, and she wants to, I won't have much left after paying the loans and bills. And, I like having the store."

He frowned. "What do you hope to get from me?" The question sounded harsher than intended. He watched Rietta sip her coffee. A hint of pink remained on the Styrofoam. He had thought she wore no lipstick. Her cosmetic efforts, like her voice, were muted and understated. She wore clear nail polish, the hint of mascara and eye shadow, along with the trace of citrus. "Maybe, we could work together on some marketing ideas, if that would help you."

A fresh percussion from nature rattled the building. Rietta jumped. "Oooh. I hate thunder."

Instinctively, his hand reached out to pat hers. When he saw her look at his fingers caressing her, and nibble her lip, he pulled back. "I'm sorry. Did I offend you?"

With the hand he'd touched, she brushed away a stray lock of brown hair from her cheek. "It was kind." Her face tilted, and her smile transformed, as if something pleasant had occurred to her. She straightened in her chair.

"So, okay. Right?"

The nod she offered in reply struck him as shy, inviting, and coquettish without being forward. It confused him. Against his professional training and the township rulebook for enrichment teachers, an interest inside stirred as he noticed her ring finger had no bands. Forcing his thoughts to slow, he told himself he must *not* let himself be attracted to her, to *any* student.

"The storm should pass soon. If possible, maybe we could discuss ideas here about how to improve sales?" Ignoring the inner cautionary signals, he hurried the words out. The idea of spending more time with her appealed more than it should have. "Can you?"

Her demeanor brightened as she nodded with enthusiasm. "Yes. I would like that very much." From her handbag she extracted a steno pad and pen. "I have several ideas I wrote down since starting your class."

Her gaze met his, ablaze with growing confidence. "You inspired me to think about things we could do."

Used to student compliments—his evaluations had been primarily glowing—a mixture of feelings cut loose by Rietta's eagerness surged through him hearing she'd found his words motivational.

He hoped his ideas wouldn't disappoint her. "Thank you. Let's hear some of them."

She flipped to the back of the spiraled pad. With hardy resolve, she sounded like a school girl giving a report while trying to impress her teacher. "Sponsor several high school and elementary plays and shows. Give them flowers or some bigger items for props, help with the sets, give bouquets to the performers. Maybe, one rose or a candle. I don't know." She shrugged and looked directly into his eyes. "Things you said helped me think about how to promote. You taught me to be more confident and to believe in myself."

Pleased at her growing resolve and sincere-sounding appreciation, his cheeks flushed. "Those are promising ideas. Always include your business cards." He smiled at her and saw her beam when she jotted that in her notebook. "It would get your name out to people who like the arts, and likely would show their appreciation."

"And, or, maybe," her tone gained more traction, "we could sponsor a float at the annual Memorial Day Parade. Berrington's is the biggest one in the area. So, folks come from around the county. It's the town's busiest day."

He bobbed his head. "Good. What else?"

"This one might be crazy, but, maybe we could have a contest." Rietta's bright face reminded him of a child's first time in a toy store. "A drawing. Monthly winners would get a figurine, and the big winner, drawn in the autumn, would win a floral arrangement once a month for a year. Hermione says it would cost too much."

"But things are going poorly now. Are the shop's profits too small or non-existent?"

Her mouth wrinkled. "Miniscule."

"It takes money to make money. Do you own the business equally?" He wondered at change in her confidence, going in a short time from timid to self-assured.

"Yeah, except ..." Her voice trailed off, giving the impression a big "if" followed.

"Except what?"

"It's like, 'All animals are created equal. Some are just more equal than others.'" Rietta frowned, as if she believed the words. "Isn't that how Orwell said it?"

He confirmed it with a nod. "So, she has the—upper hand?"

She blinked. "She acts tougher, and I usually cave."

Remy had no doubt the sister dominated decisions easily. "Since you know that, you need to change. Become stronger." He leaned toward her, and liked when she didn't retreat. "Have more faith in yourself. You have great ideas, and a clear love for what you do. Take charge."

"I know." She closed her eyes for a moment. When she opened the they squinted, as if deciding whether to believe his advice. Then, they morphed to certainty. "I will."

Not convinced she would, he avoided a chuckle. "How?"

"There is a way. I do have an idea about how to keep going—if you think it makes any sense." Unexpected strength emanated from her as she sat up straight. "I dreamt about this working, and about you helping me."

Confused, he spayed his hands, palms up. He would not invest in her little shop, if that's what she wanted.

"When I have a repeated dream about something, it happens." A new woman sat beside him. The mouse totally replaced by a huntress. "I'll buy her out. Take control. If she's not there, I won't give in to her."

"You have to be strong." As he said this he heard someone down the hall announce the rain had stopped. He looked out the window. The clouds were clearing. "But do you have the money. You said—"

"My cousin just got a big inheritance and has asked me if she could invest in the store. She is willing to split the cost of buying out Hermione. I'd have majority ownership, *and* control."

"Do it." Remy realized she had not needed to talk to him.

Her voice rang out. "We'll offer classes, like here, but about crafts, candle-making, flower arranging, things like that. It'll bring customers." Her fist pounded on the table, making her almost full cup of coffee jump.

"That could work." He hoped he had, at least, encouraged her, but she did not sound like she needed advice. Her soaring confidence meant he wouldn't be giving her counsel, so she wouldn't be spending time after class with him.

"And—" She stood up and shifted her smile to regretful. "I need to quit your class."

"Why would you stop coming? You are doing so well." His spirits dipped. He had looked forward to learning more about her, and now she wouldn't even come to the center.

Her eyes shimmered, and her face brightened. "I don't want to break the rules or cause you any trouble." With a deft move she returned her notes to her bag and while doing so her hand nudged his shoulder.

"Trouble? You haven't done anything wrong? And I haven't."

"Yet." She stepped closer. "I read page two of the township's guidelines for teachers, item 14."

"Which one is that?" Remy cocked his head, trying to remember the standard. Maybe it was the one about budgets.

"Teachers aren't supposed to date students. But, if I quit—" Rietta leaned over and kissed him on the cheek. "I have something for you at the store. You'll have to come see me to pick it up."

It surprised him to find a business card for HERS & HERS in his hand. He didn't remember her giving him one.

She turned and walked away, glancing back over her shoulder with a huge smile before she went out the door. "I dreamed about us again. It will happen. You'll come."

The Ravine

Pain shot through the fog. Lying somewhere—a ditch—a ravine—his mind made no sense of things. Where? Why? How? Questions flitted in and out of consciousness, while no answers appeared. Muck, dampness, marsh—awareness of feeling wet and cold gave no clues to what had happened to him. A disconcerting, wordless sound disturbed him, and his body ached in places he thought couldn't hurt.

His vision failed to focus, but he thought grey clouds served as a ceiling high above his uncertain resting spot. A smell, of sweat, of feces, of carrion made him gag, but he seemed incapable of even doing that. Movement seemed impossible—unthinkable. His legs, he wanted to feel them move. Nothing. Arms? Yes, he felt a finger dig into the surface around him. It felt unnatural, not of earth.

Had he been abducted? Was this how the aliens did it? A part of his mind rejected the silly notion. But, why did he think about aliens? Parts of his mind argued anything was possible. He had to figure it out. Where? Why? How?

Think, he told himself. Start with the basics. He should know some things, like his name. Only nothing came. Wrong. It struck him as wrong. Everybody knows their own name, don't they? The question hurt his brain. He had no idea, no clue.

The mental search tired him. His eyes grew weary. Sleep came.

With no concept of how long he dreamed, he woke with a quiver. That notion about names meant something, didn't it? His eyelids were heavy, but he needed to see where he was. But his vision refused to cooperate—unless he was engulfed in fog or a shroud.

The aches in his back, in his neck, in his feet—his legs! He had legs. Could he move them? Not enough to sense if he could wriggle his toes. Or was he too addled to tell?

Once again, he tried to recall his identity. If he could begin there, this might all become clearer, understandable. With no luck, he tried to remember what they called someone without a known name. Even that proved elusive. Still, he wanted to refer to himself with some label. All he could come up with was "Nameless." The exertion overwhelmed him, and his mind slowed to sleep.

Sometime later questions troubled him awake. How could he know some things, but not his own name? Why did he know about cities and towns, planes and ships, factories and farms, but nothing about himself? His mind wearied at the questions until he once again slept.

When next he became aware, he felt stronger, more alert, more aware. His eyes had trouble seeing much, but the fog had lifted. He believed he must lie in some ravine, a steep one. Whooshing sounds far below might be a river? The wind? Above him, he assumed, because he still couldn't move his head to look, there appeared to be a stiff incline to the top of whatever this place was. With a concentrated effort, he. tried to roll over—impossible. The exertion led to a shooting spasm which made him groan. At least, the pain told him he still lived. But why? For what?

Every part of him hurt. Muscles did not respond, but at last he could feel his right arm. It tingled. What did that mean? Maybe, he could move the limb? After great effort, it still refused to budge. The tiring struggle frustrated him.

But, a happy realization arose. He could move his tongue. Not to make words he discovered, but to explore his lips, to touch part of his face. Probing, he discovered he had a beard, thick, coarse, ragged. A beard? His hadn't thought he had hair on his chin.

Pulling his tongue back into his mouth, he clicked his teeth. He sensed the contact but couldn't hear the clack. All he heard was a deep hum, as though a small motor operated next to his ear. As he concentrated, the sound grew louder, more intense, more present. He grunted, but again could not hear himself.

His sense of smell had also abandoned him. Earlier, his nostrils had been bothered by odors, but those had gone, replaced by nothing noticeable. No speech, no hearing, no taste, no feeling. All had deserted.

His vision, though, cleared and he saw the sky high above. Clouds hovered, interspersed with blues. No sunshine, no darkness. Strange, the light seemed to come from various points in the expanse overhead. How could that be? What time was it? Where could he be? Like with everything else, he had no idea as to the answers.

New queries drifted into his psyche. How old was he? Did he work? Have a family? And if so, would they search for him, or rejoice at his disappearance? What about friends? Had he gone to college? Did he have a car? Could he drive? Had there been a terrible collision tossing him through the air to land in the mushy earth? What was he wearing? What about a wallet, money, keys? Had he been attacked and left to die? Or had he been running, tripped, and sprawled, falling to a forced rest?

It tormented him. He knew nothing of himself. What work did he do? Or was he retired or too young to work? Did he have hobbies? Did he love anyone? Was he loved? His mind, caught in a runaway game of twenty questions, jumped to deeper thoughts. Did he read? Enjoy sports? Drive? Did he have any talents? Democrat? Republican?

For a moment he stopped the self-inquisition. He knew about politics. He knew the names of political parties, but not what each stood for or campaigned for. Campaigns, what were they? The jumbled uncertainties piled higher.

What did he believe? He had not called out to God but understood the concept of a deity. That must mean something. If he had faith, shouldn't he have prayed for deliverance? Did he pray? Have faith? Worship? Go to church? He tried and failed to come up with any precepts of any religion. A bounty of questions, and a dearth of answers. One of the biggest—why did he know generalities, and not details? It stymied him.

Asking meant his cultural literacy exceeded his personal awareness. *Cultural literacy?* Where did that phrase come from? It suggested an academic background. Teacher, professor, researcher. Nothing sounded right. He must read—but what? His mind catalogued things he knew. Facts, absent before, started to come into focus. He listed things that returned to his memory. Cities, states, nations. Radio, television, cell phones, the web. Seconds, minutes, hours, days, weeks. Football, baseball, hockey, basketball. The weather, storms, sunshine.

Aware of the existence all of that, yet, ignorant of any substance, he wondered how he could not remember an address or an occupation.

He became aware of the growing darkness. Why couldn't it be lighter? He squinted, and then reopened his eyes. He stared up at white puffs overhead, and thought he remembered what they were called. Cumulus clouds.

Thinking of himself as Nameless, he knew Nameless wanted to live.

Someone stood—knelt?—next to him. He saw a form, but no face. She—he hoped it was a woman—pointed to movement in the sky. Something flew high above. The form next to him disappeared, but his focus studied the thing gliding in a giant loop close to the clouds. The wide swooping flight had a center point directly above him. The soaring creature was circling him!

An image from high school came to mind. He had hated biology class. The teacher—he knew the name and it echoed in his mind, a Mr. Kenstraw—bored him by giving long, droning lectures and requiring the taking of tedious notes. Nameless tuned out during the monologues, and after the exams, forgot all the facts the man had crammed into them.

With a full head of white hair, a face mapped with wrinkles and a constant sneer, Kenstraw towered over him. Was he the form he had seen a moment earlier? Nameless held a hand up—it moved a fraction—to block an assault from the man who had killed interest and curiosity. The human vision vanished.

His arm had responded! That meant strength had returned. Hope existed. To distract himself from the vulture or hawk, whatever it was, he studied his right hand. A few aging spots. He must not be young. How old? Fifty, perhaps? The fingernails looked clean, but the palm appeared discolored. Someone had told him he had a strong lifeline. He traced the crease with his gaze. It did look good. Maybe, he wouldn't die here.

The thought made him laugh. Silly superstitions like palmistry—he knew about that—had been foolishness he'd dismissed in the time before. Now, he clung to any analysis promising possible longer life. He wanted the prediction to be right.

In no hurry, the bird of prey slowly decreased its altitude, and clearly had lunch in mind. Dinner, too. Nameless let out an anemic yelp. The ground beneath his body might have heard, but nothing further could have detected any noise from him at all.

He needed to move. Trying to roll over, again, his body refused. But he noticed a change. Dampness seeped through whatever he wore.

If he was, he should have anticipated the wetness, but he hadn't. He reached down to his leg. He could tell when his fingers pressed into his thigh. Could he sense any feeling earlier? He had not. Another sign of improvement. Slow, but real.

An ache in the back of his skull announced itself. Angry it had been ignored, it started to throb. Not a good omen. Nameless moved his head. It turned. Moments ago, turning had been impossible. Mobility might come back in time to escape. Maybe.

The bird glided lower. A hawk? Nameless wondered what it would feel like to have living flesh torn from him by a predator. Unless he could scream or keep it at bay with his arm, it would soon be on him. Someone had to come. Certainly, people had to see and wonder what the winged hunter targeted. He tried again to yell. "Help!" Louder, but not enough to be heard. The effort tired him.

The creature dipped closer, still high enough to only be certain it was a bird. Not a vulture, he pleaded to himself. He hated the thought of being killed by a damned buzzard. To be devoured by a hawk or an eagle would be noble, a brave way to die. To be the equivalent of roadkill disturbed him at some deep internal level. Why? Please, be a hawk. The thought repeated itself as he noticed more darkening. A storm coming? Or did his vision fail? To die in a downpour would be fitting. To have his death cleansed by pelting rain might make up for whatever brought him here, like this. Karma. Why did he know that word? What had he done? Even if something bad, no one deserved to die trapped in a useless body.

No, the world didn't always act like that. Accidents came by chance. Bad ends came to good people. And he was virtuous. At least, he hoped so. Even if he wasn't, he wanted to believe it. Did living for years instead of hours depend on having faith he could survive? A silly thought. He was no quitter—how did he know that? Was he too stubborn to die?

He concentrated. Move one leg at a time. Wiggle the toes. Had he? Possibly. Now the foot. Bend it up, then down. Think. Believe. Do. To please himself, he assumed some muscles reacted and followed the order. Only a bit, but some. Better than before.

A person crouched by him again. The same as before? Not Kenstraw—that much seemed clear. The form became clear—a woman, not beautiful, but with a kind face. She said something. A promise of getting out? That help was on its way? That she loved him?

Not hearing was maddening.

He tried to talk, but she hushed him. "Rest. You need to rest." She stroked his arm. It relaxed him.

She moved away, ignoring his inaudible plea, "No, don't go." But she left. He hoped for a return, missing the comforting that the presence of another offered. Other than for Kenstraw, or the thing overhead.

The airborne thing looked closer, and he thought it had tightened the noose. Too close, and yet so far. Nameless squawked. "Help." A sound emerged—he had made a sound and he had heard it. If he could raise the volume, he might be heard.

The wind fought against him, as it increased and whistled above and around him. The bird adjusted its flight pattern. But still it came ever yards closer. Nameless wondered if he would taste like chicken. Did predators care? Did they prefer certain carcasses to others? Humans must be delicacies, rarely served. Nameless did not want to be a meal.

He struggled against an urge to give in to the inevitable. If the damn bird failed to finish him, what other monsters lurked when day ended? Wolves, coyotes? Not insects, please. No, let it be quick. He felt a bug on his neck. With his one good arm he slapped. Pulling his hand back, he saw remnants of what might have been a black ant. The sight made him shiver. It's starting.

He wanted the woman to come back. Where was she? He forced his vocal chords and tongue into another plea. "Help." The effort wore him out less than before. Maybe, he just needed time. "Time heals all wounds." Where had he heard that—a quotation or his own?

Either his eyes cleared, or his imagination had changed things. The bird's eyes focused on him. Under his body he felt blades of grass. Clarity reignited hope.

From somewhere, a scene unfolded in his mind. A frightened, little boy fled down a dusty lane trying to escape a snarling dog far behind. Farm fields with crops not to be trampled funneled him along the path. As the dog loomed closer, gaining at an alarming rate, the boy screamed. He stumbled and fell. A moment before the growling beast reached him, strong hands lifted him up, and the boy heard a booming laugh.

Some man—not his father, at least he thought not—had picked him up and lifted him high overhead. The voice snapped a command. "Sit, Amigo!" The dog stopped. "Amigo, lie down."

The pet obeyed. "Everything's okay. Amigo protects the cattle. You got too close, that's all. He won't hurt you. Will you Amigo?" The dog, a German Shephard, wagged its tail.

The image faded, but a memory lingered of romping across a pasture with that very dog. Nameless had laughed and wrestled with Amigo. And, he remembered, too, crying as a teen on the dog's last day. With a shovel in hand the funeral took place behind a barn where the aged pet was lowered into a hole and covered with an old blanket. The boy-not-yet-a-man filled the last resting place with a pile of earth pyramided next to the spot. Tears burned down his cheeks. He still felt them.

The flying creature swooped closer. Nameless flapped his own wing against it to no avail. He yelled, trying to shoo it away. No change in the descent. Perhaps the thing thanked its gods for this feast prepared for it.

"Help! Help! Anyone." The voice carried up into the wind, stronger, but not strong enough. No one would hear. Maybe, the hawk did, because it trumpeted its blood-boiling call. For the first time Nameless heard it. Nameless cried out again, grateful that each time he did, it took less energy. The improvement, as slight as it was, might save him yet. Probably it wouldn't, but surrender would guarantee his end. Stronger now, he developed a pattern: yell, rest for a few moments, and yell again. It had to work, despite the wind, despite the isolation, despite the hawk—it had to be a hawk—gloating in anticipation.

Nameless could move his head a bit more and examined the walls on each side what he thought of as the Grand Canyon of his life. And his demise? The woman could not be seen. He was alone, and he cried out one more time. This exertion drained him. But it sounded louder, more desperate. He needed to move, to struggle.

A new line came from sometime earlier in life: "Do not go gentle into that good night." He had no idea who said or wrote that. A saying, a line from a novel, or from a song? Wherever it came from, it motivated him. He must not surrender to the darkness. He must fight. Resist. Move. Cry out. Trust in possibilities

Had he written it? Maybe he'd been a poet or an author. Perhaps an academic, versed in great literature.

Maybe, he was a motivational speaker, inspiring clients to greater efforts, better marketing, making more money. A preacher, a social worker, a professor? Educated, as he had thought earlier.

He again wondered if he had a wife or lover. Blonde, brunette, redhead? Tall, short, skinny or with curves? Glasses or none? Not knowing added another exasperating set of questions to his life.

Did he have children? Grandchildren, too? Boys, girls? He must be old. He didn't feel young, and what did "young" feel like?

The idea he might already be dead entered his head. A hell designed for him alone? Separation not only from loved ones, but from awareness of others. Only a longing to know, certain of things missed, of people he loved and didn't know. If a god existed, he/she/it had a monstrous idea of eternal punishment.

A screech from the soaring stalker forced his eyes skyward again. The evil thing moved faster, still circling, moments from him. Time had turned ugly. He screamed.

This time his lungs and vocal chords cooperated, the plea pierced the air. Possibly, Nameless' screech affected the threatening beast, it seemed to slow? After giving his breathing a moment to recover, Nameless bellowed again. This time the creature paid no heed. Its approach remained slow, but constant.

A splash struck his forehead. Another hit his chin. Rain. Too many drops to count. The bird spiraled closer. Nameless willed his legs to move. Nothing. He tried his other arm. Useless. Sweeping his good limb in front of him, he hoped he could give himself more time. Marshalling resources, he waved his arm and shouted in a show of force. Within a moment, the efforts wore him out. His arm fell back to nestle onto the ever-dampening ground. Nothing deterred the damned thing! He closed his eyes against the wet assault from the heavens. Inwardly he cursed in resignation. What would come would come.

He felt a touch, not an attack. He looked up. The woman—an angel—cupped her hand around his neck. Her eyes assured him everything would be all right. He sighed—she had returned. At last, he could rest.

The hands slid the body onto the gurney and transported it to the autopsy room. There, the pathologist found evidence of a stroke.

When the on-call nurse heard, she shook her head. "Other than the cries for help this last week, he'd been quiet since coming here."

"Perspired a lot waiting to die." The aide sighed. "Sad no one ever visited him."

"He was adopted and brought up by a childless farm family." The nurse continued working on the man's chart. "He was widowed twice, and his only son died two years ago. A lonely life."

The aide went to change the bedding on the nursing home's latest open spot. "At least, he had a good imagination. A lot of his short stories explained gruesome ways to be killed. They were good reads." She shuddered, thinking of one story about being torn apart by a vulture. "I'm glad he got to spend time here. It's good he didn't suffer long and died in a soft, cool bed."

Match Play

So close. One, Two. *Uno, Duos. Ein, Zwei. Un, Deux.* If only. But no. Defeated, again.

The loss hurt, but not as much as the break-up with Mallory. Settled into his cushy seat, Lex Wherrett paid no attention to the others boarding the plane. Hoping no one had reserved the seat next to him, he didn't want to bother with small talk.

His defeat had followed the best tournament performance in his professional tennis career, and his mind danced between his athletic accomplishment and the rejection from Mallory after two years together. Losing on Court One in front of a huge crowd during the fourth-round of Wimbledon—to the second-seeded former champion!—meant he made it further than ever before at a grand slam tournament. His finish guaranteed the largest paycheck in his career, a hundred-thousand dollars, and significant attention from the sporting world.

But, going home without Mallory waiting for him weighed heavier on his mind than did the missed opportunities for even greater glory, if only he had won the grueling match. In the tournament he had played his best, given it his all, and lost with the respect and admiration of the crowd. The cheers had temporarily eased the agony of defeat.

Mallory's leaving still burned, Her departure before the tournament had one beneficial aspect. Instead of crushing him, the betrayal convinced him determined to prove her mistake. It added an edge to his play, like none he'd had before. He used the angst to motivate his play. It had worked.

In previous years her announcement would have ruined him—and he would have lost his only match at love. But life on the circuit, while dating Mallory, taught him to persevere. Playing against the best players on the professional circuit—and trying to prove to the eye-candy named Mallory that she had made a huge mistake—had fortified his resolve.

For two years he mistakenly believed he'd kept her happy.

Ironic, she'd replaced him with the surgeon who'd operated on his knee three years earlier.

Wimbledon, the most prestigious event in tennis, awarded him six figures for one week of play. The cutter probably made that every month. Maybe, she liked the greater certainty of consistent pay. Surgeons got paid, even if they lost.

Without Mallory, Lex played with a zest driven by the whip of the rejection. With each serve and every return, he smashed the ball imaging he slammed it at her face. Inspired, he hoped his performance made her heart droop.

Not that he would take her back. The hurt could not be forgotten. But, he had thought she understood his need to compete for recognition and a legacy, despite the almost certainty at the age of thirty his chances of winning a Grand Slam event diminished with every ache.

Lex worried he lacked the extra edge needed to transform from being a good competitor into a great one. Whatever made the difference, he'd have done it. But, and despite dedicating himself to practice and fine tuning the mental aspect of the game, the unique quality of excellence eluded him and all but a small handful of players.

With three wins in the venerable tournament he could afford to skip lesser tournaments to concentrate on the next Grand Slam, the U. S. Open. And, it meant flying First Class for the first time in his life. But the money did not eclipse the dual disappointment of the game—he should have played in the Quarter-Finals—and the hurtful betrayal of Mallory.

Maybe, if not for the mishit overhead and the last rifled return a hair wide, he could have pulled off the upset and shocked the tennis world. Those errors made all the difference in the fifth and deciding set. Lex, wanting those points back, punished himself with self-doubt. Tributes from sportswriters and praise of the fans could not dispel the agony of what-might-have-been.

Likewise, he wondered what more he could have done to keep his girlfriend. Less practice? More romance? Regular hours? The sad reality struck him. She had wanted someone else.

The cushy window seat and the warm attention from the flight attendant meant little. Mallory. Two miscues. Twin heartbreaks. Not playing in week two. No one to come home to.

The ability to focus on the moment had been a major asset during the match and all through his professional career, and he now directed his concentration on the things he could have done better. Be a step quicker. Notice her new shoes. Slow the ball. Send loving texts. Better top spin. More flowers. Follow-through. More gifts. Form. Anticipate. He hated his failures.

A soft, feminine voice sang kindness and disrupted the anguish. "The best and the worst."

He looked up. The face looked familiar. Possibly, she'd been in the crowd hoping for attention from the gallant loser. Or, could she be a woman from the hotel, the one who'd boarded the lift with him on the way to check-out? Certainly, not a tennis player on the circuit. He would have remembered. "What did you say?"

Her gaze sparkled. Not a beautiful woman, she had an appeal that centered on radiant green eyes, marked by the triangular shape of the pupils. Did she wear contacts, or simply have attractively misshapen eyes? After putting a small carry-on into the overhead, she settled into the seat next to him, lowering her purse to the floor.

With good legs, a flat chest, and shoulder-length dark-brown hair, she wore dangling earrings a touch too big for her face. "It has to be disappointing to come so close. That bad call in the fifth game cost you. It should have been overturned. Your ball landed in. It was your point." She nibbled her lower lip as her head shook. "It threw your game off."

If someone had to buy the seat, at least it was someone who understood tennis psychology. After the ball-out ruling, two double-faults and three second serves cost him a game. At that crucial point, most observers assumed Lex's confidence would fall apart. But he regained concentration and almost pulled off a comeback win. "Close only counts in horseshoes. My fault for thinking too much." He aimed a finger pistol at his temple and fired. When she laughed, he reached out a hand. "Lex Wherrett—are you a fan?"

Shrugging, she clasped his hand with warm firmness. "Aggie Mills. I only know you from afar, through your wonderful mother. She's my mentor—ever since my first class with her in college. Later, we worked together and became friends. When we're together, she talks about you all the time."

Not wanting to show surprise, he halted a rising eyebrow at the thought his mother had demonstrated interest in his life or career.

Wrapped up in her academics and research, Professor Millicent Wherrett paid scant attention to any of her three sons. Keeping his voice even, he examined Aggie's face. She wore little make-up—unlike Mallory, who never appeared without a mask of cosmetics—and Aggie's shiny skin looked clean, as though freshly scrubbed. "Are you an anthropologist, too?" Her laugh replied in a dance on his ears.

"Thank God, no. I'm a writer—hopefully, soon to be an author." A smile brightened her face. "Your mom, Dr. Wherrett, helped with information and facts for a historical novel, set north of Rome."

Lex read a lot, especially on flights or between matches on tours. Growing up with a bibliophile had made it mandatory to be a bookworm. "She loves Italy. Dragged me there more than I can remember." Lex had liked it as well. His only European championship had come at a small tournament in Orvieto. "What's the plot?"

"A mystery set in Umbria." She fished inside her purse and extracted a paperback with the word proof stamped on its side. "A bookseller and a customer race against time and corrupt politicians to recover a valuable manuscript and solve a brutal murder in the catacombs." She handed him the book.

"It looks interesting." He studied the cover. The blurb sounded intriguing, and it surprised him when he read short bio on the back cover that she lived near where he did. "Have a publisher?"

Her face crimsoned. "Unless you're famous or crazy, it's hard to get noticed by agents, so, I'm doing it on my own. It's been workshopped and edited. I'm going through it one last, tedious time before giving the final okay."

When she reached for the book, he shook his head, and opened it. "Can I read it?" The first fifty-some of the two-hundred-eighty-nine pages had multiple purple editing marks. "I mean, when it's all done, and I can buy it."

"I'd love it if you did. You can have an autographed copy." She looked so happy if she had a tail, she would have wagged it. "Your mother liked it. Said it showed great promise and a literary style. I hope the reading public likes it."

As the plane took off, he remembered his mother working long hours polishing her research into final form. It looked more stressful than playing a game, like he did.

"Impressive." Thumbing to the dedication page, he read the inscription aloud. "For Millie Wherrett, who taught me to believe in tomorrow." He shook his head. The idea sounded impossible. "No one ever calls her 'Millie.'"

The lift-off had been smooth, and his stomach had not quivered as it often did on these flights. First-class made it easier. Was it the seats, the front of the plane, or the company?

"She said I could." She offered a Mona Lisa smile.

Lex wondered if the reason his parents had divorced involved this young woman. Were they a couple? "Not even our relatives. Or, her best friends. It's always Millicent." She never had been Mom, always Mother. The emotional distance had been her doing, keeping people—and sons—at arm's length. Lex believed she had no sense of nurturing, unless she had some for her work.

Aggie leaned back in her seat, and crossed a leg over a knee, dangling a shoe near his leg. "Over the last year we spent a lot of time together, working on my project. I think she liked my enthusiastic work ethic, and my interest in what she did. We became friends."

"She hated being called 'Millie,' acted as if it was disrespectful." The frost in his tone matched his mother's when someone disturbed her concentration, which had been often during his childhood. "She must feel very close to you." A previously relaxed eyebrow arched in a challenge to the young woman.

She ignored the doubt. "She does. One evening we went to dinner to relax and recover from a lengthy work session—she should have co-author credit—and we found ourselves sharing life stories and laughing over the dumb things we'd each done." Aggie closed her eyes and exhaled a long breath. "After a third glass of Chardonnay, she told me to call her Millie. I did. It seemed natural. Millicent or Dr. Wherrett sounded much too formal for the friends we'd become."

Game, set, and match. Lex frowned at his triple agony: Mallory, a loss on the big stage, and finding out his mother had a softer side—one he'd believed didn't exist. "She *drank? Three* glasses? *She's* changed."

Over the last few years, he had avoided time with his mother. Christmas meant dinner at her parents' home—gifts no longer exchanged—and obligatory hugs. They'd meet two or three other times a year, and he called her occasionally—she never initiated the communications. When he told her he loved her, he got a muffled acknowledgment and a rote, "Love you, too."

Aggie's head tilted, eyes open now, with gaze fixed on him. "She's lonely. Her other friends are all so serious, and she shows little interest in dating. A shame for someone who looks good for their fifties. It's about time she let her walls down."

"I know." It relieved Lex to know the reserve had been evident. He'd begun to worry it existed only to keep him away. Aggie's shoe dropped from the dangle, and he reached down to retrieve it, placing it gently onto her foot. He sensed her shiver at his touch.

"I'm a little ticklish." With a shy smile, she played with an earring. "At first, I thought your mom might be a female Spock without human emotions. The facts, and only the facts, mattered." She tapped the hanging silver bauble—it looked like a stack of books hanging from her lobe—making it sway. "That day we worked so long, before our first, but not last, dinner with wine. We talked easily, even about how different our families were. I grew up with hugs and support."

His vision darkened as he remembered the chill of childhood. "Be a little man." "Boys must not cry." "Sit still—be quiet." Other children believed in Santa, but both his parents let him know it was all a fairy tale, and that they bought the presents he got.

Aggie leaned a bit closer. "I'm sure you know, she had strict, unforgiving parents, who demanded obedience and respect." Her hand reached to retrieve the novel, her fingers lingered a moment on his palm. "She wished she'd been kinder, and more encouraging. Said she'd failed as a mother."

Lex wanted to scream it was true, but his own reserve wouldn't allow it. "Are you a therapist? Seems she needed one." Quivering, he gritted his teeth at the knowledge she had discussed her shortcomings to a stranger, and not to her family.

"You worried her the most. Your brothers—an accountant and an attorney, right?—have secure jobs with dependable incomes." When he nodded, she beamed. "She said you, as the baby of the family, probably felt abandoned when she worked so much." She sighed. "It relieved her to know you have a steady girlfriend, and Millie hoped being in a relationship gave you some of what you needed."

He turned to stare out the window. "It did. But, it's over."

"What? Your mother thought you might get—engaged." She reached a hand to his shoulder. "I'm so sorry." Despite her words, another mysterious smile formed on her face. "When did it happen?"

In slow motion, he swiveled to face her.

With a patient nod, she waited as if eliciting an answer from a shy school boy.

Something in her demeanor suggested she already knew the answer. He wondered if the tabloids had run a story about his heartache. He tilted his head and tried to read her eyes. "Just before the tournament. Horrible timing. The airport, in fact. She found someone—better." He bit his lower lip and tasted the saltiness of blood. "Probably for the best. She had expensive taste."

Aggie pulled a tissue from her purse and wiped the crimson from his lips. "Foolish girl." She frowned. "And certainly, not better."

The attendant interrupted them to ask what drinks they'd like. Aggie wanted a Seven and Seven, while Lex requested a screwdriver. They held their conversation until served.

After taking a sip, Lex cleared his throat. He punched words across the net. "I doubt Mother *ever* regretted her parenting. Or worries about *me*." The edge in his voice sharpened. "Tell me more."

With the stir stick, Aggie agitated her drink. The clink of the ice cubes offered a soundtrack to her voice. "It tore at her. She wanted to write, be published, and recognized for new discoveries. I think being a mother got in the way, because when she decided career came first, she hired a nanny. She said she found a good one, but she still felt remorseful she had so little time with any of you."

The nanny for most of the years had been a Latino named Angela, who taught Lex Spanish, and how to make tacos, enchiladas, and quesadillas. He still loved Mexican food. "Never showed it." He wanted a burrito or nachos. Comfort food.

"I miss her." Not certain if he meant his mother, or his nanny, Lex stared at the drink. He suddenly wanted to get drunk, but not if it would be reported to his mother.

"She'd like to be closer. Call her when you get back, it would mean a lot to her." Aggie drained her drink. "I'd like another."

"Want mine? I don't." Lex wished he had the words back. This woman had no reason to trust drinking from his cup. He'd been silly to offer, and it surprised him when without a word she picked up his cup and nodded thanks.

"Yeah, sure. Bottoms up." She took a long drink, paused for a moment with a smile on her face, and then finished it. "I used to love these. Hadn't thought to get one until after you ordered it. Tastes good. Why didn't you want it?"

He gazed at his fingernails in his cupped right hand. "Tennis."

"Lots of athletes drink, especially after a successful effort. You did great." She raised the glass. "Celebrate."

He closed his eyes and remembered awkward lunging for a ball during practice. He'd been drinking, and the foolish move almost caused a career-ending knee injury. "After a surgery, I quit for a few months. Wanted to get back to this tournament and to the U.S. Open. I dreamed of winning. Still hope to, someday." The truth was all he wanted to do was qualifying for the major tournaments and winning some major cash. Everything else would be a bonus. At this stage in his career, the odds daunted him.

"Me too. I want my novels displayed in bookstores. To be asked for autographs by readers who can't wait for my next book. We dream big." She rattled the ice cubes. "With your performance in England, you're closer than I am."

"Not at my age. Too old. With luck I have two more years. After thirty-two, done. Best years are behind me." His knee ached. It hadn't in months, and now it told him, even repaired, it would limit his future. "Writers are never too old. You have years. Me, months. Hopefully."

"Do you really think about retiring from competition? After this impressive performance?" Her gaze locked on his face. "You're doing better than ever. I've watched. You no longer just depend on your serve—and it is powerful—but your all-around game has improved. You play smarter and react quicker."

"But I'm at my peak. It's all downhill from here." Several clubs wanted him as their professional. He'd agreed to take a job back home in River Forest as a teaching pro after he retired. The spot offered good pay and benefits. He'd still play on the senior circuit, the elephant burial ground for former tennis stars. "Depends on health, and how I play." He shook his head. "I like competing. It keeps me young but takes a toll. Lots of twinges. A few more grand slam events—then, I quit." He nodded at her. "You'll write forever."

"You're right. I don't think I'd ever want to quit writing. All these people in my head. A friend has a tee-shirt that reads 'Some of my best friends are fictional.' I feel like that."

He smiled. She had hopes. Like he used to have, long ago. "Mother's lucky. Having you."

"Thank you, that's nice of you to say. Your mom needs to date again. Maybe, find a husband." She tugged on her earring again. "I can see why she says you're sweet. Maybe, we could be friends, too. I'd like that."

The stewardess came by and the two women exchanged knowing smiles. They glanced toward an empty seat on the other side of the plane, and then the attendant clearly winked at Aggie. "Is everything going well? Anything I can get you *two*? Freshen up the cocktails?"

They both nodded. This time, he wanted his. He glanced over at the vacated seat and understood.

Silently he offered thanks to Mom, to the kind stewardess, and for Maggie, glad to have someone he liked to drink with.

The Encounters

Amen Point

With one hand on the wheel, Cos took another hit from the joint. He turned down the rocking rhythms of *Bare Naked Ladies* to blow smoke at his best friend, which elicited a cough. "What's wrong? This is good stuff. And, man, it might help you get out of your funk." When TJ just shook his head, Cos shrugged as he guided the Malibu along the road to the oft-deserted Amen Point Park.

TJ McKuhn knew the truth would sound petty and jealous. Vocalizing those thoughts, even to his best friend, could ruin his image as the school's smartest and coolest guy, a role he prized.

The new student, Gloria Judson, made him crazy. And not in a good way. Smart—as bright as TJ—*and* pretty, acting so self-assured, she had attracted nothing but positive attention from everyone else. In the first six weeks after transferring to Twin Forks, she'd become the most popular girl in the whole school.

Everyone assumed next year TJ would be valedictorian, speak at graduation, and be voted most-likely-to-succeed. Her presence threatened those honors. She needed to shut up and stop annoying him. Better yet go away. But to admit resentment would lower his standing at the top of the all-important high school pecking order.

Worse, he needed to deal with the pain-in-the-neck for the rest of the semester during his favorite subjects. For some unfathomable reason, Mr. Leister, who taught both Current Issues and Creative Writing, liked to call on her, and seemed to believe she added a lot to class discussions. TJ wondered if the old guy lusted after the girl. Dirty old fifty-year-old men should keep their libidos, and their zippers, in check.

With the highest grade point of all the juniors, TJ rarely had been challenged in academics, at least until this year. Now *she* tested him. This must not stand. TJ wanted to be—no, needed to be—number one.

Adding to her aggravating confidence, she looked attractive. And why did she have to wear apple blossom perfume—the same scent Philly used? With a shapely body and an infectious smile, Gloria drew stares from all the guys in school, watching her with mesmerized longing when she passed. Even Cos opened doors for her and curried her favor.

It surprised him girls didn't resent this too-good-to-be-true, fashionable non-bimbo. They included her in their hallway huddles and cafeteria conferences. Rather than spurning and shunning her, they'd elevated her to leader of the pack. Why hadn't they rejected her with proper envy and cruel gossip? It had to be her smooth charm.

Cos took another hit on the joint. After a long moment he exhaled and looked at his friend. "C'mon, man. What's wrong? You haven't said a word since we got out. It's not like you." The two talked about everything and went everywhere together. Cos starred, and TJ started in both football and baseball. TJ had the lead in the school play and captained the championship Math Olympiad Team with Cos participating in each. TJ topped the Honor Roll while his friend ranked third. They, along with the pleasant-if-simple varsity quarterback, pretty much ruled the junior class—at least, until Gloria.

"It's nothing man. Something I got to work out." No use complaining about the female interloper until Cos dropped his unfortunate infatuation. Making matters worse, the newcomer had arrived shortly after Philly left. TJ sighed. "I miss her."

"Who? Oh, Philly? Don't do this to yourself." Cos tapped a beat on the steering wheel. "You still text, don't you, and keep in touch?"

"Not the same." Long distance relationships wouldn't work with Philly. Hating being alone, she'd find someone sooner than he would. Not that he didn't have offers. Several girls made it clear they'd love to go out with him, but the Philly-ache still hurt too much.

Despite how cool he appeared, TJ felt empty inside ever since she left. Philly—never called her given name of Harriett—had won his heart and occupied his dreams. Life seemed lost without her. "Why couldn't her mom have moved back to Pennsylvania instead of all the way to *Alaska*? Heck, I'll never see her."

"You need a buzz. Get over her." Cos turned onto the drive into the park. "Plenty of babes dig you. Pick one and move on."

"No one's like Philly." TJ shook his head, waving off both the joint and the idea of dating someone else. "Think anyone will be here? It looks deserted, and it's cold."

The weather had been mild near the Bay, but today's blustery winds and gray snow-laden clouds threatened a big, maybe school-closing storm overnight. TJ hated missing classes, but the thought of a day without Gloria held strong appeal.

"Look for the sign at the entrance." He referred to a landmark boulder near the entrance. "If she's there, a blue scarf will be tied around the gate." As he spoke, Cos spotted the signal. "So, I'll go up to the old shack. You keep watch and call me if cops show."

TJ didn't mind. He never bought any. On the rare occasions he wanted to indulge, Cos always shared.

Amen Point had once been a popular getaway. Now, most went to the bigger parks with modern facilities. Cos preferred to make his purchases in the relative safety of this quiet county beach. His dealer, from Berrington High, planted her own pot in a greenhouse on her family's farm, and kept her business basic, not offering anything other than what she and her dad grew.

Several minutes later TJ walked the beach and enjoyed the view of the Bay. He loved the smell of late autumn along the shore. Overhead, the darkening sky promised a storm. Soon it would be nightfall, and it would be best to leave before the threatened blizzard.

A symphony of the waves, swift swishing and swooshing onto the sandy waterfront, kept TJ company while Cos went to make his deal. As thoughts of the absent Philly and the unfortunate Gloria stirred the unhappy waters of his internal lake, he zipped up his jacket. A moment later, a voice startled him. The call came again, and he turned to see someone approach.

She walked toward him. It was the she-monster herself! Bundled in layers of sweats, her blonde hair escaped below a stocking cap. He cursed silently thinking why-did it-have-to-be-*Gloria* who waved at him.

Despite his angst, he decided to be cordial. "Gloria. Hello. "Where'd you come from?" Wanting the question to sound innocent, he would not give her the privilege of knowing how much she annoyed him.

She wiped a brow, where, even in the cold air, hints of perspiration glistened. "I'm in training for track season. Four times a week, I run five to ten miles." Glancing in the direction of Twin Forks, she took several deep breaths, exhaling slowly. "I follow River Road, and then the trail along the small creek."

He indicated the ominous clouds. "A blizzard's coming. You don't want to get caught in it." Why couldn't she wear layers to school, and sweat more, like now? Part of him had to admit, even in winter garb, and, despite the exertion, she looked attractive. He pushed the thought aside and replaced it with the hope she wouldn't ask for a ride.

"I have my cell. The worst won't hit for another hour, and I'll be back before it gets bad." She tilted her head. "What about you? It's a strange time to stroll the beach, especially, if storms bother *you*. Or do you like watching them develop? I do."

He did love seeing and listening to Nature unleash her power with the winds playing angry tunes in the barren tree tops, and the waves, intense and raucous, exploding on the beach. The world decorated with drifting terrains of ivory reminded him of good times with Philly. No, the storm disturbing him the most stood next to him on the beach. "A buddy asked me to come because he's meeting a girl up there." He nodded at top of Amen Hill. "She's from another school, and her folks don't approve." That sounded lame. He hoped she believed it. He doubted he would.

"Hmm." Tilting her head, she took a step closer before turning to look at the Bay. "I love it here. In this beautifully lonely spot, one can see possibilities. The future, the good and the challenging, is coming, and we have to face it." She glanced back at him. "It renews me, helps me understand that whatever comes, I can handle it."

"This is one of my favorite spots. Not today." If he closed his eyes, he could inhale Philly. He missed her as his mind filled with wonderful memories of this park where they had made love—his first time. She used to relish the gentle warm-weather waves dancing onto shore. "In the summer and spring, it sparkles here."

Gloria pointed down the beach at large waves plummeting onto a rocky area. "I love how the bay sounds, crashing and colliding. Like a demented jazz percussionist pounding out a chaotic melody." As she hugged herself, TJ admitted to himself he valued it as well.

At least this female-devil appreciated nature.

Gloria's arm swept across the area. "Is the story about this place true? Immigrants thought they landed in Grand Traverse? How'd they go so wrong?"

Her lack of familiarity made him smile. At least, it proved she didn't know everything. He cleared his throat. "In 1847, an unscrupulous ship's captain dropped his passengers on this spot, lying about the location. Before they discovered the truth, the drunk and his crew left them stranded." The story made him laugh. "They'd named it Amen Point. The name stuck." Not knowing if she understood the humor, he added. "It means 'Let it be so.' They couldn't afford to leave, so they made the best of it. Appropriate name, don't you think?"

"Yes, it is." Her mischievous grin spread light on the dreary day. "Did *your* ancestors arrive with them?"

Had she just suggested his forebears had been stupid? No. Not her style. But with her unfortunately attractive face, even insults would sound innocent. "I'm Irish. Those folks came from Germany and stayed because of other similar communities near here."

Her smile evaporated as she shivered in her layers of clothes. "After Castro executed my grandfather, my mother's family escaped from Cuba. Grandmother and her two daughters, my aunts, fled to Florida. That's where my mother was born."

As the wind picked up, TJ noticed vulnerability beneath her veneer of confidence. Don't give in, he thought. Remember who she is. Struggling to maintain detachment, he spoke with a somber tone. "My great-grandfather got run out of River Forest in the early 1900s because of being Irish-Catholic and wanting to start a union."

She nibbled her lower lip. "That's terrible. What did he do?"

"He and his brother moved to Twin Forks and farmed until they lost their place during the Depression." Closing his eyes, TJ imagined the pain on their faces. Several long, hard years saw two children die, and another arrested for stealing. TJ did not share those stories. "After that, they lived in shanties, did odd jobs, and hunted to stay alive. My grandfather joined the army to fight the Nazis, lived through that, and came back to get a job at the factory. Things got better then."

Gloria hugged herself. "It's good you care about the past. So many at school don't know anything about history, not even their own family's story."

He had to agree. "They don't."

She shook her head. "A person should have a sense of what has been, to understand today and tomorrow. That's one of the things I like about you. You think about things."

Startled, he stammered a thank-you. Philly rarely paid attention when he talked about events and people from long ago.

She raised her voice as the winds gained force. "At my last school, we had Honors classes, and lots of bright, interesting people, who wanted to talk about life, about ideas, and about issues. Here, it's just you and me."

In class discussions, TJ found her grating, always ready to make a point, often to challenge his. Here, on this chilling day, she sounded—for lack of a better word—human. He mentally shook pre-conceptions from his brain. Maybe, she'd prove less than evil.

She raised an eyebrow. "What's TJ stand for? Danielle told me it means, 'Too Juicy.' She really likes you." Her eyes focused on him, as if searching for his reaction to the comment. She looked pleased when he shrugged. "Is it for Thomas James?"

"Got the middle name right. My parents named me Talbot." He shuddered as he said it. "Doesn't work for me. Dad went by his initials, DJ, so …" He trailed off, not wanting to go into too much detail. His given name had been the source of teasing from cousins. Fortunately, none of them lived in the area. Glancing at Gloria, he hoped she wouldn't stoop to mentioning it around his friends.

"Your family has lived here a long time. We move every year or two. It'd be weird to have roots and have *real* best friends. I miss that." Her eyes, a deep, vibrant blue, carried a sadness that looked past him into the darkening clouds billowing to the north. "I've got friends in New York, California Texas, and France. It's not the same as you, and your buddy, Cass. I've never had someone like that."

It pleased him that she messed up the name—she had flaws! "It's Cos, short for Costain."

"Costain?" She cocked her head.

"His grandmother named him after some novelist she loved. Cos's mom died giving birth." TJ shook his head at the thought of never knowing your mother. Even worse, at being brought up by grandparents, especially ones like TJ had.

"What about his dad?"

"He left the minute he found out he'd be a father. Cos never hears from him. Doesn't care to find him either. Can't blame him." TJ hoped Cos didn't mind Gloria knowing about him. It might make him more appealing to her. They would make a good couple. Both had been in Europe, and both looked good. "I don't know what's worse: not knowing or having a bad one around."

Surprised at how easily he had shifted his thinking about Gloria, TJ for a moment wondered if *he* liked her. Impossible. After all his animosity, how could he?

Gloria shifted on one foot, looking uncomfortable standing in the wind. "A mean Dad would be the worst. I've known too many girls who've been abused." Her eyes darkened. "It sucks."

In psych class, TJ had been fascinated by case studies of abused teens. How someone moved forward—carrying the anchor of being molested—impressed him. Being abused by someone who should be loving had to be devastating. "Can't imagine how hard it must be."

Her face turned from ruddy to ashen as she pursed her lips. Words drifted from her mouth, as if afraid to be heard. "I know."

Did she know? Her last two sentences had been present tense. Did that mean it happened to her? He gulped. The girl he loathed did not stand before him. This person carried deep hurts he could not comprehend. A terrible thing must have happened to her, and the realization shifted his attitude. He lowered his voice and stepped closer. "It takes strength and courage far more than I could ever muster. With so much to deal with, I'd find it hard to be around other people, happy people, sad people, unmarred people."

She nodded, a dull, damaged expression in place of her previous energy. "It—they must find it difficult." She bit her lower lip and her eyes clouded before she looked away.

A voice interrupted the moment. "Why, hello. Gloria?" Cos walked toward them, a smile hiding disappointment in his eyes. "What brings you here?"

TJ answered for her. "She's in training. Ran all the way from town. Stopped for a breather." He nodded toward Gloria, while his eyes asked Cos about the hill. "Did you see *her*?"

His friend held out empty hands. "Only a moment. Too much going on, and—" He meant cops had been watching her.

"Too bad. No date for Saturday, eh?" TJ glanced from one to the other, offering Cos a private thumb-up, indicating Gloria would be a good choice.

Gloria wiped her eyes with a tissue pulled from a pocket. "Nice to see you, Cos." She looked at TJ. "I enjoyed talking with *you*, but I'd better get back. See you at school."

"Do you want a ride?" The boys spoke in unison.

TJ, surprised at their stereo-suggestion, suddenly realized she'd smell the pot in the car if she rode with them. That might be bad. "Or, do you need to keep training?"

"Thanks, but I want to run." Her eyes focused on TJ. "Thanks for the conversation. It helped. Maybe, we could—"

Cos stepped between them with his attention on Gloria. "Are you sure? I'd be happy to give you a lift. A storm is about to hit." To support him the wind howled and whirled about them as a few flurries started to fall. "I don't want you to get too cold or caught in the snow. I checked a few minutes ago. *Six* inches."

Her eyes rolled. "I'm like the post office. 'Neither rain nor snow …' But, I should get going." She smiled at TJ. "Let's talk more soon. Get each other's number so we could text about classes and stuff. You know. Going to run back now. Bye." With another glance at him, she winked, and then trotted toward the tree-covered path, waving back at him twice.

Cos leered after her. "I'd love a piece of that." He punched TJ lightly on the arm before turning toward the parking lot. "Let's get back before it really comes down."

"Sure." Not moving, TJ watched her run. At the beginning of the forest path, the angel who had replaced the devil swiveled to yell something he couldn't understand. He raised his hand in recognition. Despite the whipping wind and fluffy flakes clouding his vision, warmth spread inside of TJ as she waved one more time before entering the woods.

J. R. Rauschert, still uncertain about what he would ever do if he grew up, considers himself a most fortunate human. He shares a home with the love of his life, Elaine, three cats (Whisper, Nelson, and Jacob), and a four-year-old golden retriever puppy named Lincoln. Having loved his career teaching in an alternative high school, he feels blessed to have time to write, to think, to travel, and to be the only thing he knows how to be, himself.

Blessed with the ability to laugh, most often at himself, J. R. writes about unfinished people, ones like all of us. He hopes his characters' journeys lead them to a better understanding of life and the possibilities that surround them. And he hopes his readers enjoy those treks.

Residing in two not-so-different places at one time, he eats, sleeps, works, and plays in rural Clinton County surrounded by corn, wheat, and beans, as well as living in fictional Forest County, filled with the imaginary folks populating his stories.

His first three novels include *Past Forgetting*, in which an anti-war protestor matures working in a nursing home, *Window Pains*, about a disgruntled Vietnam Vet doing displays for a large department store, and *Another Chance*, about an alternative education teacher suffering from PTSD. All are available online.

He is working on his fourth, fifth, and sixth novels, each in various stages of production.

Along with Larry Brown, the motivational speaker and educator, he would like to remind people to "Remember, even on your very worst day, you are somebody's best hope."

Made in the USA
Monee, IL
17 February 2025